PR(

A LORDS OF ACTION NOVEL, VOLUME 2

K.J. JACKSON

First Edition: September 2016
ISBN: 978-1-940149-18-9
http://www.kjjackson.com

K.J. Jackson Books
Historical Romance:
Stone Devil Duke, *A Hold Your Breath Novel*
Unmasking the Marquess, *A Hold Your Breath Novel*
My Captain, My Earl, *A Hold Your Breath Novel*
Worth of a Duke, *A Lords of Fate Novel*
Earl of Destiny, *A Lords of Fate Novel*
Marquess of Fortune, *A Lords of Fate Novel*
Vow, *A Lords of Action Novel*
Promise, *A Lords of Action Novel*

Paranormal Romance:
Flame Moon
Triple Infinity, *Flame Moon #2*
Flux Flame, *Flame Moon #3*

Be sure to sign up for news of my next releases at
www.KJJackson.com

DEDICATION

– As Always,
For my favorite Ks

{ CHAPTER 1 }

The thick liquid ran from the pot, rank clumps of devil-spewed muck splattering out to the ground. A blast of wind whipped between the tightly stacked buildings, sending an incomprehensible swirl of smells into the air.

Her lips drawn tight, Lady Natalia Abbingale snorted a puff of air from her nose, trying to expel the stench that had attacked with the gust. The wind chilling her arms through her thin wool dress, she ignored the shivers, shaking the chamber pot empty and stepping back to the rickety door.

Under the weak light of one lantern hanging to the left of the door, she pulled the handle, refusing to acknowledge the brown splotches that had splattered onto her hand. As much as she could stop her nose from wrinkling, she couldn't stop her stomach from churning.

Revulsion. Fear. Rage.

All of it seethed in her gut, fermenting. Not that she would unleash any of it.

If she stopped now, she could count her sister lost to her forever.

The door jerked open toward her, jamming her knuckles and sending her stumbling a step backward.

"Out ove me way, wench."

A large brute pushed past her and Talia scampered to the side, her head bowed so low she could only see the man's shoes slopping through the muck in the back alley.

A quick breath that she tried to convince herself didn't stink, and Talia stepped through the open door. Pulling it closed behind her, she yanked hard, forcing the askew door into the frame. Glancing upward, her look quickly ran across the wide main room of the brothel. The haze of smoke in the air muddied the light the many lanterns gave off, making her squint. Ignoring every one of the slovenly drunk males, her searching gaze had to pause longer than she would have liked to stare at each of the females in the room.

None of the women were Louise.

Not out here in the public area. Talia had to get upstairs.

A flurry of bodies flailing. A scream. Talia's look flew to the side of the room, searching the commotion afoot by the long bar that stretched nearly the depth of the main area. Several men—the brutes that kept the brothel from descending into pandemonium—were wrangling a writhing girl with a hood over her face. A quick scan of the girl's plump body told Talia it wasn't Louise.

A tall man with brown hair stood next to the door, waiting for the girl to come under control. Even with only being able to see his profile, Talia could see that the tall man was clearly bored with the proceedings.

Rage bubbled from her gut into her chest. The devil himself treated girls with more respect than the men in this wretched place did.

Far better dressed than most of the sailors and vagabonds in the place, the tall man turned slightly, looking across the many tables in the common room, his full face turned her direction.

Talia nearly dropped the pot in her hand. It fumbled down her skirts and onto her knees before she caught it and had it under control. She looked up just in time to see the man grab the writhing girl and disappear out the side door of the brothel.

A face she recognized. Recognized from a past she was so far removed from now.

Lord Lockston.

She lowered her head, ducking back out the alley door of the brothel into the cold. Setting the pot down, she ran along the back of the building, slowing at the corner to sidle along the side of the brothel and past the door Lord Lockston had exited.

Slipping into the shadows along the street, she followed him down the block.

The poor girl with the hood covering her head struggled the entire way, forcibly dragged to Lord Lockston's waiting carriage.

Bile hit Talia's throat, as it had the last two times she had seen a girl dragged off like this. That her sister could have been…

No. Do not think. Do not imagine.

Do not think on the possibility of what Louise could have—may be suffering somewhere at this very moment. Do not.

Her fingers running along the brick of the building behind her, Talia skulked to the corner, dipping back into a side alley where she could still see Lord Lockston's large, black coach.

Lord Lockston opened the door of the carriage and lifted the girl, pushing her inside. The girl resisted, her bound wrists flailing, her nails dragging across his hand.

Yanking his hand free from the girl, Lord Lockston shook it, rubbing a long line along the back of it after closing the coach door. His head swinging back and forth, he stood on the cobblestones, watching the carriage start to roll away from him. Talia strained, but could not hear what he appeared to be muttering. A curse, she imagined. The girl looked like a wildcat. Good for her.

The carriage rumbled down the rough street. Lord Lockston remained in his spot, a lone figure in the muck of the street staring at the coach as it disappeared. He glanced about and moved further along the block, then vanished around a corner.

Talia's breath caught in her throat.

Lord Lockston.

Was it possible? Was he the one?

~ ~ ~

Talia tugged the wet strand of red-blond hair that whipped into her eye. The bitter wind had not ceased in the last eight hours, instead, conspiring with mist to make the walk to Lord Lockston's townhouse particularly chilly.

She noticed a swath of black covering the tip of the strand of hair. Blast it. She had spent two hours scrubbing the black soot from her hair. The coal she'd used to darken her hair worked well enough, but it was nearly impossible to remove all of it using the small washstand basin in her rented room. It didn't help that she hadn't bothered to clean the soot from her hair since she arrived in London a week ago. She had been exhausted and had let the color sit day after day.

She rubbed the blackened strand between her thumb and forefinger. The hair had not been protected from the drizzle by her small black bonnet, the trimming long since tattered and removed. She sighed looking at the wet, dark smudge smeared from the strand of hair onto the thin leather of her gloves. The black coloring had only partially disappeared from her hair, making it more or less obvious, she couldn't discern.

Stopping, Talia tucked the wet lock behind her ear, hoping the dark hairs were hidden, and turned, her steps heavy up the three marble stairs. She took a deep breath, staring at the gleaming brass knocker just above her eye level. Her gaze travelled upward, her eyes squinting through the mist as her palm flattened on the front of her dark blue carriage dress—truly, her only dress, save for the one black wool maid's dress and apron she owned.

Looking up at four tall stories above her, Talia noted the middle two floors were unusually tall, if she judged by the large windows. She had not noted the impressiveness of the façade—of the home—when she had attended a dance here five years before. Of course, she wouldn't have noticed it—she hadn't noticed anything back in those days. Back when she never would have imagined her life would take this turn.

This money, this wealth was too commonplace in her world in those days—homes such as this were not impressive because every home she visited was just as elaborate as the last.

Her eyes dropped back to the brass knocker, hoping this wasn't a waste of her time. Hoping she hadn't completely misread what she had seen in the street in the middle of the night. She was giving up sleep that she desperately needed.

Lifting the heavy brass ring, she clanked it three times. It only took two breaths before the door swung wide.

The butler looked Talia up and down, his nose wrinkling before his eyes even made it up to her face. Apparently, she hadn't cleaned herself up as well as she had attempted.

She opened her mouth before he could say a word. "Lady Natalia Abbingale to see Lord Lockston on imperative business."

The wrinkle of his nose flared out, making him look like a mad bull. "You are accompanied, Lady Natalia?" His look lifted above her head to scan the sidewalk and street behind her, searching for a coach and companion.

Dammit. She had been in such a rush to make it to Lord Lockston's home that she had forgotten to consider the need for a companion. Had she lost all memory of propriety?

She smiled what she hoped was the sweet smile of a simpleton. "I was, but I lost my shoe in an impossibly large puddle of street muck a block away, and it was subsequently run over by a wagon. I only moved to the side just in time to avoid injury. I took my maid's shoes and she went back to retrieve me replacement footwear for the walk home. As we were already so very close to his lordship's residence, I thought it more prudent to approach Lord Lockston with my business, than to waste half the day chasing shoes. My maid should arrive shortly with proper boots in-hand." Talia looked to the sky, overblown distress flooding her face. "But I would much like to get out of the rain. You see, the rain as well, I did not plan upon."

The butler looked down, noting the scratched, worn leather of her boots peeking past the bottom of her skirts.

Good thing her only pair of shoes were boots barely fit for a maid.

Her story verified, the butler looked to her face, his eyes shrewd. "You will excuse me for a moment, Lady Natalia?"

She nodded, and the door promptly slammed closed in her face.

Staring at the black paint right below the brass knocker, she tried to still her heartbeat. If this didn't work, what would she do next? Stalk Lord Lockston? Accost him on the street? Wait for him to leave in his carriage and sneak onto the footman's back footboard? Or did Lockston have footmen as he travelled? From what she remembered of the man, he was not the type to appreciate displays of pomposity. He seemed the type to prefer minimal fuss— not the grandiose show of matching footmen hanging and running about his carriage.

Truly, how would any of those scenarios of her surprising him in public play out? Not well.

She had to get into his house today. She had to.

The door opened.

"His lordship will allot you five minutes, Lady Natalia, for your business." The butler's voice dropped on the word "business," making it evident that he knew she had no proper business to see Lord Lockston about.

She didn't care. She was in.

Stepping into the foyer, Talia swallowed the nervous clump lodged in her throat.

She was so close and she knew it. She felt it.

If Lord Lockston was the one she thought he was, then she had hope.

~ ~ ~

Fletcher Bartholomew Williston, the eleventh Marquess of Lockston, stepped into his lower drawing room. Having only slept for three hours, he had been attempting to convince himself to sleep longer when Horace had announced the arrival of Lady Natalia Abbingale.

Fletch had almost had Horace send her away until a faint memory of the name clicked into his mind. Her father was the Earl of Roserton. Or had been until his death several years ago.

Not that he could recall ever meeting Lady Natalia.

Yet instant curiosity had gotten the better of him and put a stake through the last thoughts of achieving more sleep.

Standing by the door to the drawing room, Fletch lifted the tumbler of brandy that Horace had handed to him, sipping as he took a quick second to observe the back of the woman warming herself by his fireplace. Her hands rubbing vigorously close to the fire, she stood maybe as tall as his mid-chest and was slight—a thin leaf that could blow away in the wind. Loose tendrils of her red-blond hair dripped wet splotches onto the shoulders of her dark blue carriage dress which was worn thin in spots.

Another step in and Fletch cleared his throat. "Lady Natalia, I do not believe we have had the pleasure of meeting. But I did wonder what would send a young lady to my door, unchaperoned, early in the day."

She jumped at his words, spinning, the blue skirt of her carriage dress swinging wide. Her initial surprise at his voice quelled by the time she faced him.

"Lord Lockston." Her head tilted with the two words, her eyes running him up and down as her hands disappeared behind her back. To hide the wringing or to continue the warming, Fletch wasn't sure.

"Your maid has not yet arrived with your shoes, Lady Natalia?"

"No."

Her eyes flickered to the side. Liar. Fletch could recognize that easily enough.

"And you are not fearful of being here unchaperoned? You know as well as I it is not done, Lady Natalia." His gaze ran over her. Her dark blue carriage dress with gold trim and a line of brass buttons had been at the height of fashion four—maybe five—seasons ago. There were swaths across her chest, at her hips, along the top and bottom edges that were threadbare, slightly tattered. Her red-blond hair was weaved into a serviceable upsweep with a small black bonnet that had been partly crushed and then bent back into place sitting at the crown of her head. The hat would be no help against the current freezing drizzle.

His look stopped at her face. Large hazel eyes with blues and browns twisting in a mad dance around her irises stared at him just as quizzically as he took her in. It was then Fletch noted she was pretty. Even if the bones of her elegant cheekbones and soft jawline were stark—stretched far too thin. Her nose was pleasantly pert and her lips, though currently purple with cold, were fairly plump. She wasn't old, yet she wasn't a young pup, and a slight wariness sat uneasy across her brow. Fletch wondered if it was permanent.

Indeed, were it not for the sweetness of Lady Natalia's face, he would have thought her unremarkable on every level. For there was certainly not the level of care taken with her appearance as he was accustomed to with his widows.

Her eyebrows arched as if to inquire if his assessment was over. Before he could react, she took a step toward him. "Being ruined is the least of my concerns, Lord Lockston."

"What is your concern?"

Her eyes dipped down to his left hand holding the tumbler and then back to his face. A visible spark ran through the dancing blue-brown in her eyes. "I am here to beg of you your assistance."

Fletch searched his mind. *Did* he possibly know her? No.

He took care with his next words. "How may I be of assistance?"

"I saw you last night."

"You did?" Fletch could not for the life of him remember this face at Lord Gregory's party the previous night. "I apologize—did I cut you in some way? If so, I did not intend harm. I am sure all can be remedied." He took another sip of his brandy.

"I saw you at the Jolly Vassal, Lord Lockston."

Brandy caught in his throat. The woman was fortunate she didn't get spewed upon.

He coughed, clearing his throat. "You were at the brothel?"

"I was."

His hand flew up, stopping her next words as he turned and closed the door of the drawing room.

He turned back to her, his eyes narrowed. "What in the hell is a lady of the *ton* doing at a brothel?"

Her hands pulled from behind her back, her arms folding across her ribcage as her spine straightened. "I was a lady. Now I am a maid. My current position is the natural downfall for a woman with a mother who has never lifted the tip of her finger in labor, and a sister that needs food in her belly."

Bitterness laced her words, even though Fletch could see her attempting to control her voice.

"What do you think happens to the family of a dead earl when the title passes to a distant, vengeful branch of the family, Lord Lockston?"

"Surely the current Earl of Roserton ensures your well-being."

She took another step toward him, her chin lifting as her look pierced him. "Surely you do not think your contemporaries are all paragons of responsibility."

"Your father left you nothing?"

She took a quick breath, her lips tightening. "He assumed we would be taken care of."

"Incorrectly?"

Her head tilted, her hazel eyes shrewd upon him. "Incorrectly."

"But a maid in a brothel, that is uncalled for, Lady Natalia—you could be a maid anywhere and support your family."

"True."

His look went hard, the true meaning for her visit surfacing. Fingers tightening about the tumbler in his hand, he took a step closer and leaned over her. "If you think to blackmail me with knowledge of my nightly activities, Lady Natalia, you had best reconsider your current course of action."

She didn't cower, meeting his glare. "Please, do not be obtuse. I care to do nothing of the sort. Yes, I can work as a maid anywhere. But I cannot find my sister anywhere."

"What do you mean?"

"I am here to ask for your help. My sister disappeared from the village of Knapton in Norfolk where we are living."

"I do not see how I can help you, Lady Natalia." Fletch took a step backward, his head shaking. "If your family situation is as dire as you say, maybe she just left to escape you and your mother."

"Do not dare to utter a blasphemy such as that." Her voice slipped low, vehement. "She would not have done so. Never. Someone took her. Another girl was taken at the same time. Another girl that returned to the village a week after they disappeared. She didn't want to tell me anything—would not admit to anyone what happened— not until she saw how desperate I was."

"Lady Natalia, I still fail to see how I can be of assistance."

"The girl—she is the blacksmith's daughter—she told me she was taken to a brothel here in London. They sold her. But the man they sold her to did not touch her. Instead, he delivered her to several women who then brought her home. Maybe you remember her? Her name is Valerie." Lady Natalia's arms unthreaded and her hand went to her chest height, palm down. "She is this short, rotund, black hair down to her waist."

Damn.

Fletch bit down on letting the blasphemy slip from his lips. He had purchased a virgin from the Jolly Vassal two weeks prior with that very description. And this waif knew of it. Knew of him.

Damn.

The business of buying virgins to save them had apparently caught up with him. No one—not a soul could know what he was doing at the Jolly Vassal. Not when the whole operation of saving the girls hinged on secrecy. Hinged on him being nothing more than a sordid lecher with an insatiable need for the virgins.

Fletch's eyes narrowed on Lady Natalia. "That is quite a tale, Lady Natalia, and I do sympathize with your plight, but I am not the man you seek."

"No." Her foot stomped, her hands balling to fists at her sides. "You are the man. Please, Lord Lockston, I have no one to turn to, no one to trust, and I have to find my sister." Her head dropped forward, and she took a deep breath. He could see her struggling with her pride, but then she looked up at him, her soul bared in her eyes, begging. "I need help, Lord Lockston. Please. I cannot do this alone.

I have looked so hard, done things I never thought I could and I…I have not a soul that can help me."

Fletch looked to the front window, unable to watch the agony in her hazel eyes. Agony or not, he could not risk being discovered. There were too many innocent lives at stake. "I am not what you are looking for, Lady Natalia. You have approached the wrong man."

She rounded him, jabbing her face into his line of sight. "No, I do not think I have. I think I have approached the one man—the only man—that can help me in my particular situation. You save the virgins. You are the one. My sister, she is my height, my build—she has blond hair and looks very similar to me. Maybe you have seen her— bought her?"

His eyes met hers and he forced his voice bland. "Again. I am not the one you seek, Lady Natalia. I cannot help you."

"You cannot or you will not?"

"Either way, I must refuse you. You will not receive my assistance."

Her lips curled into a snarl. "You are despicable."

"Possibly. But that hardly gives you the right to come into my home and say as much to me." His gaze settled on her tight lips. "Of course, what else should I expect from a lady turned brothel maid?"

"I saw what you did last night. I saw her scratch you." Her fingers whipped out to snatch his left wrist, and she yanked his hand up. Brandy sloshed over the rim of the tumbler he almost dropped. "I see that very scratch now. It is you. You were the one."

He clamped her wrist with his right hand, squeezing her sharp bones until she released his arm with a squeak. A flicker of pain crossed her face, and Fletch instantly dropped her wrist. But he did not let her escape him. He leaned down, his voice brutal. "Whatever you saw, Lady Natalia, you were mistaken. I am not in the business of saving virgins. You need to take your accusations and exit my home."

Rubbing her wrist, she stared up at him, not cowed by his words. No. It was only fire that lit her hazel eyes. Fire brewing with annoyance. Yet just when she looked ready to speak again, she instead shook her head, a muttered whisper slipping from her lips. "You are all the same. I should have never expected anything from a bloody peer." She stepped around him, quick to the door.

Within seconds, she had exited his townhouse.

Fletch spun, staring at the opening to the drawing room for long minutes, the cold blast of air from the door opening in the foyer dissipating around him.

The devil. He wanted to go after the brash chit. Wanted to help her. The urge was unmistakable—unexplainable, even as he attempted to deny it.

His heels dug into the thick maroon threads of the Axminster carpet. He couldn't risk the countless girls he could save in the future for one lost sister that had most likely long-since been sold from the brothel. If the Jolly Vassal was even where Lady Natalia's sister had been taken. No, he couldn't risk it.

Yet the waif still pulled at him. What was it that made him want to admit the truth to her—to help her?

The cut of her mouth, the tilt of her chin? Her hazel eyes drawing him in, pleading with him? She was beautiful enough, especially if she ate some meat and filled out her cheeks. But beauty had never swayed him before.

His eyes closed, and her face flashed in his mind. The one moment when her soul was bared to him. It was the fire burning in her. Her vitality. Her spirit drawing him in.

Youth.

Youth against all odds.

The thought hit him with uncharacteristic boldness, for he attempted at every turn to avoid self-examination. But there it was. Her youth was the thing drawing him in. Her youth was what he wanted to possess. Possess just a tiny bit of it while he still could, before death came for him.

Fletch shook his head, swallowing the last gulp of brandy in his tumbler.

Her hazel eyes were dangerous. And not at all simple. Complex blue strands twisted with brown in her irises, yet there was a modicum of innocence sprinkled into her intelligent gaze. A determined gaze that had pierced him with expectations that he be the man she needed—that he deliver the world for her, even though they had just met. Expectations he had no doubt he would disappoint.

He couldn't get involved. And she would involve him. He had known her for little more than five minutes, and he already fully understood he could not throw her away like he did so many of his trysts.

There was a reason he liked the company of widows. He liked them not only for their easy lack of commitment, but also for their acquaintance—their comfort with death. Nothing was permanent. They knew that.

And he knew Lady Natalia was not one to be tossed aside.

He was not about to do that to her spirit.

He was a dead man, after all.

{ CHAPTER 2 }

Talia set her shoulder to the wall, head bowed to make herself small as she moved to the next tiny room on the second level of the Jolly Vassal.

Chamber pot after chamber pot she had emptied during the past three hours, but at least now she had finally been allowed upstairs in the brothel. After receiving a few propositions, the last maid assigned to this floor of rooms had decided she would be better off making her coin on her back. So the witch that ordered all the girls about and doled out the pittance of pay for labor had sent Talia to service this floor.

Progress. At least in the fact that Talia could search for Louise in all the rooms of this floor. The guards at the end of the hall ensured Talia didn't move to the upper two floors of the brothel, where only the "experienced" maids worked. But if she kept her head down and emptied enough pots, Talia hoped she could find just one moment when she could slip past them and search the rest of the upper rooms. If Louise wasn't here, she needed to move onto the next brothel. She had already heard some patron's downstairs talking about the auctions at the Robin's Roost five blocks to the west.

Her knuckles hit the peeling paint on the door in the middle of the hallway, giving a quick knock. It took a moment before Talia heard a grunted "yes."

She opened the door and stepped in, only to see a naked woman standing, bent over at the waist and staring at her. Talia froze in the doorway. A half-dressed man, his dark jacket hanging off from only one arm, was straining right behind the woman, his face to the ceiling and hands on her hips as he grunted, thrusting.

Talia ducked her head, her eyes on the floor as heat swamped her face. "Me 'pologies, lady." The working women all insisted the maids call them "lady." Talia always adhered, even as she recognized the sheer ludicrousness of the hierarchy instilled in the most derelict of places.

Talia's feet shuffled backward as she tried to silently back out of the room.

"Stop, ye wench. Yer 'ere, take 'e pot."

Talia stilled, both horrified and humiliated. Without disengaging from the pumping man, the "lady" leaned to the side, grabbing the chamber pot. "Girl—'ere. Bloody litt'e idiot."

Talia took a quick step forward, holding out her hands while trying to avert her eyes to the floor by her toes.

Not close enough to hand it to her, the woman grunted, flinging the pot at Talia. "Out with ye."

The pot hit Talia in the stomach and she fumbled to catch it, the contents sloshing up and onto her chest. Talia swallowed instant bile, stumbling backward out of the room.

Clear of the doorway, she jumped sideways, kicking the door closed with her foot.

She could hear the guard at the end of the hall chuckling. Arse.

Her chin deep on her chest, the rancid smell of the pot filling her nose, Talia sped down the hall and past the guard.

It wasn't until she had made it to the darkness of the back alley that she took a full breath.

After dumping the chamber pot into the cesspit, she set it onto the squish of muck by her feet as she tried to scrub her hands clean on her apron. Lifting a mostly clean corner of her apron, she tilted her face high to the sliver of sky she could see between the rooftops, and she wiped the wetness that had splattered onto her neck, her tongue still deep in her throat to stay back the bile.

"Ain't worth payin' fer this bitch."

The garbled words reached her ears only a second before she realized they were about her.

In the next second a brute was on her, shoving her against the far wall, his thick mitt of a hand wrapped around the back of her neck, choking her to the wall, her face smashed into the rough brick.

Rage sent her body into a frenzy. Twisting, her arms thrashed. No matter how small, how unattractive she had tried to make herself—she smelled like dung, for heaven's sake—all these bastards saw was a hole to abuse.

Cold air hit the backs of her legs, her skirts lifting. She clawed against the brick, her throat crushed against the wall, cutting all sound. She tried to kick backward without losing her footing. No contact.

The struggle made his hand go tighter around her neck. Breath left her.

No air. No air. No air.

Her skirts still moved behind her. But her arms had gone so heavy. No air. She thought she was still flailing her hands, but she looked down along the wall only to see her arm had slowed, no longer reacting to her panic.

Her body ignoring her.

Her body leaving her.

No air.

She fought to keep her eyes open as she felt her body slide down the wall, slumping into a heap, her cheek sinking into muck.

Boots. Shiny boots, the glare showing even in the dark. Boots half buried in dung directly in front of her eyes.

The boots disappeared, blackness taking over.

～～～

Talia cracked her eyes open. The ball. She was going to make them late to the ball.

She had promised Mama she wouldn't fall asleep in the tub again, and now they would be late. Mama hated tardiness. Disrespectful, Mama always said.

She would just have to smile with extra innocence at Papa. He would defend her. He always did and he knew exactly how to erase Mama's sour moods. Papa would be her way out.

That meant she could sleep a little while longer. Her eyes slipped closed.

The warm water. So soothing. A wet bubble popped under her chin. Lavender.

Lavender?

Mama sneezed around lavender. They didn't keep anything of lavender in any of their homes.

Talia's eyes opened.

Panic wrapped her. Not her tub. Not her home.

Her body froze, even as her eyes flew about the room.

Do not panic. Do not panic. No sudden movements.
Memory shot through her mind.

She had no home. She had a nearly starved mother in Norfolk and a missing sister. She was a maid in a brothel. And she was in a tub?

The panic she was attempting to ignore turned into terror.

"You are awake."

The voice came from behind her. Where did she recognize the voice from?

Lord Lockston.

She moved her chin up a sliver, truly taking in the room. Dark wainscoting covered the walls, rich sconces evenly spaced within the panels and lighting the room. A green marble fireplace with high flames to her right. Tall, hunter green drapes closed off a window to her left.

And Lord Lockston behind her. She glanced down. She could feel she still wore her thin chemise. But the few bubbles covering the surface of the water were quickly disintegrating.

Pop. Pop. Pop.

What was she doing in a tub?

She swallowed, a lump sticking just past her tongue where sharp pain cut around her throat. The choking. The bastard in the alley. She must have fallen unconscious.

Talia opened her mouth, hoping her words would make it past the painful clamp around her throat. "Why am I in a tub?"

She heard rustling behind her. Boots clicking on wood. Lord Lockston was standing, moving.

He appeared to her right, his thigh hitting the lip of the copper tub. A quick glance upward, and Talia gave a slight exhale of relief. He was fully clothed. Trousers, waistcoat, jacket—even his cravat was neatly in place. Not a drop of water on him. Someone set her into this tub, but it wasn't him.

Or he had changed clothes.

She shifted uneasily.

Pop. Pop. Pop.

Her eyes lifted to meet his and she was struck at the grey of them—so unique in their lack of color that she wasn't able to read them.

"You are in the tub because you smelled like…shit. Please excuse my language, Lady Natalia, but there is no other proper word for it."

Talia laughed at the absurdity, both of his words and her current situation—whatever this situation possibly was. "I was covered in it. Of course I smelled of it."

His stony façade did not crack, nor did his eyes veer from her face, and for that, she gave him credit. He did have a madwoman sitting in his tub.

She glanced down at the water past the popped bubbles, verifying what she imagined—her soaked chemise had turned undoubtedly transparent. Her forearms slid over her chest. "Who stripped me and put me in here?"

"A maid helped me."

She nodded, her chin tilting upward so she could meet his eyes—read them—read anything about why he had brought her here and plopped her into a bath. In her old life, she would have been ruined ten times over by merely imaging this current situation. Good thing she was now just a maid in a brothel. Yet her arms tightened instinctively above her breasts.

He stared down at her, his grey eyes now nearly vibrating. Vibrating with…outrage?

The credit she had given him a moment ago disappeared with his next words.

"Look at you, you stupid girl. Look at what you have done to yourself."

"You have no right, Lord Lockston. No right at all to judge me." She shifted in the tub, water sloshing as instant hostility burned through her veins. She looked up at him, the side of her lip pulling back. "I will go to any depth to find my sister. I have only myself to do so, if you recall. And being a damn maid is the only way I can get into these places. I will find her—I will not be stopped."

"So you will heave shit and piss? Get buried in it? Have you no pride?"

Talia exhaled a seethed breath, shaking her head. A man of his station would never understand. "Pride will not find my sister, Lord Lockston. I have no other choice. Bring forth all your arrogant judgement, but there is no action beneath me when it comes to finding her."

He leaned down, his face dangerously close to hers. "You will be raped?"

Her mouth clamped shut.

He straightened, pulling to his full height, but his glare did not leave her face.

She shook her head, meeting his stare. "I do not think you understand the depths to which I will go to find my sister. I will do anything—anything it requires of me to find her."

"I am beginning to understand that."

"There is nothing for you to understand. You have no desire to help me, Lord Lockston. You made that perfectly clear yesterday morning. Why do you feel the need to interfere now?"

"I would not come upon the scene that I did in that alley and not interfere, Lady Natalia."

"Yes." Her eyes narrowed at him. "But you could have very well left me in that brothel."

A flicker flashed through his grey eyes, a flicker Talia didn't understand, nor had the energy to even try to guess at.

He shrugged. "I have decided to help you. You were right about what you saw two nights ago when I bought that virgin. You did find the right man, and I will help you to find your sister." He paused, his eyes leaving her face for the first time to look at something behind her head. His look dropped back to her. "But it will come at a price."

He spun away, walking to the door next to the fireplace where he stopped, but he did not turn back to her. "The bubbles are almost gone, Lady Natalia. There is a dress on the chair behind you that should fit. Wash the rest of that black crud and stench from your hair, and then put it on. I will speak to you downstairs in my study."

He left the room.

Talia stared at the closed door, fury steaming with each exhale.

The man was pompous. Insufferable. Overbearing. Condescending. A cad.

And also going to help her find Louise.

And aggravatingly handsome.

And respectful as possible, given the situation.

Talia heaved a sigh, grabbing the lavender soap from the tray next to the tub. She knew she should have been highly offended at his notice of the disappearing bubbles. But she couldn't quite conjure true offense at that particular infraction.

Yet what exactly was going to be his price for helping her?

~ ~ ~

Talia tugged the span of silk down along her hips. The cerulean blue dress had been made for someone shorter than her, without as ample a bosom, and she had to keep tugging the fabric down as it was wedged awkwardly under her breasts. The sleeves were short on the dress, the lace trim ending in the middle of her upper arms—completely inappropriate for the chill outside, but Lord Lockston's home was unusually warm. Or maybe it was just that she had grown accustomed to the constant chill on her skin.

Practicality aside, the silk almost made her feel like a lady again, though she had foregone the slippers that sat on the floor near the dress and tugged on her boots instead. Silk slippers would do her no good against the sludge on the London streets—especially the streets near her boardinghouse.

She had waited for a few minutes in the washing chamber for a maid or Lord Lockston to appear, but as she had apparently been abandoned, she was now tiptoeing her way through the darkness of the townhouse. Two lit sconces by the curved staircase were the only illumination against the night. It was still early in the morning—so early she heard no movement in the house—not even a cook clanking about several levels below.

From the foyer at the bottom of the stairs, Talia recognized the drawing room from the previous day. She spun around the hefty newel post and went down the center hall, peeking into dark rooms. It wasn't until she neared the back of the townhouse that she saw a warm glow of light past a half-closed door.

Stopping alongside the frame of the doorway, she leaned forward, peeking into the room. It was a study. A large, but not ostentatious room. Full bookcases lined one wall across from Talia, several large windows along the back faced a garden, and a wide fireplace with a black marble surround anchored the wall opposite the garden.

Lord Lockston sat in a dark leather wing chair facing the fire, his feet propped up on a leather-encased ottoman footstool. His thumb and forefinger balanced a tumbler of amber liquid on the arm of the chair. Talia could only see the edge of his profile, but his eyes were open, staring at the healthy fire.

She watched the flicker of light from the flames dance off his face. He was handsome, she had not mistaken that earlier. He possessed a strong but not too big nose, a chin that cut sharply to his neck, not a hanging jowl in sight. His brown hair sat slightly longer than fashionable, but it stayed off his face due to a natural swirl at his brow, setting his hair back. Individually, everything about his face was hard—intimidating—yet as a whole, he still radiated approachability.

The man was approachable, but clearly not by the likes of her. That was made apparent by their conversation yesterday. So what could he possibly want from her? She had not a thing he could not buy for himself.

Talia braced herself, adjusting the few pins at the back of her head valiantly trying to hold up her wet hair. Lord Lockston was about to demand a price, and she was about to find out if she could stand by her words—that nothing was beneath her when it came to finding Louise.

Clearing her still raw throat, she stepped into the room.

At her footsteps on the wood floor, his face turned to her.

Talia clasped her hands in front of her belly, wishing she had tugged once more on the dress before stepping into the room. "Thank you for your assistance in the alley, Lord Lockston. The happenstance of you or some other stranger coming upon that scene was my only escape."

"You are welcome. How is your neck?"

"Bruised. Nothing more." Talia swallowed. Talking felt like she was swallowing jagged rocks, but he did not need to know that.

With a nod, he stood, stepping behind the chair, his hand patting the top of it. "Please, sit, Lady Natalia."

"I would prefer to stand."

"I would prefer you to sit."

Talia eyed him. For all his approachable charm, his grey eyes were quite solidly set on this demand of her. She swallowed her innate defiance that her mother always chided her for possessing. She would be no closer to finding her sister if they stood at a ridiculous impasse in his study.

She walked forward, stepping widely around Lord Lockston's form as she tried not to notice how closely he watched her, his eyes consuming her every move.

Dipping down, Talia sat at the edge of the leather chair, her spine straight, her chin tilted slightly up as she watched him.

"You still sit like a lady. That is good."

"Why is that good?"

The left side of his mouth lifted in a wry grin. "We will get to that."

"You would like to start elsewhere?"

"Yes. I would like to start with what you saw at the Jolly Vassal the other night. With me buying the virgin."

"The reason why you buy virgins to save them?"

He moved to stand next to the fireplace and faced her fully. "Yes. But only if you can promise absolute discretion."

"I would no more want my current station in life to be discovered, than you would your business at the brothel."

"I imagined that to be so. Then we can agree to mutual confidence?"

Talia nodded. "We can."

"Very well. I do purchase the virgins to save them. You are right about that."

"Why?"

"I inherited this business from a close friend, and I do it because it is something of value I can contribute to the world." He shrugged. "My part may be small, but it is an act I can do for the way of good. How my friend's involvement in this business began is another story, but as it stands now, I purchase the virgins from the brothel, and then I hand them over to women who work for me.

The girls that are saved are given a choice—they can start a new life here in London with our assistance, or they can be delivered back to their homes from where they were stolen."

He tilted his forehead to her. "Which is what I assume must have happened to the girl from your village you spoke of—the one that told you of me."

"You do not know what happens to the girls after you buy them?"

"No. I deliver the girls to the women who can either guide them home or through starting a new life in a much better way than I ever could. That is what you saw when I set that one girl into the carriage the other night." His thumb rubbed the scab on the back of his hand. "I doubt that any of the girls ever even see my face, as they almost always have hoods over their heads until they get to the carriage."

A chill shot down Talia's spine. She had seen the hoods over the heads of the girls on the stage in the brothel—saw how they quaked, could feel their fear. She had vomited into the chamber pot she carried the first time she had seen it. Louise could have gone through that very thing.

Talia's head dropped, her chin tucking into her shoulder as bile threatened upward.

No. Do not think. Do not imagine.

"You are thinking about your sister's fate?" His question came soft, wrapped in concern.

She forced a breath deep into her lungs and looked up at him. Shaking her head, she couldn't stop the tears from welling in her eyes. "I cannot afford the energy wasted on imaginings. It does not bring me closer to the reality of finding her."

His grey eyes pierced her, waiting several breaths, waiting for her tears to fall. Talia held them in place, tilting her face upward. Tears meant defeat. And she was far from defeat. She would find Louise. She would.

"Exactly. Concentrate on reality." Lord Lockston took a sip from the tumbler in his hand. He shifted, setting his elbow on the fireplace mantel. "So the girls that choose to stay in London, they build a new life here, learn a trade or marry, whatever they desire to do. We have a home on Baker Street where they live as long as they see fit to."

"You think Louise may be there?"

"No. I am the only one that buys virgins, and I have not purchased any in the past weeks with the description you told me of your sister. There is no other way to find the Baker Street home except through me."

Her shoulders slumping, Talia's head cocked. "So why tell me of it?"

"I want you to live at the Baker Street house."

"No. I am quite comfortable in my room at the boarding house."

"That you are staying at a boarding house alone tells me it will not only be much more convenient, but also safer for you at the Baker Street house."

"Yes. But it is not mine—it is charity." Talia's shoulders straightened. "I have paid my own way at the boarding house. I will continue to do so."

His elbow slid off the mantel and he took a step toward her. "With what? You have already admitted you lack funds."

"I can afford the room with the pittance I get from the brothels." She bit down on her tongue. No matter that she had missed last night's pay after falling unconscious and ending up here in Lord Lockston's home—she could make her last coins stretch. Beg for more time from the landlady.

He took another step toward her, his knees almost touching the skirts of the silk dress. His voice hardened as he looked down at her. "You have worked at more than one brothel?"

"What?"

"You said 'brothels.'"

"Yes, there was the first one I worked at, the Seahawk Den, until I assured myself Louise was not there. Then I moved on to the Jolly Vassal." Her hands clasped together on her lap. Must the man know everything about her current situation?

"How did you find work at them?"

"I show up, talk to the barkeep. I came to realize quite quickly that establishments of nefarious dealings are always in need of maids to do the dirtiest work. It is hard to keep a girl emptying chamber pots when she is surrounded by a much more lucrative profession. The brothels hire and pay nightly."

"So you are concerned as well about being paid?"

Her chin jutted out. "I will not accept charity, Lord Lockston, nor be dependent upon any man."

His grey eyes narrowed, and Talia stretched her spine tight. She would have to fight him on this.

Instead, his eyes softened. Softened almost to coddling, if she believed the man capable of coddling. Which she didn't.

"Fine, Lady Natalia. Stay at the boarding house. That part of the deal was merely for your comfort."

"So we are finally to speak of the deal." Her forehead crinkled. "What is the price of your assistance in finding my sister?"

Lord Lockston turned from her, stepping around the ottoman to stand before the fire, his back to her. Several moments passed before he spoke, his voice low. "It starts with my great aunt—my Aunt Penelope. She raised me, my older brother, and my sister after my father died when I was seven."

"Where was your mother?"

"My mother died when I was four."

Talia eyed the long stretch of his dark jacket along his back, shoulder tip to shoulder tip. "You need me to do something for your aunt?"

"She desperately wants to see me wed. See the Lockston line continued."

"So do so."

"I would prefer not to."

"So then, do not do so. You are a marquess—with all the wealth and power that accompanies the title—no one controls you so what care do you have?"

He spun to her, his grey eyes skewering her. "My care is for my aunt. I love her dearly, and I do want to assuage her worry for me."

Talia shrugged. "So then do so. What do I have to do with any of this?"

"I would like your assistance, Lady Natalia. I would like you to accompany me to several events. I would like it to appear as though I am seriously pursuing you as my wife."

Talia jumped to her feet, hearing, but unable to believe his words. "You want me to what?"

"It will soothe my aunt's worry. It will merely take a few hours of your time every few days. You are the perfect candidate for the role, as you are a lady, even with your recent disappearance from society, but you are not attached to an overbearing family that would insist upon moving forward with a wedding."

A coarse chuckle erupted from her ragged throat. "You do understand I am a maid at a brothel, Lord Lockston, and so far removed from the *ton* it is entirely laughable?"

"Yes, but that is hardly common knowledge. And you have disguised yourself well—I barely recognized you in that alley tonight."

"So I appear as your possible intended, and you will help me find my sister?"

"Yes. That is the price I am asking. I do not think it too great a burden for you to bear. I will supply the clothing, and you will receive a few hearty meals at the events." His eyes dove to her left arm. "And from the looks of it, your body would appreciate a few full meals."

Her fingers flew to her upper arms, wrapping around the bare skin. Yes, her arms were skinnier than she would like them to be. But she didn't care for the gall of his opinion. "None of this, Lord Lockston—including seeing me in that bathtub—entitles you to make judgements upon my person."

Eyebrow cocking, he looked her up and down. Talia attempted not to fidget under his stare.

Silently, his eyes settled on her face.

"No judgements."

"I said nothing." He gave a half-hearted shrug.

Talia drew a breath, attempting to ignore the judgement running rampant in his look. She was skinny. Haggard. No longer representative of a lady. She knew it. But she also didn't need the fact tossed in her face. His help had better be worth this humiliation. "If I accept your trade, when will these events I am to attend take place?"

"The first one is tonight."

"Tonight—no, I have to work at the Jolly Vassal."

"It is an early event, a dinner. We will be excused to move on to the next affair while the eve is young, which will give you plenty of time to make your way to your…job."

Talia's eyes fell to the fire as her fingernails dug into the muscles in her upper arms.

Two choices. She could continue forth as she had been, alone, with no progress. Or she could accept his absurd offer and pray that the trouble of him was worth it and he could truly help her find Louise.

A week ago—days ago—she would have rejected his offer. But every day that passed with no evidence of her sister, with no lead to follow, was another day that Louise slipped further from Talia.

She looked up to him. He already knew her answer—the twitch of his lips told her so. She almost changed her mind.

Instead, she nodded. "I will play the part."

A restrained smile touched his lips. "Splendid. Then I would like you to call me Fletch. Only close personal friends do, and it will add credence to our relationship if you do so in front of my aunt. So you may as well begin."

Her eyes closed, her head shook in disbelief at what she had just agreed to. She opened her eyes to him. "I will do so."

He stepped toward her, setting his palm at the small of her back as he began to usher her out the door. "Do you prefer to be called Natalia? Or some other term of endearment?"

"Talia. It is what my family calls me."

"My carriage will take you to your boarding house so you can sleep. The maid should have already cleaned your clothes and placed them inside." They stepped through the doorway of the study. "Can you arrive back here early—six—by way of the mews? If you wear your maid's clothing, no one will note your presence. Plus, your clothes will be readily available to change back into after we are done and you leave. I will have a gown and a maid available to work your hair."

He opened the back door of his townhouse, his hand going to her elbow as they descended the three stairs into the pathway going through the dormant gardens.

"I will be here." She craned her neck to look up at him in the early morning darkness. "And you swear you will help me find my sister?"

"I promise. I will begin posthaste and I will do everything in my power to find her."

His voice held such conviction, Talia had no cause to question it.

His feet stopped as he looked down at her, his jaw slipping to the side. "I did not figure on this cold with that dress."

Talia looked down at her bare arms, goose bumps covering her flesh. She hadn't even noticed the cold with Lord Lockston's heat next to her.

He shrugged out of his jacket, draping it on her shoulders before she could protest. Just as she opened her mouth to do so, he started propelling her forward as he leaned down to her ear.

"I do not want to argue about my jacket. I rarely have to choose clothing for a woman, and I was the one that chose that dress, so I am the one remedying the problem. I will not send you home cold. But if you must argue it, do so quickly, as I am tired."

His words took every bit of resistance from her mouth. She offered one slow nod with a smirk as they stopped by the open carriage door. "As I am tired as well, I will save my defiance for another time, and instead, thank you for your chivalry."

"Chivalry?"

"Something akin to that. It has been a long time since I have been around a man with honor."

A frown settled on his face at the word honor. He grabbed her hand, helping her up the carriage step. "I do not know that it is honor that you see, Talia, but as far as our farce of a love affair goes, this banter will do nicely."

Talia settled into the plush velvet seat. "Find my sister, Lord Lockston, and I will banter with you until the end of days."

"Then, 'till the end of days, Talia." With an incline of his head he closed the carriage door.

Only at the last second did Talia see his frown deepen. Curious.

But she meant her words.

If he found her sister, she would trade her soul—do anything this man demanded of her.

{ Chapter 3 }

"You look most presentable tonight, Talia."

Talia's eyes shifted from the carriage window to Fletch. Her white-gloved hand ran along her lap, smoothing the rich peach silk of the gown she wore. "I am impressed you produced such a beautiful gown that fits me as well as this does. You did not know my measurements or have much time to do so."

He shrugged. "I took note how the earlier dress fit you, and had adjustments made accordingly. Quite simple, truly. You wear it well and look every bit the part."

A part. She had to remember that. She was playing a part in a show. She was not back in this world. This world of fine fabric that slid luxuriously across her skin. This world that offered the comfort of travel in a well-sprung, spacious coach. This world that demanded her hair be properly combed and piled high upon her head.

A part. That was all she was. An actress playing a part. She was still a maid. Still searching for her sister.

She offered a tight smile. "Did you not know it was this easy?"

"What is easy?"

"To transform from maid to lady? A fine dress and artfully weaved hair. It is all that is needed."

Fletch's mouth lifted in a half smile. "I do believe there is a little bit more involved. If not, I could have enticed any young maiden to accompany me before my aunt." He glanced out the window before looking to her. "Repeat to me how we met. I want to ensure our stories align in case my aunt corners you without me nearby to intervene."

"She would hound me?"

"And not think twice on the matter. You are forewarned—she is a canny one."

"It is good to know." Talia nodded, her bottom lip tucking inward. She wished she had slept more during the day, but the boarders beneath her were pounding about all day, creating what, she could not discern. She knew she wasn't at her sharpest.

Taking a breath, she set calmness to her face. "We met a month ago on Bond Street. I was in front of an apple cart, and I slipped on an apple core under my heel. You caught me as I fell, saving me from the mud of recent rain. You then set aside all propriety and offered to walk me to the Western Exchange. We walked, you purchased me an iced lemon, even though it was chilly that day. At the end of our first encounter, we agreed we would like to speak again."

"You might want to say you were besotted at first sight. That would play well." His mouth serious, Fletch's eyes twinkled in merriment.

"Do not stretch it." Talia's look went to the tight black fabric across the ceiling of the carriage as she held in a chuckle. She didn't want to encourage him. The man knew he was handsome and didn't need her verifying that fact. Her look dropped to him. "And must I truly admit to falling? I have excellent balance, and it is a strike against my dignity."

"I am afraid that is part of the story I told my aunt of our meeting. So yes, your ego will have to suffer the blow."

"It is not my ego. I just would appreciate to not be seen as a clumsy ninny upon our first meeting. Assumptions of my character will be made."

"Such as?"

"That I cannot stand upon my own two feet." Her gloved hand flew up, fingers waving. "That I am a simpleton that cannot look down to find sure footing. Or that I slipped on purpose to garner your attention."

"All that derived from a simple misstep of your foot?"

"Do you know nothing about how the female side of the *ton* conducts themselves, Fletch?" Talia leaned forward, her eyes determined. "I worked extremely hard to fit into this world, to adhere to the strictest of bounds when I moved within it. There was not a person that could mar my name or reputation. So I do know of what I speak."

Fletch smiled, his hand turning over, palm up to her. "And therein stands my point—not just any maid can become a lady. You, Talia, are the only one for this particular farce."

She sat back, groaning as she slumped against the plump, velvet-covered squabs. Instantly remembering her current clothing, she shot upright, her back straight. A lady's spine never touched the back of a seat. No matter how tired she was. No matter how aggravated she was by the man across from her.

Fletch chuckled. "You need not worry on your atrocious sense of balance. My aunt is not your normal matron of society, and she judges by only what she sees before her."

"Yet she judges. And therein stands my point."

"Understood." With a smirk, he tilted his head in deference. "We can add to the story that you were shoved by an overzealous pickpocket. It will add both drama and danger to the story."

Talia laughed. "Perfect. A pickpocket. That will do nicely and make you appear even more the hero."

"If it does, it does." Fletch smirked with an innocent shrug.

The carriage slowed, the clomping hooves of the horses ceasing.

Fletch quickly glanced down at his own attire, smoothing his lapels, and then he looked across to Talia. His grey eyes took in the whole of her, and with a satisfied nod he leaned forward, swiping an errant strand of hair across her brow back into her upsweep.

He approved, and it was strangely heartening to know that she could still look the lady—that he believed her to be one. His fingers leaving her, her heart started to pound in her chest as he sat back.

Talia watched Fletch pull on his gloves as they waited for his driver to escort the maid he had commandeered to act as Talia's companion from her outside seat to the townhouse. Fletch's trousers, jacket, waistcoat, and cravat were impeccable—the only thing out of control was his slightly unruly hair, which lent a rogue charm to his person. He was completely at ease in his power, completely at ease with his surroundings.

Talia could not help the spark of jealousy that ran through her—Fletch was not even aware that he enjoyed the luxury of complete control over his own capacity to care— or to not care—on everything in life.

Glancing out the window, prickly heat started to flood down Talia's back, her heartbeat flying even more erratic. What was taking the driver so long?

Time slowed.

Every movement Fletch made, slow.

She looked down. Her own fingers moved in a crawl. No, shaking. Her fingers were shaking.

The carriage door opened and Fletch stood, starting to exit.

Her arm weighing a thousand stones, Talia reached up to grab his elbow, stopping him.

He looked back to her and then immediately grabbed the carriage door and swung it closed. He shoved his body next to hers on the bench, crushing the side of her beautifully pressed skirt.

She stared at his leg. Not her smooth silk. Not now. Not the wrinkles.

"Talia?"

The word entered slowly into her head, but she couldn't lift her eyes to him. She could only stare at the dark threads of his trousers in the dim light of the carriage lantern. "I…I think I am going to be sick."

"Talia, a moment ago you were laughing at me. What is it?"

Her head started to spin. She was losing the threads of his trousers. Spinning. Her head whirling around her eyes. Her trembling fingers lifted, trying to reach her throat but were so heavy they could only make it halfway, falling to rest on her bare chest. "Hot…I am hot…breathe…I cannot breathe…cannot…"

Air stopped. Not a breath could make it downward to her lungs. Only to her throat. No air.

His hand went under her chin, lifting her face. "Talia. What is happening? Tell me. Now, Talia."

Her head shook, her eyes shutting as she forced what little air she had left from her lungs. "I—I cannot go back to this world. Cannot be in it. It betrayed me. It was my life and then it abandoned me. I cannot—cannot go through it again. The cuts. The pleas that were never answered."

She gasped, searching for air. "What we were reduced to. The begging. The fear. Just to have a place to sleep, to have food. It—this killed everything my mother was—once so proud—begging."

"Talia—"

Her eyes flew open, her breath speeding, gulping, as words flew. "You cannot imagine what that did to me, Fletch. I promised to never want this life again. To give these people the kind of power that they had over us. And I cannot—"

Her words cut as she jerked her chin from his grasp, the last of the air in her lungs gone, even as she panted, trying to breathe. Her eyelids squeezed tight, the heat invading every pore on her body as her stomach flipped.

"Open your eyes, Talia."

The spinning of the blackness in her mind intensified. She shook her head. Or she thought she did. She was going to vomit.

"Talia."

The sharp command snapped her eyes open. A hand. She had to force her eyes to focus on it, to understand what it was. Fletch's bare palm positioned right in front of her eyes.

"My hand, Talia. Concentrate on this. Trace the lines on my palm. From underneath my pinky to above my thumb. Don't think about anything else. Only my palm. Nothing else. Start on the right. Go to the left. Yes. Slowly. That is it. Now back and forth on just that one line, Talia. Back and forth."

She followed the sharp crease on his palm, across and back again. But then she lost it, her chest tightening. Her eyes slipped closed.

"Open them, Talia."

She cracked her eyelids.

"The line on my hand, Talia. That is the only thing there is. The only thing to concentrate on. Count the crosshatches along the line. Tell me how many there are. Count them out loud."

She gulped a mouthful of air, her eyes finding the line on his palm again. "One...two...three...four." What started as cracked whispers grew more solid with each expelled breath. "Five."

"Trace it back, keep counting."

"Six...seven...eight...nine...ten..."

"And back again."

Talia did so. Did it again and again until she had counted to fifty-seven. At fifty-eight, she realized her breath had calmed, her body no longer seized in unyielding panic.

She leaned back, collapsing against the cushions, every muscle in her body drained. It squished the back of her upsweep, but she didn't care. She wasn't about to pretend to be a lady at this point.

"You are back?"

Talia looked at Fletch. Concern was evident in his grey eyes, but beyond that, he didn't look the slightest bit bewildered. She had just acted like a madwoman, and he appeared to have taken it in stride. She exhaled a long breath. "Yes. I think I have recovered. I do not know what just happened to me."

He turned from her, drawing the curtain aside to look out the window. She hadn't even noticed him closing the curtains. "Are you ready to go in?"

"Yes." She wasn't sure that she was, but she didn't want to add any more to her current mortification by refusing to go into the party.

Fletch turned back to her. His eyes swept her face. "Good. But we will walk around the block before we enter to make sure you have your proper legs about you first." He leaned across her lap, grabbing her warm shawl from the opposite side of her and sliding it over her shoulders to wrap her.

Talia lifted herself from the cushions, eternally grateful for the few extra moments she would have to collect herself.

The cool evening air settling about her, calming, they walked in silence around half the block before Talia's fingers tightened on the crook of Fletch's arm. She looked up at him, watching the night lanterns cast bouncing shadows across his face. "How did you know how to do that for me in the carriage—your palm, the counting?"

"My sister was always anxious at balls. What happened to you was very similar to what often happened to her. She would be fine, happy one moment, and the next, she would not be able to breathe. Shaking." Fletch looked down to Talia. "That was what I would do to calm her, give her something tangible and solid to concentrate on. I took the chance it would work with you as well."

"It happened to your sister?" Talia scoured her brain. Fletch had mentioned a sister, but Talia didn't remember her. Had his sister been present at the one ball she had attended at the Lockston townhouse? She couldn't recall.

"Yes. Rachel. You are of similar age." Even in the shadows, she could see how his eyes softened.

Talia smiled. "It is clear you adore her. She is married now?"

Fletch's gaze flew from Talia, his eyes straight ahead. "She was married. She died."

His pace quickened, and Talia had to hop an extra step to keep up. Her fingers tightened around his arm. "I am sorry for your loss. Was it long ago?"

"Two years."

His stride went longer, and Talia had to stretch her legs to keep up. Evidently, he was done talking about his sister.

Minutes later, her breathing now quickened by the rest of the fast walk, they entered the dinner party. In the drawing room, Fletch made a straight line with Talia to his aunt, politely dissuading the many men stopping him for a discussion.

A bold yellow turban wrapping her head, Fletch's aunt pounded her cane on the dark wooden floors the moment she saw her great-nephew come into view across the room.

The banging rose above the general din of the crowd, producing an instant smile on Fletch's face.

He leaned down to Talia's ear as they weaved through the crowd. "That is the third cane I have gotten for her this year, as she keeps splintering them with all the battering she does. Her knees may be weak, but her arms more than make up for it."

Talia swallowed a giggle. She hadn't even met Aunt Penelope, yet she already liked her.

They halted in front of Aunt Penelope as she waved away a lady in midsentence sitting at her side on the long sofa. Miffed, her mouth half askew, the woman departed, glaring at Fletch. Aunt Penelope took no mind.

"This is she?" Aunt Penelope jabbed the air with her cane, almost touching Talia's belly. A wide swath of piled-upon necklaces sat upon her chest, the jonquil yellow turban matching the bright yellow wrap and gown she wore. Age had set wrinkles deep into her skin, but her eyes were the same lively grey as Fletch's—even more mischievous, if it was possible.

"Yes, Aunt Penelope, this is she." Fletch gently pushed the end of the cane down to the floor as he leaned forward to kiss his aunt's cheek. He stepped back to set his hand on the small of Talia's back, sending her a step forward now that the cane had safely been lowered. "May I present to you Lady Natalia Abbingale."

Aunt Penelope fished about her many necklaces, finding the blue ribbon attached to her quizzing glass. She squinted, one eye closed as she looked through the glass, her inspection running up and down Talia three times. Talia tried to keep the smile on her face tranquil under the scrutiny.

With a harrumph, Aunt Penelope leaned forward, the quizzing glass dropping from her eye. "Your cheeks are flush, my dear, and it was repeated to me that you two were in the carriage for quite some time before entering the event." Her shrewd eyes flew to Fletch. "Do I need to box your ears, Fletcher?"

He coughed, his hand flying up to mask the chuckle he attempted to cover. "You need do no such thing, Aunt Penelope. A short conversation we had in the carriage, that was all. Not even one unseemly moment was had."

"I'll believe that when I believe man can sprout wings and fly." Aunt Penelope turned her attention very pointedly to Talia.

Talia watched Fletch's mouth open with a retort, but then he clamped his lips shut, a wry smile settling on his lips.

"We are done with you, Fletcher." Aunt Penelope lifted her cane and poked him in the thigh. "Go. Leave me with Lady Natalia for a moment. I cannot speak to her with you hovering about, ready to muzzle a hand across my mouth."

With a nod, Fletch took several steps away, disappearing into the crowd and abandoning Talia to stand in front of Aunt Penelope. A composed smile on her face, Talia forced her hands to remain open, casual at her sides.

Aunt Penelope watched the back of Fletch until she was satisfied his location was far enough away. Her grey eyes moved to Talia. "I wish to speak plainly, dear. I am too old for anything less. Let me know this instant if you cannot handle what I say, and I will excuse you from my company."

Talia's smile froze in place. "I believe I can endure whatever you have to say. I prefer honesty as well."

Her cane hit the floor in a smack, sending vibrations under Talia's silk slippers. "Excellent, dear. Let us get to it, then. You are much different than the widows my nephew is partial to. I want to know why."

"Widows?" Talia glanced to her side, already wishing Fletch hadn't moved so very far away.

"Do not look over your shoulder for him." Her cane pounded onto the floor again. "Come, my dear, you must know of Fletcher's loose associations with women. He is partial to widows—exclusively, I believe—he likes to brush against death. But now he is not partial to them. He is partial to you. I want to know why."

Talia dragged a deep breath in through her nostrils, her smile unwavering. What did it matter what Fletch's aunt thought of her? She would be leaving London as soon as she found her sister, so she would likely never encounter Fletch's aunt again. She may as well tell the truth as far as she could. Her smile slipped away. "I am afraid I do not have an answer for you. I have only been back in London for a number of weeks, so I have not been privy to…whispers of Fletch's associations."

"No? Well, that is uncommon." Aunt Penelope's head tilted, the turban going slightly askew on her head. "Maybe you are uncommon. Perhaps that is the appeal."

Talia offered a smile. "Perhaps."

"Fletcher said you fell in the market and he caught you. Besotted you both were. The start of every fabled love story." She waved her cane in a wide arc, the end of it hitting a man to Talia's left in the shoulder. He whipped around, annoyed, then saw who was attached to the cane and merely took a step away, returning to his conversation.

Aunt Penelope's penetrating eyes sank into Talia. "But the story is a little too perfect, my dear. So tell me where you truly met my nephew."

"I…" Talia took another deep breath. What had she just decided? Tell the truth as far as she could. She braced herself. This was either going to go horribly awry, or awfully awry, so she may as well start forth. "I saw Fletch one day on the street, and I remembered him from a ball held years ago at his townhouse."

Aunt Penelope nodded, both of her hands wrapping atop the gold gilded pigeon with ruby eyes on the top of her cane. "I remember that. It was the last ball held in the Lockston house—the only one in the last six years. It was to celebrate his older brother's engagement."

Talia nodded. She hadn't remembered that particular fact, but she couldn't let that show to Aunt Penelope. She couldn't recall when his older brother had died, only that he had, but she wasn't about to show ignorance and ask about it. Her smile widened. "Yes. So after seeing him on the street, I approached Fletch a day later, as I need assistance with my sister and I imagined that maybe he could help me."

"What assistance does your sister need?"

"I am not at liberty to discuss her current situation, but suffice it to say, Fletch was very accommodating to my needs. And now here we are."

Aunt Penelope's grey eyes went to slits, her voice hissing. "That story possesses more crevices and cracks than the garish one Fletcher told me about your meeting."

Talia's heart sank. She had hoped to say enough to sate the older woman, but had only floundered in her explanation. And if Aunt Penelope hated her, that meant Talia held no use for Fletch. He now had absolutely no reason to help her find Louise.

"But I can see it is also the truth, dear, as far as you are willing to tell me. That, I do respect—the keeping of confidence you have been entrusted with." She patted the seat next to her on the Gothic-inspired sofa, its fabric an ostentatious damask featuring a mass of golden swans. "You may sit now, dear."

Talia's eyes went wide.

"Do not just gawk at me, dear. Sit."

Talia blinked, realizing she was standing still. Spinning so fast her skirts flew wide, she sat next to Aunt Penelope. She could not help but feel she had just managed an enormous victory where Fletch's aunt was concerned.

Aunt Penelope leaned toward her with a sharp tap of her cane on the floor. "Though you must understand that, at some point, you will tell me the full truth on the matter of your meeting my great-nephew. I will demand it, dear. But not tonight."

Talia squarely met her look. "I expect that you will. Thank you for the courtesy."

Fletch's aunt nodded, her eyes sweeping the many faces in the room. "I understand you arrived tonight with a young companion instead of your mother. Tell me, dear, how does your mother fare?"

"Oh." Talia's look snapped to the older woman. "I was not aware you knew my mother."

"She was a friend of Fletch's mother, Margaret, when they were young debutantes." Aunt Penelope shook her head, then righted her turban so it sat straight once more. "So very dreadful, the death of your father. And that new Earl of Roserton—do not get me started on his machinations. That is what happens when a far-removed relation is plucked from obscurity to head a title. A debacle ensues. That man has taken parliament by quite the angry storm."

"He has?"

Aunt Penelope's grey eyes went shrewd again. "Why yes, dear. Do you not keep up on politics?"

"I only just came in from Norfolk and am a whit behind in my knowledge of town business." She swallowed a longer exaggerated excuse. In truth, Talia hadn't bothered to keep tabs on politics in a long time. She had been far too busy finding food to eat.

"You have missed an abysmal show of the man, then, Lady Natalia." Her cane cracked into the floor. "Ridiculous, what the man has demanded of ancient families. Shame he is your family."

"Cousin Arnold is not my family." The words blurted out, irrepressible rage bursting forth before Talia could curb it. Her mouth clamped shut.

"You do not care for the man either, dear?"

Talia shook her head.

"You are in good company." Aunt Penelope's focus went back to the crowd. "So your mother, dear. How is she?"

"She is in Norfolk."

"Fine. Fine place to be this time of year. Excellent sport in Norfolk."

Talia's chin jutted out, her lips tightening. Norfolk was not fine with the bitter cold and a dwindling stack of scarce peat logs. Talia nodded.

"Your sister, Lady Natalia. When will her coming out be? This upcoming season? I understand you and your mother and sister withdrew to grieve, but as you are back in London, I can assume your sister will be presented soon? She is past age, is she not?"

Natalia froze, all moisture leaving her mouth. As boiling hot as she had been earlier in the night, an opposite chill swept her, draining all blood from her face.

They withdrew to *grieve*? That was the story Cousin Arnold floated about?

Aunt Penelope looked at her, her head cocking to the side as she stared at Talia's face. "Your sister, dear, what of her plans?"

"Aunt Penelope, tell me you have not extracted every last piece of information from Talia so there will be nothing left for me to enjoy in the wonder of discovery." Fletch's hand went onto his aunt's shoulder, drawing her attention away from Talia.

Aunt Penelope's gaze swung to her nephew, clearly miffed at the interruption. "I was just getting to that, Fletcher Bartholomew, and I do not appreciate your interruption in the matter."

"Alas, they are ready to go down to dinner and I would be honored to help you to your feet."

He leaned down, setting his hand under his aunt's elbow. She patted his cheek.

Fletch glanced over his aunt's yellow turban to catch Talia's eye. She mouthed a silent "thank you."

He lifted her elbow, and with both hands pressing down on her cane, Aunt Penelope made it to her feet. Talia stood next to her, hands at the ready in case she faltered. Fletch was right—for how very hard she wielded her cane, she was slight, almost fragile.

"I do not care for you trying to control me, Fletcher."
Aunt Penelope looked up at him as she steadied herself.
"But I am pleased you have finally brought a lady to me.
Impeccable lines, this one. Her father was a fine man. As
was her grandfather."

They started walking across the drawing room. Talia
trailed Fletch and his aunt, staring at the height disparity
between the two. He was tall—two heads taller than Talia—
and his aunt was a head shorter than Talia, even more so
with the stoop of her back. Yet the comfort with which his
aunt held his arm, and the way Fletch tilted his shoulder
down to her to ease the height she had to reach, told Talia
more about their relationship than words ever could.

She just hoped she had performed well enough tonight
that Fletch would not see fit to dissolve their deal.

~ ~ ~

Talia leaned back on the cushions in the carriage,
exhaling the breath she had held in the depths of her lungs
the entire party.

She watched Fletch move onto the seat across from her.
He had said little to her the entire night, leaving her to her
own conversations with people, but she had still felt the odd
security of him always just within reach. Always ready to
step in and save her from an uncomfortable conversation.
Or at least, she thought that was his intention. He could
have just as easily been ready to swoop in to save another
guest from her.

Loosening his cravat, Fletch settled his wide frame on
the bench, stretching his legs straight out on either side of

her calves. The man did take up a lot of room. The carriage started to roll forward.

"Was that overwhelming?" Fletch asked the question without judgement and without mentioning her earlier anxiety. "It appeared you did well."

"No. It was easy enough to act the lady in the life I once led." Talia tugged at each of the fingertips of her white gloves, loosening them from her fingers before she pulled her hands free of the fabric. Her belly fuller than it had been in years, guilt sliced through her. What had Louise had for dinner this night? Her mother?

She looked up at Fletch, ignoring how her stomach had started to churn at the thought. "I had assumed our expulsion from society was well-known. But apparently, the new Earl of Roserton has wanted to keep his reprehensible exploits far from the light of the gossipmongers."

"Just what, exactly, did the earl do to your family?"

Talia's lips drew in as her head dropped, fighting against the years of shame. But then she glanced up at Fletch. His grey eyes held only genuine concern. "Cousin Arnold was polite enough to wait until the day after father's funeral. Then he had a horde of men remove us from Rosevin, our estate in Suffolk. Our home. Nine men to remove three small ladies in mourning." Her throat caught on her words. "Mother pleaded with him, but it did not sway him. We could take nothing. Nothing. The clothes we wore."

She swallowed hard, her look going to the top left corner of the carriage. "It was the home I grew up in. Land I loved. Horses I loved. Chickens. Goats. Sheep. Dogs. I loved all of it. Every corner of that home. My bed. My room. And then…then it was just gone."

Her face tilted upward, the crown of her head hitting the cushion as she attempted to drain back tears that threatened. She never thought of Rosevin. Never.

"But surely your father provided for you? Your mother's thirds at the very least, dowries for you and your sister. A trust. A home for you to live in."

Talia's gaze remained on the ceiling of the carriage. Her head swayed back and forth. "He overlooked the necessity of it. Or it was destroyed—I do not know. My mother's dowry was tiny—we went through it quite quickly. And then father's solicitor died—he was the only one who offered to help us demand her share, and even at that, it was pity on his part. Since then, Cousin Arnold has effectively blocked any attempt we have made to claim her thirds—he has tied all the land into mortgages that must be satisfied— cutting all income. Even the provisions father made for Louise and me were verbal—nothing written. Nothing signed."

"Your father—what kind of a man does that to his family?"

Talia's eyes whipped down to Fletch, her voice harsh. "Do not. My father loved us. He was kind and he took the utmost care with us. You do not get to speak ill of him."

"Leaving a wife and daughters penniless is taking care of nothing."

"You do not understand who he was." Her fingertips went to her forehead, rubbing it. "Papa never would have imagined—he did not know this would transpire. If he had…he would have…he just never wanted to consider death."

"And he failed you in the process. He did not take care of you."

Her hand fell from her forehead, and her arms clamped across her ribcage. "He loved us."

"Love and responsibility are very different things, Talia."

She looked away from Fletch, staring out the window to the passing buildings. She didn't want to think on this tonight. Didn't want to defend against the same argument she'd had with herself countless times since her father died. Especially not after having to enter back into the world she had been ripped from.

"I meant no disrespect to his affection for you, Talia."

She nodded, unable to look at him.

"It is just that I am conditioned to think about death and all it entails."

Her eyes crept back to him. His aunt had mentioned his preoccupation with death as well. Now knowing he had lost a sister, as well as an older brother, Talia assumed it was hard not to be preoccupied with death.

"Your aunt—I am the first woman you brought before her?"

"The only one."

"She mentioned you like the attentions of widows."

Fletch bolted upright, his eyebrows high. "She what?"

Talia shrugged. "She said you like widows. She found me peculiar in contrast to them."

He groaned. "And now you know why I have never brought a woman before her. No one should be subject to her devilry."

"She adores you. Anything she says clearly comes from that particular place."

"I do not think I want to know the details of the rest of your conversation." He could not stop his head from shaking. "She approves of you thus far, that is the important fact."

"She said so?"

"No. She would never admit to such a thing. But I could tell."

Talia nodded. "Is there any news on my sister?"

"Not yet. Where can I drop you?"

"The boarding house. I have to change and darken my hair. My maid's clothes are with us?"

"Yes." A frown set onto Fletch's face. "So you are still determined to work at the Jolly Vassal this night?"

She nodded.

"I did not say anything earlier, but after tonight, after seeing you in that drawing room…it is not right."

"What is not right?"

"You working in a brothel. You are a lady, Talia—bred to be so."

Her chest tightened. He wasn't going to try to stop her, was he? That was not part of their bargain. "What you saw tonight were clothes, Fletch. Nothing more. Clothes and clean hair. I am the exact same person that appeared on your doorstep the other day. The exact same person slopping a chamber pot behind the brothel. I am far removed from the lady I once was. I have seen and done and heard too much to be the innocent flower I once was. Nor do I have any desire to rejoin that world. My only desire right now is to find my sister."

He nodded, but she could see very well he was arguing in his mind against every word she uttered.

"But the brothel, Talia, the danger. Do you think it wise to return there? You do have my assistance now."

"Yes, yet I am still woefully short on time, Fletch. Louise has been gone for a fortnight. And I cannot depend solely upon you to find her. Every day I do not find her is another day she…"

Her voice cut, unwilling to speak the possibilities she did not want to give credence to.

"I cannot convince you to let me handle the investigation?"

"Do not think to even try."

He sighed. "Then you should know, if you do not already."

"What?"

"Have you been to the top floor of the brothel?"

"No."

"I fear telling you this." Pausing, he rubbed the back of his neck. "The top floor—that is where they keep the girls when they come in, if you can make your way upward. There are three rooms, as far as I have been able to piece together from the Baker Street house women. The brothel does not want soused patrons stumbling in upon the girls, thinking they are free for the taking. So they keep them far above the other rooms. For all the horrid business of it, they do at least attempt to keep the girls pristine until they are auctioned off."

Talia gasped air, not even aware she had been holding her breath. "The top floor?"

"Yes. But do not do anything dangerous, Talia. If an auction happens tonight, I will be below, ready to buy her. You will recognize her, and you will pass by me, whispering to me which one is Louise. It is the safest way to remove her."

Talia nodded just as the carriage came to a stop in front of the boarding house. The carriage door opened and she gathered her skirts.

Fletch leaned forward, grabbing her wrist to halt her, his voice hard. "Nothing dangerous, Talia. Promise me."

Her eyebrows arched at his vehemence, at the intensity flowing from his fingers into her wrist. She nodded. "I promise."

He released her wrist and she stepped down from his carriage with something she had not felt in a long time.

Hope.

{ CHAPTER 4 }

Tip of boot. Skirt. Tip of boot with a new hole at the big toe. Skirt. Tip of boot.

All her renewed hope lost. Gone. Decimated in three short minutes in the top floor of the brothel. No Louise.

Skirt. Tip of boot with a new hole at the big toe. Skirt. Tip of boot.

In the twenty blocks she had walked, Talia had looked nowhere but at her feet. So deep into the night, she hadn't needed to watch for horses or carriages. The darkness heavy on her shoulders, she couldn't even manage to lift her chin.

Twenty blocks, and she didn't have a plan. Every step along the way for the past four years, a plan had always come to her instantly. Find somewhere to live. Plan. Find food. Plan. Find heat. Plan. Find work. Plan. Find Louise. Plan.

But now, in that very moment, she had nothing. Absolutely nothing. An empty well with not a scrap in it.

And the twenty blocks of walking had not sparked a single idea. There had to be something more she could do. There had to be. This could not be the end. She could not allow it.

Her toe caught on a chunk of wood from a broken barrel, and she stumbled.

She looked up for the first time since leaving the Jolly Vassal. Spinning, she tried to recognize her nearly pitch-black surroundings.

Hell.

She was in the alley she always took during the day and never at night. Never at night.

And now she stood in the exact middle of it.

She lifted her foot just as panic sent a shiver down her spine a mere second before a slight shadow to her right lurched. She jumped away, scampering.

A meaty clamp went around her wrist, yanking her to a stop and swinging her into a stack of crates. The crates tumbled around her and she fumbled, trying to wrench her arm free.

Her wrist was jerked upward and it lifted her off her feet before her hand slammed into the brick wall. She could hear pounding feet and crates flying into the air.

A silver blade flashed past her eyes.

A flurry of limbs swung around her.

Talia twisted, the blade searing through flesh along her side. She screamed but heard it only come out as a whimper.

Her hand dropped from the wall, freed, just as a black cloak wrapped around her, a strong arm along her shoulder propelling her out of the alley and onto the street.

Her feet stumbling to keep up the speed she was being pushed at, Talia shoved the top of the cloak from her face so she could see.

"Fletch?"

"What the hell were you doing walking down that alley, Talia?"

"You were following me?"

"Yes. All the way from the Jolly Vassal. Your fool head was down the entire time—you were taking no care at all— what the hell were you doing?"

"I—I take that alley during the day—but never at night—I didn't realize I had turned there."

"Why not?"

"I was…I was not paying attention."

"It is the darkest hour of the night, Talia. Why in the devil were you not paying attention?"

Her feet stopped.

Fletch's arm pushing along the back of her shoulders didn't halt fast enough, and he dragged her forward. He caught the front of her only a second before she sprawled face-first into the empty street.

His hands around her ribcage, he righted her. "Damn, Talia. What is this?" He pulled his left hand from her ribcage, holding it close to his face to look at it.

"What?"

"Is this blood?" He flipped his fingers to her.

"I…I don't know. The blade I saw must have nicked me."

Both of his hands went onto her shoulders, his eyes searching her face. "Nicked? If there's enough blood to get onto my fingers, it was more than a nick, Talia."

"It is nothing."

"Nothing?"

His forearms next to her jawline, Talia grabbed both of his wrists, meeting his eyes. "I don't care a whit about the nick, Fletch. I made it to the top floor of the Jolly Vassal."

"You what?"

"I made it to the top floor. I carried a pot and mumbled to the guard and he let me by. I found two rooms with girls in them. Frightened girls. But Louise was not there. They said she was taken away days ago."

The words spoken out of her own mouth jarred her—brutal reality she hadn't wanted to acknowledge slamming into her consciousness. She swayed, her eyes closing.

Fletch's hands dropped from her shoulders, catching her around the waist and ushering her further along the street before she could open her eyes.

"She is gone, Fletch. Gone." Talia wedged her hands up from the side of him and pushed, shoving at the side of his torso for no other reason than he was right there to shove.

His grip around her waist tightened, his gait not slowing.

"If she is gone, there may be record of it somewhere, Talia. Who bought her. They keep some sort of list of men that they invite to the auctions. I know because my name is on that list. That list exists, so it is very possible they also keep record of who bought which girl and when."

Talia stumbled. "She was there, Fletch. There and I missed her by two days. Two. Two bloody days. If I had gone to that brothel first I would have found her."

Fletch stopped.

Talia glanced up at the building to her right. They had reached the boarding house.

She looked to Fletch. He was making no motion to leave her. "You cannot come in with me. Mrs. Beezler will hear two sets of footsteps and come to investigate and I cannot lose my room here. She is very strict. She does not want her boarding house turning into a whorehouse."

Fletch looked up at the clapboard building, the front porch at a decided slant that gave evidence to the whole building sinking on the west side. "Where is your room? What is so special about it that you cannot lose it?"

"It is quiet. In the rafters. The only one at the top of the stairs. I can sleep during the day."

He nodded, his arm swooping down and picking her up before she realized his intention.

Talia swatted at his chest. "Fletch, what of you? Put me down."

"You are injured and there can only be one set of footsteps on the stairs, Talia," he whispered in her ear. "Now hush, or your landlady will hear us and you will be evicted."

Her teeth gritting, Talia held in the words she wanted to skewer him with.

Silently, Talia opened the doorknob and Fletch carried her up the three sets of stairs. She noted he made his toes sound light on the wooden steps. Already abashed at her current position in his arms, it only aggravated Talia more that he did not display even the slightest strain in carrying her weight. Not even a furrow in his brow. High-handed arse.

She opened the door to her room at the top of the stairs, and Fletch had to duck his head under the frame to step into the dark space.

Setting her down lightly, Fletch straightened next to her.

Thunk.

The darkness of the room hid her smile at what could only have been his head knocking into a beam. Not that she wanted her smile hidden. She wished he could see her smirk. The man deserved it after barging his way into her room uninvited.

"Let me light the lantern." Talia moved across the tiny room to the lantern on top of a small chest of drawers. Her fingers working the flint box nimbly, light flickered into the room as she lit two rushlights.

"This is a room?" Fletch whispered.

Talia turned to him. He was still hunched over, his head at an angle and his hair brushing the boards of the roof. "I am not as tall as you, so it suits me fine." She removed her apron and then unwrapped the long black handkerchief covering her head, her fingers staining black from the coal powder coloring her hair dark.

"Sit. I am looking at your wound."

"I will be fine, Fletch." Scratching free her hair, Talia set the handkerchief next to the pitcher of water on the chest of drawers. "It is just a gash. I can feel the blood on my skin, and it is not too deep."

"Pray tell me I do not need to explain to you the many things wrong with that statement." He glared at her. "Sit. I will check it. And I will be the judge as to whether or not it is too deep and needs further attention. I will wake my surgeon if necessary."

"It is not necessary. None of it."

"Sit." He glared. "Or I will be forced to be extra loud on my exit and wake your landlady."

Scowling, she tiptoed past him and sat on the bed. "Not fair."

"Nor was you getting sliced in that alley. I should have been quicker on that wastrel. Lift your arm."

Talia lifted her right arm, the skin along her side stretching and reopening the wound. She grimaced, searching the room for something else to concentrate upon as her fingers clamped onto the rough wood of a low-angled beam above her.

She twisted her side toward him. "And you did not need to follow me from the brothel tonight, Fletch." Her gaze settled on his face. "But I do thank you, in that you did so."

His right eyebrow cocked. "That is gracious of you."

"Just because I am miffed at you for forcing your way up here, does not mean I cannot be polite, especially when you helped me in the alley."

He nodded, dropping to his knees in front of her. His fingers went to the torn wool on the side of her black dress. Tugging at the fabric, he tried to see through the hole. He looked up at her. "The top of your dress, can we pull it down? I can see nothing through the wool and the layers beneath."

She jerked away, her right arm clamping down over her bloody side. "No."

"No? Shall I get the landlady to assist you instead?"

"A bloody devil you are," she muttered under her breath.

"What was that?"

"I was remarking upon what a fine gentleman you have turned out to be."

"You would not have asked for my help in finding your sister if I was a true gentleman, Talia. Fine gentlemen do not frequent brothels, purchasing virgins." He smirked, flicking his fingers upward. "Off with your dress. Just the top. I swear I will keep my eyes averted from delicate areas."

Her cheeks flaming, Talia turned on the bed. "Then unbutton me, please."

Fletch's fingers quickly swept down the line of buttons along her spine.

Gingerly, she peeled off the right sleeve from her arm and then shrugged the top of the dress off her other arm and down to her waist.

Sitting in just her chemise, she lifted her right arm again, aiming the area of the wound to him. She stared at the far corner of the room, refusing to acknowledge the fact that she was now sitting half-naked in front of this man.

Fletch looked at the side of her ribcage, his fingers rustling the fabric. "Your chemise is all bloody, and what is all this cloth?"

Talia hadn't thought she could be any more mortified than she had been a second before. She was wrong.

Her right arm dropped to her side, her elbow shoving his hands away as her left forearm went in front of her breasts. "It is binding. I do not want anyone in the brothel to know I have…"

"Breasts?"

The heat in her cheeks went hotter, spreading to her forehead. She nodded. "As much as you think me crass and an idiot for going to the depths I do, I do attempt to protect myself from my surroundings. I have made myself as benign as possible. Darkening my hair, wrapping my head, ill-fitting clothes, hiding my bosom, dirt on my face. I have tried to be as unattractive as possible so I am not approached."

"How has that worked for you thus far?"

Talia hedged her reply. "Other than the man behind the brothel and the man tonight in the alleyway, the few times I have been thrust into a situation with a forceful man, I have always escaped without a scratch."

His right cheek lifted, disbelief evident. "You do realize you forgot your teeth."

"My teeth?"

"They are far too white, too straight—that they even exist in your mouth is an obvious indicator you are not exactly what you pretend to be."

Her fingertips went to her lips, nails tapping her teeth. She had never considered her teeth. She should have been blackening them all along.

"Do you carry a knife?" Fletch asked.

"No. But that is a valid idea. I just do not own a knife. I have escaped those other men by acting very interested in what they propose to do to me. I talk fast and loud like a simpleton, and then I tell them I am diseased. They have always instantly dropped their hands from me."

"So what happened the other night behind the brothel when I had to remove the brute from you?"

"He closed off my throat before I could speak."

Fletch nodded, looking down at the red-soaked linen along the side of her ribcage. "The binding has to go. I cannot see the wound through all of it."

"No."

"Talia, you can see how blood-soaked all of this fabric is. I have to remove it. Or I can wait until you faint from lack of blood, and then do so without resistance."

He wasn't going to leave her room until he saw her wound—his grey eyes had hardened, telling her as much.

She exhaled, giving in, even though the thought of being even more exposed set her nerves on end. Silent, she slipped her arms out of her chemise, letting it drop to her waist and expose the binding wrapped around her chest.

She closed her eyes, lifting both of her arms and resting her wrists on the top of her head.

His knuckles slipping along her skin, he unknotted the tie of the long strip of linen on the side of her chest. Going tall on his knees, his head peeked through the crook of her arm to her back as he began to separate the tangle of the strip. She could feel his breath on her neck as he slowly unwrapped the length of the linen from her body.

His hands moved gently as they went around her torso again and again with the wrap. Taking care, she supposed, not to jostle her wound.

Talia wished she hadn't wrapped it six times around her chest—she barely made it through the first two torturous unfurls by Fletch's hands without pushing him away. His hot breath stayed even on her neck, his hair tickling her bare arm. The cold of winter was creeping into the room from the small window behind her back, but his heat warmed her against it. A fortress against the chill.

Her eyes still closed, she managed a shallow breath, but she was too close to him, and the scent of pine, brandy, and a sharp spice she couldn't name filled her nose. A scent that sent her back. Sent her to years ago, when she would twirl in ball gowns, drink punch laced with giddiness, and clasp hands with handsome men, fluttering her eyelashes. The men had smelled like Fletch. Clean. Crisp. Power. So simple and fun, the game of it all.

And then her world had imploded, scattering beneath her silk-slippered feet.

Fletch loosened the fourth layer, and her breasts won the fight against the fabric and stretched plump before her, aching against the submission they had been forced into.

The rest of the fabric fell to her waist. His head still over her shoulder, Fletch jerked back slightly as her breasts bumped into his chest.

Air hit her nipples, and Talia froze, her breath held, her eyes squinting shut.

But she could feel his continued breath on her neck.

The binding was off, and he was not pulling away. Her mind screamed at her arm to move. To cover herself. But she couldn't force even her pinky to twitch.

His hand moved up, his fingers wrapping around her left wrist on the top of her head. Talia jerked. Gently, Fletch pulled her arm down, setting it between them, her forearm covering her nipples from the air.

"May I pull away, look at the wound now?" His words were soft in her ear, his lips almost brushing the skin of her cheek.

Air still lodged in her chest, she nodded.

He pulled away, setting himself to her side, his fingers running along the bloody skin over her ribcage. With an incoherent grumble, he shifted to his feet and went to wet a cloth that hung next to the small basin of water on the washstand. Talia cracked her eyes open, watching him.

He came back to her, dropping to his knees once more to dab at the skin around the wound.

It stung, but Talia bit the inside of her lip, refusing to loosen from the statue she had coerced her body into.

In silence, Fletch dabbed at her skin for minutes, cleaning the wound.

He cleared his throat. "You did not scream when the blade sliced you in the alley."

Talia stared at the top of his head, focusing on the haphazard swoop of brown hair near his forehead. "Screaming does me no favors. Not in my life now. Not in my world. Screams announce weakness, and there are too many that prey upon weakness." She said it without bitterness, just simple acceptance.

He glanced up to her, his eyes falling quickly back to her side. "Life has reduced you to that viewpoint?"

"Life has opened my eyes to that viewpoint."

His fingertips slightly pulled at the skin aside the cut to see the depth of the wound.

Pain shot through the nerves to her belly, and Talia closed her eyes, sucking in the sharpness with a hiss.

Fletch grabbed the edge of the linen wrap, tearing off a clean swath of the fabric. He folded it, holding it over the wound. "The cut is not too deep. It does look like the blood has slowed. But you should lie down and hold this over it until it stops completely."

Keeping her forearm in front of her breasts, Talia shifted her left hand under his to clutch the wad of linen to the wound. She stretched out awkwardly onto her left side, still trying to cover her breasts.

Fletch stood, picking up the bloody linen wrap to set it on the chest of drawers. He swished his fingers in the bowl of water.

Talia watched the back of him as he rinsed the blood from the linen in the bowl, surprised he bothered to stop to do so. Even in these movements—the smallest task—he was at ease, so sure of himself.

"Do you know that we danced once, long ago, Fletch?"

He glanced over his shoulder at her. "We did?"

"Yes. It was at a ball at your home years ago. Your aunt said it had to have been your brother's engagement celebration. Your name went onto my dance card early in the evening, but by the time the dance came about, your eyes were glazed over and you had settled on a widow—Countess Gillison, I believe it was. She was beautiful. I do not think you looked at me once."

He twisted the fabric above the bowl, squeezing the water from it. "I do not remember that."

"No. But I do. I liked your eyes, even if they never settled upon me. The grey in them. That was how I recognized you at the Jolly Vassal. Even in that dim light, I recognized the grey. It was why I followed you down the street after you bought the virgin. I could not believe it was you."

Fletch opened the top drawer of the chest and draped the linen over it to dry. He turned around to her.

"Sleep, Talia. We will discuss your sister tomorrow and what the next course of action will be." He walked over to the foot of the bed, quickly untying her boots and setting them under the bed before grabbing the one thin blanket and setting it over her body, tucking the top edge on her neck.

"My carriage will be by at four to pick you up for the event you will be attending with me tomorrow evening. I will have a new dress delivered during the day for the occasion, and I will procure the same maid to act as chaperone for you. The last thing I want is to have scandal touch your reputation."

She smiled up at him, drowsiness hitting her as the tight hold across her breasts finally loosened now that she was covered below the blanket. "You have thought of everything."

"At least as much as I can foresee. Even as you continue to toss mayhem my way."

"Mayhem. Generous of you." A soft chuckle floated from her lips. "Thank you, Fletch, for looking at the wound."

He stepped to the doorway, his hand on the doorknob as he looked back and winked at her. "Thank you, Talia, for letting me look at it."

He slipped out the door, quietly clicking it closed. She could not even hear his feet creaking the floorboards as he moved down the stairs.

She hadn't thought he would do it. Remain a gentleman. But he had kept his promise to not look.

Now she just hoped he could keep his other promise to find her sister.

{ CHAPTER 5 }

"We are to be outside?" Talia asked, lifting the edge of the thick wool cloak draped over her arm.

Fletch looked across the carriage interior to her, a smile playing on his lips. "We are."

Talia nodded, her attention going to the window as the coach jolted to the left after hitting a deep rut in the street. It was a pleasant enough evening—the bitter wind had finally ceased, but darkness was quickly stealing the warmth the sun had created that day.

"Where?"

"Vauxhall Gardens."

Talia's throat instantly tightened. "It is not closed for the season?"

"It has opened for a special exhibition of cold weather animals. They have turned it into a fair that will last five days. It would not be my first choice of entertainment for the evening, but my aunt's friends are gathering there. All will want to look you up and down."

Talia glanced to the window. They were crossing the river. Fingers clutching her skirts under her cloak, she looked to Fletch. "I do not think I can go in there."

"The gardens?"

She nodded.

Worry creased his brow. "You are concerned with the people or the venue?"

"Both. I am sorry. Had I known this was the event you wished to go to, I would have told you before you went to all this trouble."

Fletch leaned forward, his forearms balancing on his knees. "Talia, I think you can do this. It is near winter, so the gardens resemble nothing like their appearance in summer. As for my aunt's friends, first, my aunt has decided she likes you, and second, I will not leave your side. I will not be drawn away by acquaintances that I must chat with here. Tonight, you need only to smile and nod your head."

His tone was soothing, yet her heart started to speed, thudding hard in her chest. Fletch was logical. Too logical, and for that alone she didn't want to disappoint him. She had to ignore the fear gripping her. She had promised him she would help him, play this role. She could do this for her sister.

Her head tilting to the side, she gave the smallest nod, her eyes skittering to the window to avoid his stare.

A role. She was a besotted admirer of Fletch's, hoping for a marriage proposal. She needed to concentrate on that. Concentrate on acting the role.

Think of nothing else. Just Fletch.

His grey eyes. The humor that easily crinkled his cheeks, drawing dimples. His calm. His strong jawline, always sprinkled with stubble late in the night that her fingertips ached to trace out of sheer curiosity. His uncanny prowess to appear at the right time to save her from danger. His ability to take the utmost care with her. His gentle hands.

The list of Fletch's fine qualities manifested far too easily in her mind and Talia shifted slightly on the bench.

Apparently, the role of a besotted admirer was not going to be hard to play.

The carriage stopped, and Fletch stepped down from the interior. He took her fingers to help her descend, and she could feel the warmth of his hand through her kidskin glove. Light snowflakes had started to float through the air, sparkling under the line of lit lanterns along the front brick wall of the gardens.

It was the warmest she had been in the cold air in years. She wasn't sure whether it was due to Fletch's well-chosen dress and cloak for her, or if it was due to Fletch's solid arm next to hers as she slipped her hand into the crook of his elbow.

Either way, she was warm, her teeth not gritting hard against clattering.

Her hand tucked along Fletch's arm, they started walking and Talia could hear the music and liveliness inside the gardens.

Her feet stopped.

Fletch paused, looking down at her.

"You can do this, Talia. You can walk in here with me." For as demanding as his words were, his tone was nothing but soft and compassionate. "You already know my aunt and I swear I will not leave your side. You can do this."

"I…I…"

"You cannot avoid everything of your past life, Talia. It will always chase you, and eventually, you will need to meet it and resolve it."

He was right. Logical. She knew that. She looked up at the proprietor's house that held the entrance to the gardens, staring at the Vauxhall sign above the doorway. Yet logic didn't make her steps any easier. Didn't make her heart slow to a normal pace.

She gave herself a quick shake, taking a deep breath. He would soon start to think her insane if she didn't collect herself. She met Fletch's eyes and nodded with renewed will.

He patted her hand on his arm and tugged her forward.

Inside the gardens, rather than to find his aunt directly in the crowd, Fletch strolled them past the exhibits of penguins, seals, a walrus, three foxes, white hares, a family of puffins, and a polar bear. As much as she found the animals interesting, Talia guessed it was a consideration by Fletch, giving her time to ease into the situation before he brought her in front of his aunt.

Fletch's kindness of stalling almost worked, but the knot in her stomach refused to ease. Vauxhall did look decidedly different, as all but the most stubborn of leaves had fallen to the ground, lending an airy, open look to the gardens. But she still knew this place. The buildings. Could not forget what happened here.

Fletch leaned down to her ear. "Brace yourself. We approach my aunt and her stable of dragons."

He pointed them to several tables set on the grounds near the tall orchestra building. Talia quickly spied his aunt, seated at the side of the longest table, watching the crowd with hawk eyes. Six other matrons sat with her, their furs piled high against the cold.

Talia leaned into Fletch. "Dragons? You said your aunt liked me."

"She does. But I did not include her friends in that assessment. They are an entirely different mountain to scale."

She swatted his arm, the motion pulling at the wound on her side from the previous night. "You could have warned me."

"I was trying to calm you, not aggravate your anxiety."

"You just did." Her hand tightened around the crook of his elbow, her feet slowing as her eyes drifted up. The orchestra building. The musicians had broken from their last set of music, standing and stretching their legs in the open upper level of the octagonal structure.

Not here. Why did Fletch's aunt have to be sitting here?

Talia made her gaze drop from the musicians to his aunt at the table.

Play the role. Do not look up. Do not remember. Play the role.

She forced her cheeks to pull back, forced the corners of her mouth to lift.

"Fletcher, what has you dawdling so?" Aunt Penelope was already jabbing her cane in the air at Fletch. "I have been waiting for you to make an appearance."

"And you have forced us to bear the brunt of her impatience," an elderly woman to the left of Aunt Penelope grumbled, frowning.

"No more harm than me having to bear the brunt of your current infatuation with your first great-grandson, Edith." Aunt Penelope knocked the side of her cane on the table. "Come, sit with us, Fletcher and Lady Natalia. I had to send Doreen and the dowager duchess away to procure some mulled wine—truly, just to gain their seats when I saw you approaching."

Fletcher and Talia stopped in front of Aunt Penelope. "As much as you would like us captive in chairs, Aunt, we are not about to steal seats from those two. Must you insist on antagonizing them so?"

"They deserve it," Aunt Penelope said. "They had the gall to make the animal keeper bring a penguin over to me. Atrocious little animal. The little bugger pecked at my leg."

"Not the one with gout?"

"Yes, the one with gout, Fletcher."

"Talia rather liked the penguins." Fletch looked down at her, a side smirk on his face. Devil. "She thought they were delightful."

Talia's eyes dropped from Fletch and she conjured an empathetic frown as she looked at Aunt Penelope. "I did, but I was not close to them. Now that I know they are entirely rude with their beaks, I have changed my opinion thusly."

The cane slammed onto the ground, but only a thud emanated from the cold dirt. Aunt Penelope frowned, though it appeared to be more at the lack of sound from her cane than at Talia. "Do you lack steadfast opinions, dear? Or are you patronizing me?"

Talia smirked. She should have known Aunt Penelope would hold her to honesty. Rather why she liked the woman so. She offered an apologetic smile. "I do still think the penguins are rather adorable. But best to be admired from afar, I suppose is the lesson."

The end of Aunt Penelope's cane tapped on a leg of the table. "That it is, dear. Come, step closer, I must introduce my friends to you."

Above Aunt Penelope's head in the open-air orchestra building a violinist pulled his bow across his strings, warming to the next set. Just as Talia stepped to stand in front of the first woman next to Fletch's aunt, the grumbling Edith, Aunt Penelope's voice was drowned out as the musicians began their next set of music.

A fast quadrille, the notes sped to Talia's ears.

Instantly, she stumbled backward, her hand dropping from Fletch's arm.

But the music didn't stop.

Whirling dizziness set into her head, and Talia spun, trying to escape the notes. Yet the notes only surrounded her louder, smothering.

Pushing through the crowd, Talia ran. Through the people. Twisting down the lanes of the gardens. Slipping on the frozen ground.

Still the music gripped her, clutching and tearing at her sanity. Her heart flew out of control and she gasped again and again for air, clutching her stomach as she sped past the dormant trees into a dark lane of tall evergreens.

Still, the music held her captive.

Her feet flew out from under her, an arm clamping around her waist.

"Dammit, stop, Talia." Fletch's voice was in her ear.

She tried to twist out of his arm, the tips of her boots pointing, scraping for the cold ground.

"Stop, Talia. Stop. Why didn't you stop? I've been chasing—yelling at you."

She jerked, trying to contort her arms free from the cloak, her fingertips jabbing behind her into his stomach to free herself.

"Stop. Stop twisting. Stop running and I will put you down."

No air. There was no air to breathe. Talia's eyes went frantic, her panting out of control. Where was the air? What did Fletch do to the air?

"Hell, Talia." Not letting her escape his arm around the front of her waist, he set her onto her feet, his free hand pushing down on her neck so she folded in half.

He bent with her, his mouth near her ear. "Close your eyes, Talia. Close them. Breathe. Breathe. Open your eyes and look at your feet. Breathe. Hold that breath. Try again. Breathe. Hold it. Longer. Hold it. Let it go. Another one. Hold it."

His words made it past her panic and slowed her. Talia latched onto the last breath, holding it as he commanded. Only when he told her to exhale did she do so. He repeated it eight times until her breathing was controlled once more, if not her heart or head.

His hand moved from the back of her neck to her shoulder, and he pulled her upright. His arm left her waist and he rounded her, both of his hands clamped on her shoulders as he bent so his face was level with hers.

"What was that Talia? Why did you run away?"

"I am insane, Fletch." She craned her head to the side, needing to escape his look. At least this lane was empty, no one but Fletch to witness her madness. "Leave me. I can make my way home. I will return the clothes. I will not bother you again."

"No, Talia, I am not leaving you."

She tried to duck and spin away from his hold.

His grip on her shoulders tightened, and he gave her a little shake. "Talia. Answer me. What made you run?"

She wanted out. She needed to leave here. But Fletch had her captive. She needed to escape him. Her gaze crept to his face. His grey eyes looked hooded, dark in the shadows of the lane. She looked away. "I am mad—crazy. Just leave me."

"Or you can tell me what made you run and I will decide if you are deranged or not. I will not—"

High-pitched laughter floated through the air to them, interrupting Fletch's words. A deep baritone chuckle joined in, and a partially entwined couple passed by the end of the lane.

Fletch's eyes went above Talia's head, searching the evergreens. "Here." His hands dropped from her shoulders, but only to slip an arm behind her waist and steer her several steps to a small alcove denoted in the evergreens with a white wooden arbor.

He turned her to him in the relative privacy of the nook, blocking the entrance as he lifted one hand to rest lightly on her shoulder. The music became muffled with the surrounding evergreens.

"Was it my aunt? Why did you run, Talia?"

Under her cloak, her arms clasped together over her belly as she realized that Fletch now had her even more captive. She drew a breath that shook her chest as it descended into her lungs. *Tell him.* If she told him, he would let her leave this place. "The music. It was the music, that piece." Her words were barely audible.

"The orchestra?"

For all the times she had refused to allow herself to remember, Talia now had to force her mind to acknowledge the memories that were threatening to drown her.

She closed her eyes, her voice a whisper. "I was here when Papa died. I was here and happy and laughing with friends. Our butler appeared. He told me here. In front of my friends. In front of everyone."

Her head dropped, her words shaking. "He told me during a break in the music so I could hear him. He told me and then they started that same tune. The exact same one. The music drowned out his words. My friends. It drowned out everything."

Silently, Fletch's fingers tightened on her shoulder. To steady her or to keep her from running again, she wasn't sure.

She lifted her head, her eyes opening to him. "Everything stopped that day. My friends stopped talking to me. The laughter stopped—the happiness. And the sadness became so overwhelming I could not bear it. So I went numb. Numb, and I have only been surviving since that moment." Her arm swung out to the direction of the orchestra building. "Since that moment in that very spot where your aunt is, I have not felt a thing. Just survival. I know what I should be feeling, but everything is numb. Everything is nothing except for the panic. And the panic is huge and it was exactly where your aunt was and I just needed to escape it."

Fletch nodded and his right hand lifted from his side. Achingly slow, he dragged his thumb across her cheek, wiping a rogue tear away.

"I am a madwoman, Fletch. I know this." Her eyes fell closed as her head shook, his thumb rubbing along the side of her face. "Do not burden yourself with me, Fletch. I cannot help you. You picked the wrong woman for this."

His hand on the side of her face slipped downward, wrapping along her neck.

"Tell me if you feel this, Talia."

Before she could open her eyes to his words, his lips were on hers, his heat an instant fire to her chill. She didn't resist—couldn't resist for the fire that spread through her body as he opened his mouth, his tongue slipping past her lips.

He teased her, gentle as he took control of her senses, took all of the panic that was threatening to pull her down to hell. He pulled her back to the present. Pulled her into the moment where there was only him right in front of her. His breath weaving with hers. The leather of his gloves slipping under the back of her cloak to caress the bare skin of her neck.

He pulled away. "Did you feel that, Talia?"

She dragged her eyes open to him, not wanting to leave the moment. The light flakes of snow fell about his head, melting the second they touched his hair. As much as she didn't want to—as much as everything was wrong in her life—this she felt. She couldn't deny it.

She nodded.

"Good. I did too."

He bent again, capturing her mouth without preamble. Harder this time, control evident in every movement. His teeth caught her lower lip, sucking, playing with the delicate skin. The rawness of the scruff along his chin should have hurt, but instead, only elevated her senses, helping her to take in every nuance of his mouth on hers.

Her arms lifted on their own accord, wrapping around his neck. She damned her gloves in that moment. She wanted to feel his skin, feel his warmth under her fingertips. Fletch had no such problem, for his suddenly bare fingers danced along the back of her neck as his left hand found the front opening of her cloak and slipped inside, wrapping around her waist.

He pulled her into him, his arm pressing her hips into his body. Hard—every bit of his body hard against hers.

A low sound, softly guttural, escaped from the recesses of her throat with the motion. Sound she didn't recognize but fully owned as her lips met his, aching for more of his fire. His fingers traced down the side of her neck, slipping down between their bodies to breach her cloak. Finding her left breast under the heavy fabric of her dress, he cupped it, his fingertips collapsing around the nipple, rolling it through her dress and stays.

He swallowed her gasp at the touch, and she could feel him smile at her reaction. His fingertips moved, finding bare flesh above the cut of her gown. They slid downward, teasing skin alive and shoving stubborn fabric. Cold air hit her nipple for the merest second before being captured by his palm, by his thumb and forefinger playing, making her strain.

She could feel him revel in how he could make her body react to his touch, arch into him. Fleeting wonder flashed through her mind at how she had so quickly and completely surrendered all control to him. Yet she could not pull away. Could not abandon the first true feeling she'd had in years.

Heaven help her, she didn't want her feet to land on this man, to find footing in his world.

His world—her old world—had betrayed her before.

It would again, she had no doubt.

But was it already too late?

~ ~ ~

"I raised you better than to maul a lady in the gardens, Fletcher Bartholomew." Aunt Penelope's voice cut sharply into the night air, her cane swinging at the evergreens behind Fletch and sending needles flying through the air.

Damn.

Fletch jerked away from Talia, his hands dropping from her body after instantly yanking up the top of her dress. Talia stumbled a step backward at his sudden lack of support, but she caught herself before he could reach out to steady her.

What could have been seen from the angle? Everything? Nothing?

He turned to look out of the alcove. Leaning heavily on her cane, Aunt Penelope took two steps toward him.

"Aunt Penelope, you have come upon—"

"I know exactly what I have come upon, Fletcher. We thought to follow you and offer assistance to Lady Natalia, as she was overly distraught. I imagined it was your doing and it would be better if I comforted her. Yet, perhaps it was a farce so you two could escape to the deep corners of the gardens. Despicable. I thought Lady Natalia a fine miss, but

I can see now she is somewhat suspect as a lady. Perhaps she has lost her sense of propriety in the years since her father's death."

Fletch stepped fully in front of Talia, his hand lifting behind him to grab her arm and hold her in place when he felt her start to move around him. "Talia has lost nothing, Aunt."

"Do not take that tone with me, Fletcher."

"The fault of that display was mine alone, Aunt," Fletch said. "It does not and it will not besmirch Lady Natalia's reputation."

"No?" Aunt Penelope slammed her cane into the cold ground. "My friends just saw the very same thing I did, Fletcher. Who do you think walked me back here?"

His hand still pressing Talia backward, Fletch took a step forward to look around the corner of the evergreen alcove. The devil. The dragons were already converging. A growl rumbled from his chest.

Before he could turn back to his aunt, Talia tore his hand from her arm and skittered around him to move out of the alcove. She stepped into the lane, and he saw Talia's face fall as she spotted three of Aunt Penelope's friends at the end of the walk, moving away slowly, their three heads bent together. He could only imagine the conversation.

Aunt Penelope moved her fragile frame in front of him, skewering him with her grey eyes. "Idiot boy. You do that business in a hallway. A coach with the curtains drawn. A dark study. In the carriage house. Hidden in a willow tree. Behind draperies. You do not do that in public. At least go farther into the gardens, Fletcher."

His aunt knew far too many places for a clandestine tryst. He glanced over his shoulder at Talia. She was still watching the dragons at the end of the walk and he could see her anxiety rising, starting to spin her head. Dammit. He had just calmed her, and now this.

Fletch's eyes swung down to his aunt as he turned to her. "I did not imagine an audience, Aunt."

"No. But there you have it. You had one." She swung her cane up to point at her retreating friends. "You say you do not want this to besmirch Lady Natalia's reputation, then you make good on your lewd actions, Fletcher."

Grumbling to herself, she spun as fast as her ancient bones would let her, hobbling away, her cane digging with fury into the ground with every step.

"Walk away, Fletch. I meant it earlier. More so now." From behind him, Talia's soft words floated up to his ears.

"What?" He didn't turn around to her, his voice coming out through gritted teeth.

"Walk away from me right now. Walk down this lane with your aunt. I do not have a care for my reputation. You know that. I am so far removed from what this is—this life—what your world is. It is not where I belong anymore. So walk away, Fletch."

He stared at his aunt as she joined her friends at the end of the lane. "I am not about to abandon you in the middle of Vauxhall Gardens, Talia."

"So take me home and walk away."

He turned around to face her. "I am not about to abandon you at all, Talia."

She shook her head. "If you happen to find the man that bought Louise, you can send me a note with any information. But I hold you to no obligation. You can be done with me. I have not fulfilled my end of our deal, as I have not helped you at all. And now I am no longer of any use to you. Do not let misplaced honor hinder what you need to do. Walk away, Fletch."

He leaned down, his mouth next to her ear. "I am not abandoning you, Talia. So you can cease your attempt to be rid of me this instant." The vehemence in his own words startled him.

She blinked hard, her head craning backward.

He stepped to her side, holding his elbow out to her.

Her hazel eyes wide, she nodded, lifting her hand. She let him place her hand into the crook of his elbow.

Without another word, he marched them straight past his aunt and her dragons, and out of the gardens, his head held high.

He gave Talia no choice but to follow his lead, and out of the corner of his eye, he noted that she lifted her chin as well. Her steps were unsteady, he could feel it as she gripped onto his arm. But her eyes were level. Her face serene.

Still the lady.

And he found himself inordinately proud of her.

CHAPTER 6

A man snatched her upper arm, stopping her, and he leaned in front of her to spit into the chamber pot she was carrying as she weaved her way through the tables. She stood, waiting for him to hack up whatever putrescence was in his lungs, her eyes trained on the doorway next to the long bar that filled one end of the Jolly Vassal's main room.

Talia counted the guards coming down the steps beyond the door and into the main room. She had waited all night for this. One, two, three. Only two guards had gone up to relieve them. That meant there was one floor without a guard at the end of the hall.

Her palms went sweaty around the pot she was about to empty. The owner was behind the bar, chatting with the barkeep. She also knew they would never leave the third floor unguarded. If she was lucky, the floor above her was the one without a guard. It was where the owner's office was—she had been in there to empty the pot the first night she had been allowed onto the second floor—and she recognized this may be her only chance that night to sneak in there. She needed to find that list Fletch talked about—a ledger, she guessed, of all the virgins purchased and who the purchasers were.

She hurried through the tables to the back door, slipping out into the night. Dump this pot and then she could pretend it came from an upper floor. A quick scan told her the alley was empty.

She hurried through the shadows to the cesspit. Taking a deep breath and holding it, she flipped the wooden lid to the side with the toe of her boot. She dumped the pot, shaking it until she could hold her breath no longer. Kicking the lid back in place, she turned her head, scooting several feet to the side before she opened her mouth for a gasp of air.

A quick scratch at her itchy hairline under her handkerchief, and she started back to the door, only to be suddenly yanked to the left.

The pot dropped to the cold ground, shattering. Blast it. Another blackguard to deal with and her chance to get up the stairs broken at her feet.

Lesson learned from her neck that was still bruised, Talia started babbling in her ill-bred accent before the cur behind her could get his hand around her throat. "Aye, 'bout time 'e sees me pretty muff—it be primed 'n ready fer ye."

The man clamped an arm around her chest, dragging her backward and deeper into the alley as she kept blabbering. "I be awaitin' all night fer ye to take me. Me itch ain't bad tonight—no pus, so I be ready fer a good clangin' with ye. Don't charge like 'e whores inside accountin' on me bloody sores. Them bloody bast'rds pull me from the rooms cause of 'em. Make me change their pots, they do, when I be better on me back."

A thick hand clamped over her mouth, cutting her words.

Time to panic. The second she mentioned sores, the men always dropped her to the dirt. Talia twisted, trying to free herself from the arm dragging her backward on her heels.

"Cease, Talia."

Talia froze. Fletch.

Her heels scraped along the muck of the alley as he dragged her to the next street over. She didn't move. Couldn't move for the vise he had her in. He may as well have tossed her over his shoulder for all the control she had.

The clamp around her chest tightened as Fletch's voice, growling, filled her ears. "Truly, Talia—'muff,' 'clanging'?"

His gait sped, jostling her as blood rushed to the tips of her ears. He had heard everything she said. She recognized he knew very well why she had said the words, yet still. Vulgar. He had heard her vulgar. Her only saving grace in the humiliation was that darkness hid her red face.

Fletch stopped at a black carriage, opening the door and lifting her. He tossed her—with a distinct lack of gentleness—inside onto the floor and jumped in after her.

He slammed the door closed behind him, sending the unlit interior into darkness as the horses jumped to a trot. Talia could feel him sit down, his legs brushing her arm. He didn't bother to help her from her heap on the floor of the carriage.

"You are done here, Talia." His voice came down at her from the blackness, seething.

Her fingers found the edge of the bench opposite him and she clasped it, yanking herself up onto the seat. "Why? But I—"

"No discussion, Talia. No pleas. No argument. You are done at the Jolly Vassal. You are done from ever setting foot near a brothel again."

"But—"

"Done."

The word left no room for explanations. No room for argument.

The carriage rattled down the street, taking a sharp turn that sent Talia onto her side. She righted herself, scooting along the bench to the side of the carriage to open the black velvet curtains. Flashes of dim light made it into the carriage from the random street lanterns.

She looked from the window to Fletch, almost afraid to witness in his face the violence that was in his voice. A flash of light verified his glare was exactly as furious as she imagined. She looked out the window. "You are taking me home?"

"I trusted leaving you at the boardinghouse earlier tonight after the gardens. I am not about to make that mistake again. I am taking you to my home so you can bathe and change out of those clothes that stink like the ass of a pig."

Rage sent hackles along the back of Talia's neck. "Of all the bloody high-handedness, you overbearing ogre." She lunged to the side, reaching for the handle of the door.

His hand swift, Fletch snatched her wrist, stopping her movement before she could turn the brass handle. "So now you think to jump from a moving carriage, Talia? You are not that stupid."

"And now you dare to call me stupid?" She wrenched her wrist, only managing to slightly jerk him forward.

"I said you were not that stupid." He dropped her wrist, his eyes boring into her. "Prove me wrong."

Talia glanced out the window. The carriage was going much too fast for her to jump safely. She was that angry, but not that stupid.

She shoved back onto the cushions, crossing her arms over her ribcage. "I do not care for your presumption that you can order me about, Lord Lockston. Our deal entailed no mention of your boorish tyranny."

"I suspect you do not care for anyone ordering you about, Talia." His head tilted, and he stared at her in silence for several blocks.

She refused to look at him as she was too consumed with attempting to stop her body from shaking in indignation.

He sighed, loud, filling the carriage. "Please, Talia. Please will you come to my home, wash the smell from your person, and change into a clean dress so that we may talk without a wall of stench between us?"

Her shaking eased, but it did not disappear completely. She looked across to him in the shadows. He had asked. And Talia guessed that Fletch rarely asked anyone for anything.

She swallowed the rage still wanting to send her tongue to lashing. "I stink that badly?"

He nodded. "I do not exaggerate. I will have to bathe as well after holding on to you."

She shrugged, looking out the window. "Fine, I will come with you."

One hour and one bath later, Talia sat in Fletch's study, warming her bare toes by the fire. Fletch had procured proper stockings and slippers, but as she rarely got to indulge in a true fire to heat her feet and dry her hair by, she had foregone putting them on.

Waiting for Fletch to finish his own bath, she stared at the fire, trying not to look at her surroundings. The room was rich, she had noticed that the first time she had been in here. Elaborately carved woodwork framed the fireplace. A deep mahogany coffered ceiling loomed above. Bookcases filled with row after row of leather-bound tomes.

Fletch's gleamingly polished desk alone took up a quarter of the room.

She didn't want to look at it all, because she didn't want to remember. Her father's study in Rosevin had been much like this one. And she had spent countless hours in there, playing on the floor, interrupting her father every ten minutes.

She had loved his study. Loved how safe, how warm it always was.

It was just another thing lost to her that she couldn't afford the energy to miss. Not when she still had to find Louise.

So she stared at the fire, racking her brain for how she could get into the brothel again to find the list of virgin purchasers. Fletch had taken it upon himself to know her every movement, and she was going to have to ignore his order that she stay away from the Jolly Vassal if she was going to find that list. She needed to find it, needed to hang onto the last vestiges of her tattered hope.

She would talk to Fletch and then leave. Return to the brothel, his anger be damned.

Talia was weaving her hair into a braid when she heard the study door open.

She popped up from the wide leather chair by the hearth and picked up the stockings she had draped on the ottoman.

"I should not be here, Fletch. Your staff has seen me and it is only a matter of time before their gossip reaches hungry ears."

He closed the door behind him, pausing with his hands behind his back. Foregoing full dress, he stood in dark trousers that sat tightly about his waist and a simple white linen shirt that opened wide on his neck. Still wet from his bath, his brown hair looked dark, almost black in the shadow by the door. His feet were bare.

His left eyebrow cocked at her. "Should you not have been worried about my staff's discretion days ago when you were here?"

She waved her hand in the air, the silk stocking she gripped fluttering. "That was before you set me in front of your aunt. She would be destroyed if she knew you were harboring me here in the middle of the night—even more so if she knew you were lying to her. That I was a farce in your life. Especially after what she witnessed at the gardens."

He gave a slight incline of his head to her and stepped fully into the room, stopping within an arm's length of her. "My staff will not breathe a word of your presence. They were hired long ago for their ability to be discrete."

She rolled up one of the stockings and set her bare foot on the ottoman in front of the leather chair. She looked up at him as she slipped the stocking on and unfurled it up her leg. "Do you have need for discretion often?"

Fletch looked at her without answering, his face notably blank.

The left side of her mouth lifted in a smirk. "Ah, yes. I suppose you are just as discrete as your staff."

"Why did you go back to the brothel, Talia? Your sister is not there."

"It is possible that she may land there after…" At a loss to finish her thought with what she didn't want to acknowledge, Talia cleared her throat as she tied the garter and then switched her feet on the ottoman. "And you said there was a list of buyers. I was on my way to sneak into the office of the owner to search for the list when you so rudely stole me from the alley."

"Dammit, Talia." Fletch ran his fingers through his wet hair. "I didn't tell you about the list's bloody existence so you would go a fool and risk your neck looking for it."

She stood straight. "Oh. I thought that was exactly why you told me about the list. So I should look for it."

"What? Why would you not think I would handle it? Get the list by my own means?"

"It is just, in my position, I can move about the brothel much more covertly than you can." Her fingers drew together in front of her, intertwining. "I was going to deliver that chamber pot into that office—make it look as if that was all I was doing in there, just in case someone came in. I was only in a little danger. The owner and the barkeep do think I am quite stupid. I am positive they do not believe I can read, so I could have easily prattled my way out. Whereas if you somehow made it into that office, your presence could not be easily explained. You cannot deny my logic, Fletch."

"I cannot." His chin jutted out, his tongue visibly pressing along the inside of his cheek. "But there is one rather large folly in your plan, Talia."

"No. There is none."

"There is—it is the fact that I already have the list in-hand. I received it this morning."

"What—how?"

"I hired an investigator to get it for me."

Talia's teeth clamped tight, grinding. Of course. Money. Money would buy one anything. A virgin. A list. Whatever one fancied.

She stepped toward him. "You had it all day, when we went to the gardens—why didn't you tell me?"

"I didn't think I needed to, Talia." He exhaled an aggravated sigh. "I told you I would find your sister, and that is what I am doing. I didn't think you would not trust me at my word."

"It is not my trust that is in question. It is your trust in me, Fletch. Why did you not think it a necessity to tell me what you found?"

"I did not want you preoccupied at the gardens and I in no way imagined you would take it upon yourself to go back to the Jolly Vassal. Especially when there is nothing that can be done at the moment."

His mouth closed.

Talia suppressed a groan. The man was purposefully not sharing anything of value.

"You are telling me absolutely nothing, Fletch, and I need to know. What was on that list? Why can nothing be done at the moment?"

He hedged for a moment before sighing. "I have the name of the man that bought her."

"You do? Who is it? We must visit him, make him tell us where Louise is." Her hand flew over her mouth. "Or does he still have her—no—what would he have done with her? We have to go, Fletch."

He turned from her, going to the sideboard and pouring himself a glass of brandy from the heavy cut glass decanter. He took a sip before turning back to her. "That is exactly why I did not tell you, Talia. You cannot go half-cocked and show up on his doorstep. You approach him as a bull, and he will deny everything."

Her hands flew up in the air. "This is my sister, Fletch—do you have a better plan?"

"I plan to put myself in a position to speak in private with him. The man is Lord Drockston."

"Lord Drockston? I have not heard his name before. I must accompany you."

"No. You will not."

Talia stepped across the room to him. "I will. If he has Louise, Fletch—"

"I understand your frenzy, Talia, but I am bound to get much more honest information from him if I approach him without having to hold back a rabid big sister looking for the girl he bought."

"I am not rabid."

"I fear what you will become if you are in the same room with the man."

"He deserves whatever I can inflict upon him."

Fletch lifted his glass to her. "Exactly. While I do not disagree on what he deserves, there will be time for that another day. Today, I am to approach him alone. You forget that I have sat in many auctions with the man. He knows me to have the same peculiarities as he, so is much more likely to speak openly with me."

Her hand flew to the door. "So go talk to him."

"Talia, it is only a few hours until daybreak. I am sure he is ensconced in his bed at the moment. Aside from the fact that I cannot approach him at his home. I must first discover where his calendar is going to place him during the next few nights. If we are lucky, he will be at an event that I can bump into him, sequester him in a private room or alcove."

"But we do not have time for that, Fletch. Louise is heaven only knows where. She...she..." Her chest tightened at where her sister might be at that very moment—at what she might be forced to be doing.

Fletch gently set his hand on Talia's shoulder. "I know it is hard to wait. But we cannot ruin this one chance I have to get honest information from Lord Drockston. As despicable as it is, he is our best option to find your sister. But we have to be cautious about approaching him."

It was common sense. Talia knew it, even if she didn't want to accept it.

She looked up at Fletch, meeting his eyes. "But I cannot just wait. I cannot just pace holes into the floorboards, waiting, not doing anything to find her."

Fletch smiled. "No. I do not imagine you can, Talia. But it is what the situation calls for. So in the meantime, I have a suggestion."

"What?"

"Marry me."

{ CHAPTER 7 }

Talia jumped away from Fletch and his hand fell from her shoulder.

Not exactly the reaction he imagined from a woman he just proposed marriage to. He took a sip of his brandy, watching her face contort in a myriad of emotions.

"What? Fletch—what?" Her hands at her sides twitched manically, her fingers clamping down over her thumbs again and again.

He shrugged. "My aunt is expecting it after the gardens. And I find the idea intriguing."

Her look snapped to him. "You find the idea, *intriguing*?"

"Mayhap that is not the right word. I find it convenient."

"You find it, *convenient*?"

"Also not the right word, I can see." Fletch held in a grin at the indignant ire sending Talia's cheeks red. He hadn't figured her for flower petals and sweet poetry, but maybe that was where her dreams had aspired to. Very possibly so—at least back in the days when she danced among the *ton*.

She spun away from him, walking over to the fireplace. Slowly, silently, she bent, sliding on the black silk slippers he had set out for her. She stood, wrapping her arms about her belly as she stared at the fire for long moments.

Fletch considered saying something more. Some further encouragement for her to consider the proposal, but he wanted to observe how her thoughts played out. Granted, he knew her current troubles, knew where her mind and her energy were focused—on finding her sister.

But he also knew how her body had curled into him in the gardens—how her mouth had conformed to his control, how the tip of her tongue had tangled with his, how the soft moan had escaped from her throat when he stroked the curve of her breast.

He swallowed another gulp of brandy. No use letting his mind go to those thoughts. Not tonight.

Talia's head swiveled to him. "Your mangled proposal aside, Fletch, I do not think I can answer you."

"Why not? Aside from the obvious current matter of finding your sister—which I am working diligently to do— why not?"

"You need the thousand reasons why not?" Talia looked back to the fire, her hazel eyes downward to the flames. "My feet have not landed on solid ground since my father died, Fletch. I have been jumping, scampering from pieces of a broken, fragmented world, to pieces of a world filled with squalor and hunger and desperation. Years of flailing. Years of scratching for survival. I have never found solid footing, and I need my feet to land somewhere that I can control."

"So let me give you solid ground."

She shook her head and then looked at him, the corners of her eyes crinkling, sad. "You cannot give me that."

Fletch walked across the room to stand before her. "I can, Talia. For the next year, let me give you footing. You will want for nothing. You can discover the person you are now. Your mother will have security. And we will find your sister, I promise you that. You will have an actual home to bring Louise to—much better than cramping her into your room at the boarding house—or did you think to bring her back to Norfolk? Do you even have enough coin for the journey for both of you?"

Her mouth twisted to the side. She didn't care for his assessment of the situation, but her silence admitted to the truth of his words. Her hands went to her hips. "And then what?"

"What do you mean?"

"You said for the next year. What happens after a year?" Her hands lifted, palms up to motion around her. "It all— this world, this security—gets yanked from me again when you have tired of me?"

"No. You will be free to do whatever you wish to with your time, with the estates and holdings that I will transfer to your name alone. No one will be able to take them from you. You may come and go wherever and whenever you wish. I will have the transfer documents drawn up before the wedding to assure you of their validity."

Her hands landed back onto her hips, her eyes narrowing. "Why would you do that?"

"Because it is what you need."

"What about you?"

"What about me?"

"What do you need, Fletch? What happens to you after this year? Do you get the same leave of me? Are you just doing this to soothe your aunt, knowing she will pass soon? Then you can be free of me—I am merely the price you pay to appease an old lady?"

Or I will be dead.

Fletch gave himself a slight shake. That fact, he wasn't about to share with her. He drew a sip of brandy.

Her eyes opened wide. "Or is it that you…you like men? That is why you do this?"

He sputtered the brandy that had slipped past his lips, dropping the glass down to his side. "I what?"

"You enjoy men…more than women." A flush crept up her neck. "I did not know this before I worked in the brothels, but there were a few special men in those houses that serviced other men." She coughed, her eyes slipping to the side to look past his shoulder. "Sometimes they worked with another woman and the customer. Sometimes it was two men and the customer. It took me several passes of it to understand what was happening with them."

"The devil, Talia, what did they have you doing in those places?"

Her head leaned to the side, her eyes still avoiding him. "I emptied chamber pots, mostly. All of them. They did not care if I was in the room during…acts." She winced with the word. "As long as I was in the shadows, they just wanted the work done."

The thought of Talia being subjected to the most vulgar of scenes curdled his stomach. That she was forced to put herself in that situation. He needed to find her sister before she felt the need to do something even more drastic.

Her hazel eyes finally pulled from their avoidance and landed squarely on him. "But that is it. You enjoy the company of men, yet you would like to appease your aunt. I see how much she means to you."

A guffaw flew from his mouth. "No, Talia. You are very mistaken in that regard." His look settled on her, running down her body, and slowly returning up to her eyes, his gaze slicing into her. A stare meant to make her squirm under his heat, and she did.

He repeated the path of his eyes, enjoying too much her fidgeting intensifying and sending a flush up her neck. "No, Talia, my tastes are very much in line with what is before me at this moment."

A slight gasp escaped her before she clamped her hand over her mouth. It took several breaths before her hand slipped from her mouth, fingers dragging along her lower lip. The instant indignation in her hazel eyes faded, turning into droll defeat. "In our particular situation, I fear I cannot scold you for your forthrightness, can I?"

A smile lifting the left corner of his mouth, Fletch slowly shook his head. "You cannot."

She exhaled. "Just know that were it four years ago, I would have cut you long ago for your ongoing impudence."

"I expect you would have."

"But still, the question remains, Fletch, why have you offered me this? You do not know me, not truly, and I have not a thing to offer you."

"Some of the finest marriages in history have been forged upon much less than what we have shared together, Talia."

She shook her head. "Yet what we have shared together—you cannot possibly want a wife that will collapse upon you every time you bring her in front of society—a madwoman running at the slightest memory."

"I do not think you mad, Talia. And if that is your fear, then we will not move amongst the *ton*."

A deep-set frown settled on her face, and she took a step backward, sinking to the edge of the leather chair as her eyes went to the fire.

She was remembering. Remembering her past life. He was beginning to recognize the gaze, the far-off look in her eye when she remembered what it was like to live life as the daughter of an earl. The look ached. Dreams unhinged. Happiness stolen away.

He couldn't blame her. She had the world. And then she had nothing.

But she had survived. And as much as Fletch didn't fully understand his own desire to marry her—he knew it had much to do with that. Talia was a survivor. She always would be.

She looked up to him. "I do not think you understand how I will harm you, Fletch. How I will sully your reputation. I have strayed so far from the lady I once was that I felt no shame at what we did in the gardens—where your hands were on me." Her fingers lifted, rubbing the back of her neck as she dodged his eyes. "No shame. That is not the wife any lord wants, or can afford."

"Have you considered the possibility that you did not feel shame because you wanted it—wanted me to do exactly what I was." He stepped to her, invading the space about her knees. "To touch you. To make you feel fire in the pit of your belly. Fire lower."

Her look lifted to him, startled. "How...how..."

"I know, Talia. I know because I felt it. I felt it in my own body. I felt it in your skin, how you reacted to my touch. You want me. Yet you have not strayed far enough away from being a lady to actually admit to it."

The hand wrapping the back of her neck slid forward, splaying along the bare skin above the lace trim on the bodice of her dress.

"Why do you conjure so many reasons for the contrary, Talia?"

"I do not trust." Her answer was immediate. "Not after what was done to my family by the current Earl of Roserton."

Fletch nodded, pulling the ottoman closer to him with his bare toe. He set his brandy glass on the floor and sat, facing her at eye level. "I know you do not trust, Talia. But I hope that I have given you enough reason to at least contemplate trusting me." He reached out to grab both of her hands. "Here is what I can promise you, Talia. You will always be taken care of. From this day—this year—to the rest of your days. I swear it."

Her eyes closed as she drew a deep breath that shook her entire being. She opened her eyes to him, the twisting blues and browns vibrant in the light of the fire. "You can swear you will not die on me, Fletch?"

His body froze.

It only took a second to recover. A second he prayed she didn't notice.

He stared her straight in the eye, refusing to display anything but resolve. "Yes. I can promise you will always be taken care of, Talia."

A lie. A half-truth. As honest as possible. But Fletch could reveal no more.

She exhaled a long breath, nodding. "Then I have only one last question."

His hands tightened around hers. "What is it?"

"Why me?"

Fletch looked to the fire, contemplating the question. His gaze swung to her. "I think what happened to you and your family after your father died was atrocious. It makes me wonder how very often your situation happens as titles move to distant relatives. It was wrong, what happened to you and your mother and sister, and I would like to right that wrong."

"It is not your wrong to right."

"No. But I am in the position to do so, so I am. Aside from that, I admire your fortitude." His eyes dipped down to her chest with a wicked smile. "And your other assets as well."

She groaned, unable to squash the smirk that was determined to surface in response to his obviously lascivious gaze.

He leaned forward, his eyes meeting hers. "That is a yes?"

Her lips drew in, and she nodded. "Yes. As long as all that you have promised me you will stand by."

"I will."

"Then yes, I will marry you, Fletch."

His chest expanded in a relieved breath. He hadn't fathomed her answer would mean so very much to him. But it did. It did immensely.

Yet the warning, the dread that constantly gnawed at the back of his head, grew frenzied.

She was asking the impossible from him—asking him not to die.

He knew his promise was hollow.

He only wondered if she did as well.

~ ~ ~

His forearm stretched along the white marble mantel, Fletch stared at the dragging movement of the minute hand on the ornate French ormolu mantel clock. Five minutes until three.

He had given the clock to his sister on her wedding day. She had been delighted and then teased him that she would give it back to him on his thirty-third birthday and he would have to be prepared to stare at the thing until he was eighty and he was forced to admit he had been wrong about everything.

His finger traced the delicate gold filigree that adorned the frame of the clock face. Rachel had been so very happy that day. Glowing like he had never seen her before.

It was almost like the glow she effervesced toward the end of her pregnancy.

"Lockston. I did not expect a visit from you, though I welcome it."

Fletch's hand fell from the clock, his jaw hardening. He turned from the library mantel, his arm dropping from the marble.

"Reggard."

Moving into the room, Fletch's brother-in-law pointed at his empty hand. "You have not poured yourself a drink."

Silently, Reggard went to the tall mahogany sideboard and set two glasses upright, filling them with port. The whole of him disheveled, his dark blond hair sat rumpled upon his head, his black jacket crushed like he had slept in it. Even given the hour, Fletch guessed bed was exactly where Reggard had just stumbled in from—if he had actually made it to his chambers after the night.

Reggard walked across the room, his size, even bedraggled, swallowing the room. He handed Fletch one of the glasses and then took a long swallow from the one left in his hand.

Fletch's left eyebrow lifted at the sudden disappearance of half of Reggard's port. He usually didn't care what the man did, but at the moment, he did. He didn't need Reggard drunk today.

"What brings you by, Lockston?"

"I wanted to speak to you before you left for the club tonight."

"Oh?" Reggard tipped his head back, finishing the port.

"I need you sober, Reggard."

"If you need me sober, then you, more importantly, need me functioning. How I get there is no concern of yours." Reggard left Fletch to pour himself another full glass, drinking half of it before he refilled it and turned from the sideboard to Fletch.

Fletch stifled a sigh. "I need your help tonight, Reggard, and there is not another I can go to with my request."

"Newdale cannot help you?"

"Caine is not in town. I need someone today—tonight."

Reggard took a step toward him, interest angling his head to the side. "What is it you need me for?"

"I need you to purchase a virgin at the Jolly Vassal. It is a brothel in the East End."

"You what?"

Fletch's fingers curled at his sides. The last thing he wanted to be doing at the moment was explaining why he bought virgins—and to his brother-in-law, at that. But he had no other recourse. He had no one else to trust with this business at the moment. "There is an auction at that establishment tonight. I purchase virgins to save them from the lechers. I buy one at every auction I can, and then I turn them over to several women waiting in a carriage that will take care of them. I have the guards and the women ready to help with a purchase tonight. I am on a list in which I am invited to the auctions, because I pay high and purchase frequently. I am able to save quite a few innocents in this way. But I need someone to attend the auction tonight and buy a girl."

Reggard shook his head. He took a long swallow of port and shook his head again. His fingers ran over his eyes, rubbing them. He finally looked to Fletch. "Why can you not do it?"

"I have to get married tonight."

"Married? But I thought—"

"It cannot be helped, Reggard."

Reggard stared at him for a long moment calculating. Finally, he offered one curt nod. "But tonight? You arranged a wedding for the evening?"

"A special license from the archbishop. Aunt Penelope and her dragons have made it so. The wedding will be in three hours. You can see how I cannot make it to the Jolly Vassal."

Reggard tossed back the remainder of his second glass of port, his bleary eyes making their way to Fletch. "So I am sure I am not misunderstanding—you want me to buy a virgin in a brothel in order to save her?"

Fletch eyed him, considering going to the sideboard and tipping over the decanter of port. It would at least slow Reggard for the moment. Fletch's voice took a hard edge. "You are the only person in town I can trust with this, Reggard. Trust to have the utmost discretion about the business. No one can know the virgins are not purchased for their…purpose. You are the only one I can ask this of. But you cannot do this soused."

"I thought you hated me, Lockston."

Fletch sighed, his fingers tightening about his glass. "I thought I did too. But my options are limited. And I need someone I can trust. I trust you more than I hate you. Buy a girl. Turn her over to my women. That is all I ask."

Reggard nodded, rubbing his eyes once more. He pinched the bridge of his nose. "I miss her, Lockston. Rachel."

"You do not get to speak her name to me."

Reggard's hand dropped from his face and he met Fletch's glare. "So you still blame me."

A statement, not a question.

Fletch fidgeted, stepping to the side of the room to set his glass on a table. He looked Reggard dead-on, his voice cutting. "She was the one in the family that was supposed to survive, Reggard. The one to live. The one to keep memory of all of us."

"I did not kill her."

Fletch saw the pain in Reggard's eyes. Heard the tremor in his deep voice. None of it curbed his own tone. "No. You merely put your babe inside of her. A babe that did kill her."

Reggard blanched. For his size—a head taller than Fletch with a battering-ram chest—the man looked fragile, about to break.

Fletch tried to ignore the visceral rage that surged from the deepest part of his soul. "I am here for your help, Reggard. Nothing more. Will you do as I ask?"

It took a long moment for Reggard to compose himself, to draw himself to his full height. "I will, Lockston. Your sister would have demanded I help."

{ CHAPTER 8 }

Talia stared at her reflection in the tall mirror at the corner of the room. The chambers in Fletch's townhouse that she had prepared herself in were feminine—his sister's or his mother's, she did not know. She tugged the outer edges of the silver lace trim along her bodice, adjusting the soft, smooth silk below it along the slope of her breasts. A robin's egg blue, the fabric had been pressed to impossible crispness—so much so Talia was afraid to sit and wrinkle all the hard work of the maid.

She captured a stray blond hair, tucking it behind one of the several braids that started along her forehead, whisking back to an elaborate upsweep that highlighted the many shades of her red-blond hair.

She almost didn't recognize herself. It had been so very long since she had looked like this, shined to a twinkling star of the *ton*. She recognized the veneer now like she never had. Four years ago, she would look in a mirror and see this, and know herself. And then she would skip out the door.

But now. Now she knew what she saw in the mirror was not who she was. Far from it.

Three quick taps rapped through the door, and before Talia could answer, the door swung open.

"I assume you are proper, Lady Natalia, for how long that maid was primping you?" Aunt Penelope bustled into the room, her cane flicking behind her to bang the door closed. A red turban covered her head, a matching red shawl draped over her dark blue dress.

Talia turned to Aunt Penelope, a smile on her face. "I believe I am, but I will let you be the judge on whether I appear an appropriate bride. I do not think I can judge it on my own eye."

"Nonsense, dear." Aunt Penelope stomped with her cane into the middle of the room. "I put no stock in appearances. I am here to see you, child, before you commit to what is downstairs."

"Before I commit to Fletch?"

"Yes."

Talia's hands landed flat on her belly, her fingertips twisting together. "That sounds like a warning. Do I need to know something?"

"I am the one that needs to know something. I found you acceptable in our first meeting, but I want to know what he is marrying."

A flush skittered along the back of Talia's neck. "You now think me a woman without morals? I understand your concern. What you witnessed in that alcove at Vauxhall was inexcusable."

Aunt Penelope waved her cane in the air. "Please, child. I know that nephew of mine is as handsome as sin. You cannot possibly be to blame for that untoward scene."

"But what you saw—"

"I have seen worse in the middle of a ballroom, dear. That scene in the gardens bordered on innocent."

Talia's brow furrowed. "But your reaction—what you said to him."

Aunt Penelope cackled. "I did feign quite the scene, did I not? You can wipe free the worry from your eyes." Her cane tapped on a honey hued-floorboard with glee. "I have never been able to pin Fletcher into a commitment. He is as slippery as an eel, and he has never taken seriously his responsibility to the title. I merely saw an opportunity in the gardens to blast him fully, and quite possibly, spur him into action. I do not let opportunities pass me by, child. Not at my age."

Talia's fingers relaxed from their frantic twisting, yet she couldn't quite believe Aunt Penelope. "So your sensibilities were not offended?"

"Too many years have passed me, my dear—my sensibilities do not shudder at a mad kiss coupled with a wandering hand."

Talia nodded, exhaling. "Thank you for understanding."

"Do not give it another thought." Aunt Penelope's hawk eyes sank into Talia. "I do know about your past, child, how unfortunate these years have been for you and your mother and sister since your father died."

Talia blinked hard at the sudden switch of topic. "Fletch told you?"

"No. The dragons and I know everything. But I was not about to impress upon you I was privy to gossip about your family in our first meeting. Especially given that nephew of mine has never brought a woman before me." Both of her hands clamped onto the top of her cane, tapping it on the floor. "It is unfortunate, your past, but it has also given you character. I can see that. You are a very fine match for my nephew. Or so I think."

Talia read the question in her grey eyes. "You still have reservations about who I am?"

"Why did you say yes to him, dear? Your eyes are too canny to harbor fantasies of love at first sight."

"I…" Talia bit the inside of her cheek. This woman would accept nothing less than the truth. "I am not positive why."

"That is not an answer I want to hear."

"I understand," Talia said. "But when I think upon it, I do not know how he convinced me. Regardless, at the end of our conversation, I agreed to the marriage."

"Fletcher had to convince *you*?"

Talia nodded.

"I would have thought it the opposite. Ladies have been trying to twist his thumbs into marriage for ages—none even neared success in that endeavor."

Talia shrugged, her hands unconsciously smoothing down the fabric she had just wrinkled about her waist. "I tried to express upon him what a horrendous wife I would make. The years removed from society—it has changed me. I do not see this world as I once did. I do not trust this world—being surrounded by the wealth, by the security of it."

"Why then, dear, did you say yes to his proposal?"

"I trust Fletch." The answer came easily from Talia's lips, surprising herself. Her head cocked in wonderment at the realization. "For all I do not trust everything around me, I trust Fletch. That is why I said yes."

Aunt Penelope's grey eyes sat upon Talia, shrewd, for long seconds. She gave one curt nod. "That will do. That, dear, is an answer worthy of a marriage."

~ ~ ~

Fletch stepped into his bedroom, closing the door as he scanned the note Horace had just handed him.

"All is well?"

Talia's voice startled him.

He looked up to find her sitting at the edge of his bed, a black night rail, sheer, held tight to her body with a row of tied pink ribbons down the front center. Her hair unbound, soft red and blond waves hung past her shoulders and disappeared onto her back.

The sight took his breath, took all thought from his head.

He hadn't expected his new wife to be waiting in his room. He had thought she would hide in her chambers until he knocked on their adjoining door. For all she had witnessed during her time in the brothels, he still saw the innocence in her eyes. Still saw the flush that invaded her cheeks when pleasures of the flesh were mentioned.

But there she sat. A goddess. Looking at him with wide eyes. Slightly fidgeting, but willing. He saw that in the way she looked at him. She was willing to be in his bed.

She trusted him.

And he suddenly found himself standing by the door to his room, his cock rock hard and not even a simpleton's thought in his head, except for stripping off that wispy black piece of cloth and gorging himself on his wife's body.

"Fletch? All is well?"

"What?"

"The letter in your hand." She pointed at his arm. "Is something amiss? Your forehead was scrunched in concern."

Her words not making sense, Fletch looked down. The note in his hand. He had completely forgotten he was clutching it.

"Oh. No. It is just a note from my brother-in-law." Fletch moved into the room, setting the note down on his inlaid walnut writing desk by the window. "Lord Reggard was taking care of business for me tonight. It went well, that is all."

She straightened, scooting to edge of the bed. "Is it about Louise?"

"No." Fletch could instantly see his one word answer would not suffice. "There was an auction tonight at the Jolly Vassal. I sent Reggard in my place to purchase a virgin."

She nodded, her face slightly blanching as a frown crossed her face. "Good. I am glad you are still ensuring help for them. I had not considered how my monopolizing your time could affect others…other innocent girls. If you need to go…"

"One, Talia, you need not worry that some girl wasn't saved because of you. This is the first auction they have held since I have met you. And two, Reggard was there in my stead. He got the girl out of there without the slightest hiccup."

Fletch's look ran up and down Talia's body, full of heated intention. "So three, I have absolutely nowhere else to be at the moment, than with my new wife. Alone with my new wife. Alone. In a bedroom."

His openly salacious gaze drew the smallest smile from her.

Talia fingered the edge of the gauzy fabric that ran along her chest and up over her shoulder. "Then four,

Fletch, I am glad you do not have to attend to other business. Your aunt had this piece delivered for me to wear tonight. And I must admit, if you did have to leave, I do not know that I would be brave enough to put it on again."

Fletch stripped off his jacket and his waistcoat, watching her. "A woman who poses as a maid in a brothel, and *this* is the thing that requires your bravery?"

She shrugged, a nervous smile twitching at her lips. Fletch recognized it instantly. She wanted to please him. Even with everything askew in her life, she wanted to please him. Him.

Damn. He wanted to tell her, tell her everything.

Tell her of his brother, his father, his grandfather, his great-grandfather. Tell her of the burden. How he would be dead within the year.

But he could not. Not in this moment. Not when that knowledge would rip away the very foundation she thought she was getting by marrying him.

It was the only reason she had said yes to him during their quick wedding ceremony downstairs in the drawing room. And he wasn't about to shake that foundation mere hours after they were wed.

Fletch turned from her, composing himself as he pulled off his boots and dragged his white linen shirt over his head.

"Should I be helping you?"

He glanced over his shoulder to her, only to see she had stood from the bed. If he had thought her a goddess before, her standing in the dark night rail, statuesque, made him revise his assessment. Not a goddess. No. This woman was the moon and the stars and the sun and the earth all in one. And she was now officially his.

He turned to her. "Helping me?"

Her hand waved in front of her. "Undress. Is that done? I am in this rail and I did not think about your clothing, or removing your clothing, or…" She shrugged, her voice trailing.

Fletch stepped to her, swallowing the distance between them, but he kept his hands at his sides as he looked down at her. Close enough to smell her. Lavender and honey. His mouth started to water. "Do you want to help me undress, Talia? The work is almost done, you realize."

She met his gaze, the blue flecks twisting alive with the brown in her eyes. "Your smile could be less wicked about it."

"I pray for nothing but wicked with you, Talia." He reached down, grabbing her hand and pressing her fingers onto the top button of his trousers. "And I tend to think we are of like mind on the matter. Am I wrong?"

She paused with an intake of breath, hesitating for only a second before she shook her head. Without looking from his eyes, she popped free the first button and then made her way downward along the flap.

Every button freed, every brush against his shaft a torture like he had never imagined.

His trousers loosened, she traced the top of the fabric along his waist with her fingers. Her hands curving along his back, she pushed the fabric down, baring him fully.

She bent, picking up his trousers and tossing them behind her onto the bed. Yet she refused to look downward. Her hands landed softly on his sides, trailing on his skin, her fingers flipping as her caress went across his abdomen. Close. So very close.

Her hands stilled and Fletch looked down between them. He grabbed her fingers, bringing them upward with a frown. "Your knuckles, Talia."

"What of them?"

His thumbs traced along the bumps of her knuckles. "They are rough. I do not like that."

She jerked her hands away, stepping backward. "I have not had the luxury of keeping them soft."

He snatched her hands into his grasp again before she could escape. "No, Talia. I do not like that they are rough because it reminds me of what you have been forced to do. The injustice of it. I do not find it a flaw in you."

"Oh." Her chin jutted out. "You could have started with that statement."

He smiled. "I can see I should have." He pulled her close, curling her hands and setting her knuckles onto his belly once more. "But I do not mind it at all, the feel of them on me. They are real. They are you."

He leaned down, nuzzling into her hair until he reached her ear. "And you touching me is exquisite, Talia."

Her chest expanded into him, her nipples already taut through the sheer fabric of her night rail. "Fletch."

The word came as a whisper, fighting for sound. He had never heard his name uttered in such an innocently carnal way. And it only inflamed the blood that had been pounding through his cock for the past ten minutes. The devil in hades, he did not have it in him to ease into this.

"Yes?" He forced the word, rough, from his mouth.

"I still have clothes on."

Fletch ripped the top two ties apart in one second, not bothering with the insanity of the rest of the row of knots as he dragged the night rail down her body. Down her flesh. All of her flesh. Naked.

His hand went deep into her hair and he yanked her to him, his mouth searching for hers, searching for her body to press into his. True to her like mind, her arms wrapped around his neck, her leg lifting to pull him closer as their mouths met, dissolving into each other.

He slipped downward from her mouth, his lips devouring her neck, needing the taste of her on his tongue. With every brush of his teeth against her skin, she shuddered, her leg tightening along his backside, demanding him onward.

She exhaled a vibrating moan, and Fletch reached his capacity for patience. He moved forward, dropping them onto the edge of the bed.

He pulled up, finding Talia's swollen lips parted for him, her eyes half open, glazed.

"The devil take me, Talia, I am going to attempt to do this slow."

Her hand reached up, finding the back of his head, gripping his hair. "No. Not slow. Fast, Fletch. Fast."

He growled, her words only inflaming his impatience further. "Then you have to come for me, Talia. Now. Do you trust me?"

Her eyes flew open. "Yes."

His hand went between her legs before her word ended, spreading her flesh, his fingers sliding along her slick mound. Her hips bucked, a wispy scream pulling from her throat.

One finger, two, into the tightness of her body. His thumb circling her nubbin as her writhing grew more insistent.

"Fletch?" She whimpered his name, almost terrified.

"Come for me, Talia. Come for me." The growl in his command was borne out of his own need to plunge into her. "Trust me, Talia. Don't fight it. Come for me. Now."

She screamed, her body curling, fingernails digging into his shoulders. Fletch shifted above her, and drove deep into her in one long motion, breaking through her body's long held barrier.

Her body jerked at the intrusion, a whimper of pain that dissolved into a breathy moan as the rolling shudders continued, ravaging her body.

Fletch lifted his hips, removing himself almost to the tip, then propelled downward, filling her again. So tight, and her body constricted again and again around his cock with every second, with every thrust.

Pulling at him and forcing him to the edge of control he didn't know existed.

He lost himself.

Lost himself so deep within her until barely at the last second did he pull out of her. He only half managed to get his cock onto his discarded trousers before he came with such brutal force that his seed spread into a mess, half on her thigh, half on his trousers.

She was still shuddering, her back arched, her fingers digging into his back. Fletch made a quick swipe with his trousers to clean what he could, and then he drove his arm under her back, flipping them on the bed so she was on top of him.

His arms wrapped so tightly around her body he thought he might crush the air from her, he stared at the grey damask canopy above them.

What in hades was that torture?

Being inside Talia had shattered him.

There was no other word for it.

Shattered.

He hadn't known it would happen, so he had no defense against it. So shattered he had barely pulled out in time.

Before he could even begin to comprehend the loss of control over his own body, Talia exhaled a soft groan, rife with satisfaction, and stretched her body out on top of him.

Her arms wiggled free from his clasp and her palms found the bed on either side of his chest. She pushed herself up, looking down at him. "Do I leave now? That is what seems to happen in the brothels. One of the two people—or three—always seems to leave posthaste."

Fletch laughed, his belly shaking her. "I forget what you have seen. Be assured, Talia, there is a whole world apart from what you have seen in those brothels."

She frowned, poking his chest. "You do not need to laugh at me."

He clamped an arm around her backside, pulling her back down onto the length of his body. She only resisted for the merest second. He kissed her forehead. "I mean no offense—it is as I said, I just forget what you have witnessed and how that shapes your viewpoint."

She relaxed on top of him. "So I should remain?"

"Only if you would like. But I have no wish for you to leave this bed."

"Good." She nodded, the side of her cheek rubbing on his chest. "I like lying on you. I like what we just did. What you did to me."

His fingers twined into her hair, his voice serious. "You felt it?"

"I did."

"Good. I did too."

Her answer pleased him, but did nothing to soothe the agitation wreaking havoc in his own chest. Their bodies joined. Talia lounging on top of him.

He did feel it.

Too much so. Too deep. Feeling that wasn't ebbing.

He gave himself an invisible shake. He couldn't very well gain control with her naked body on top of his.

"Did you see the berries?" Fletch pointed to the table next to the head of the bed. "I had them brought up here after dinner."

"I did, but I did not know they were for me to snitch." She rolled off his body, going to her knees next to him as a scold set upon her lips. "I do hope you are not still making judgements upon my person."

"Your person is perfect." He kissed the side of her waist as she stretched over his chest to reach the bowl. "But I saw how little food you were able to eat in between the conversations below."

He stuffed a pillow behind his head to lift it. Talia set the bowl on his chest, sitting next to him as her fingers dug through the bowl to find the perfect blackberry. She popped it into her mouth, an instant smile radiating across her face.

Her naked thigh pressed alongside his chest as she looked down at him. Fletch set his forearm atop her thigh, his fingers playing along her hip bone. It jutted out slightly. She was perfect, but she did need to eat. And eat more than the berries she was currently munching on.

Decorum swept aside, she snatched an obnoxiously large handful of berries, devouring them, berry juice escaping down her chin. Her tongue slipped out, licking the dark streak with a giggle. "Not exactly becoming of me, I am aware."

She dragged a thumb from the bottom of her chin upward, capturing the bead of purple juice. Sucking it off her thumb, her eyes danced at him.

His chest twisted. Damn, if he didn't want to possess her. Her youth, her vibrancy, her enthusiasm for the simple pleasures life could afford.

This, right in front of him, was the answer to the question that had been plaguing his mind since he had asked her to marry him. Why had he offered for her? He didn't need a wife and had planned on never having one, no matter what his aunt's wishes were.

But Talia. He wanted her. Her ability to survive. To not wait for life to happen to her. To be present in determining her own course. To writhe underneath him. To eat berries with unapologetic gusto.

Maybe he was trying to steal that from her. Steal what she was. Steal her pluck. Her youth.

The blue in her hazel eyes darkened at him—reflecting his own look, he imagined.

She ate the last berry in her hand. "I should leave to my bed now."

Fletch wasn't sure if it was a question or a statement. Though he had never kicked a lady from his bed, he had always preferred to sleep alone. But a distinct jolt flew up his chest at the thought of her warm, naked body crawling from his bed.

His hand tightened around the side of her hip. "Or you could stay."

A smile, almost shy, crossed her face. "You would not mind? I had grown accustomed to sleeping with my mother and sister in one bed. But the bed at the boardinghouse was lonely and cold. I never slept very well there." Pulling the coverlet and sheet down, she slipped her legs under the bedding, her calves sliding down the length of his body. She snuggled her cheek onto the crook of his shoulder. "This is nice. You are far warmer and much more comfortable than an empty bed. I missed this."

Fletch's fingers curled into the bottom strands of her hair. "Please tell me sleeping with your mother and sister was nothing like this, or I shall die of serious wounds to my ego."

She laughed. "You are nothing at all like them. You are immensely better naked, and I can only dream on wicked acts with you. Besides, you will not die. You promised me that."

Fletch stiffened. Talia didn't notice, already reaching into the bowl on his chest for more berries.

Had he promised her that? Directly? He thought he had skirted the exact statements about death.

Hell.

Maybe he had promised her.

If so, he was beginning to wonder if the whole of this had been a grievous mistake on his part.

His arm tightened around her back.

Not that he was ready to correct—or give up—the mistake quite yet.

Balancing the pile of berries on her hand, Talia attempted to single-handedly drop them into her mouth. Three blackberries rolled off the pile onto Fletch's chest and then down along his neck. Fat streaks of juice came with them, stripes marking his skin.

Chuckling, she wedged herself up onto her elbow and dropped the ones in her hand into the bowl. Fishing the three rogue berries from the crook of his neck and shoulder, she tossed them into her mouth. A smirk lined her full lips as she chewed, pointing to his neck. "May I? It would be sacrilege to waste even a drop of these. How you procured them at this time of year is beyond me."

Fletch shrugged. "If you must."

She leaned down, her lips finding his neck, sucking, remaining far too long in one spot, and then her tongue dragged across his skin, lining his neck. Fletch felt himself grow hard again, and he adjusted the sheet pulled across his waist.

Distraction. He needed a distraction. She would be far too sore to take him on again.

She popped up, her eyes twinkling at him. "It dribbled quite a bit down your neck."

"I could feel that."

She grinned. "We are doing a lot of feeling today."

"It would seem we are."

Her eyes glanced down to the sheet at his waist. "Is it appropriate to ask for more feeling?" Her look ran up his body, landing on his gaze.

Lusty. A temptress, pure and through.

Fletch groaned, his cock straining, refusing to be ignored. Picking up the bowl from his chest, he set it on the side table. "You are sore."

She smiled, lascivious wickedness lining her eyes.

He sat up, grabbing her wrists and flipping her onto her back, his face hovering above hers.

"Do not make judgements on my person, Fletch. I am perfectly capable of anything at the moment."

He kissed her hard, leaving no ambiguity about what they were about to do. "That you are, Talia. That you are."

{ CHAPTER 9 }

Her arms crossed, her fingers tapping on her elbow, Talia paced over to the study window once more to look past the gardens to the mews. Only several flickering lanterns lit the darkness. No movement.

Where was Fletch? He should have returned hours ago.

Her fingertips lifted, touching the glass to feel the cold seeping in. Cold she should be feeling. She should be with him, doing everything possible to find her sister.

"You should be sleeping." Fletch's sudden low voice made her jump.

Talia spun. Fletch was whole—rumpled and tired—but whole. She hadn't realized until that moment her worry had included not just her sister, but Fletch as well. "I did not see you come in."

"My driver dropped me at the front walk. I told you not to wait for me."

She sped across the study to him, picking up and handing him the glass of brandy she had poured for him an hour ago. "You knew even when you said those words I would not listen to them. I would have disguised myself as a man and accompanied you to that club tonight if I thought I could have managed unnoticed."

"I am thankful for small favors, then." He lifted the glass of brandy up to her. "Wifely attentions already?"

"Why would I not have a tumbler ready for you?" She swatted at his chest. "Do not dawdle. Was he there? Why did it take so long? What did you learn?"

"He was at the club." Fletch took a sip of the amber liquid. "I had to wait until Lord Drockston was deep in his cups before setting myself next to him. And then I had to lose a good deal of coin to him to get his attention."

"So what did you discover?"

"Lord Drockston has the girls he is done with delivered to Rupert Redrock. He sells them, recoups some of his costs."

"Redrock?" Talia blanched, stumbling a step backward as her arm clasped the front of her belly. "But he—he rules the eastern end of the rookeries."

"You know of him?"

"I have heard his name. Heard the women in the brothel discuss him. Many worked for him."

"Yes."

Her eyes went wide, her voice shaking as she recalled all of the snippets of conversation she had overheard. "He...he is not kind, Fletch—a cutthroat—ruthless. That is how they spoke of him."

Fletch's eyes flickered, and Talia could see the unease in his look.

He shook his head. "It does not bode well that she is currently in that den of depravity, Talia."

She stepped to him, her hand going to his chest. "So I need to go there. Find her."

"Talia, your sister..." He hedged his words, his voice careful. "She was sold at the Jolly Vassal, and now—if she was sold into Redrock's clutches."

Her eyebrows drew together as she looked up at him. "Yes?"

"Have you thought about how your sister will be… affected by all of this?"

"Affected? What do you mean?"

"I mean I do not know if you are prepared for what you will find when we recover your sister. What has become of her. The state of her mind, of her person, with the damage that has been done to her."

Her hand shoved slightly on his chest. "She is my sister, Fletch. Nothing has become of her."

"Talia—"

"No. Do not even—I am heartbroken I failed Louise—I got here too late. I failed her by two days. I cannot even imagine what she has gone through, Fletch." Talia spun from him, going to stand before the fire, her arms wrapping around her body. "But she is still my sister. No matter what. That has not changed. And I will move heaven and earth for her if I have to."

She looked over her shoulder at him. "If you think her now a lesser person, Fletch, then I cannot have you near her, near me, when she is found." Talia looked back to the fire. "Maybe even now we need to end our business together."

"You are my wife, Talia. Our business is nowhere near to done."

She heard the clink of the glass being set down, and Fletch moved behind her, his heat inundating her space. "I do not think less of her, Talia. But I do not want you believing you will find your sister as you once knew her. I need you to be prepared for the harsh truth of how she may be now. The reality of what has happened to her."

Talia fought against his words.

He was only telling her what she knew, yet didn't want to acknowledge. But it stung. She wanted to hold onto the hope that her sister was unscathed. Still innocent. That Louise had somehow survived the past weeks without irreparable harm done to her mind or person.

Fletch's hands landed on her shoulders, his fingers sliding forward to press into her flesh. "I know you want to, but we cannot go tonight. It is only hours until daylight, and we know nothing. I will find out all I can tomorrow. And then, armed with knowledge, we can search for her tomorrow night."

Talia nodded, silent, her chin dropping to her chest.

"We will find her, Talia. Do not lose heart."

~ ~ ~

The three street urchins slipping into the alleyway behind him, Fletch motioned for his driver to stay in his perch.

"Home," he said.

His hand reached the handle on the carriage door and a split second of dread shot through him as he wondered if Talia would still be sitting inside, waiting.

She had insisted on coming along to talk to Fletch's bow street runner, and when the man had directed Fletch to the three boys several blocks from Redrock's main brothel, Talia had refused to be let off at his townhouse. He didn't have time to waste arguing with her if he was to reach the boys before nightfall, so Fletch had begrudgingly let her accompany him as long as she swore to stay in the carriage with the curtains drawn.

But he did not put it past Talia to sneak out on her own and go wandering the streets in some fool-headed search for her sister. His wife had an aggravating lack of concern for her own safety.

He opened the coach door with an exhale of relief to see her sitting there, and he jumped up into the carriage. Her eyes whipping to him, she almost leapt up the second he gained his seat. Instead, she stopped herself, perching on the edge of her bench. The carriage started moving.

"Tell me."

Fletch pulled the curtains open and settled himself, taking one moment to breathe. "There are three brothels that she could have been placed in. The Pink Filly, Oak's Pleasure, or The Surf Oasis. She is in one of them, those little pups assured me."

"Can they be trusted?"

"They run for Redrock. But Redrock just killed one of their brothers, so they are none too loyal at the moment."

Talia slid backward on the bench, nodding, her mind obviously churning. "Then I am going to work for the brothels. It is the way in."

Fletch leaned forward, shoving aside the fabric of his black great coat that had tangled about his legs. "Like hell you are, Talia."

"Fletch, it is the only path to get inside the brothels without arousing suspicion. I can search the rooms. This is the fastest way to find her."

"Absolutely not. I am not letting you near those hell holes."

His glare didn't give her the slightest pause. "Fletch, truly, do not be stubborn. You do not know what my sister looks like. A maid moving about with chamber pots is the smartest plan."

Fletch shook his head, his teeth gritting. "Aside from the obvious lack of safety, I do not want you hauling shit, Talia."

"I will go to any depths, remember that, Fletch?" Her eyes flashed defiance. "And this is the safest way for me to search for her."

"Except you are not searching for her. I am not allowing it. You are my wife and it would bode you well to remember that."

Her shoulders snapped back as her eyebrows stretched impossibly high. "Bode me well? I did not become your wife so that you could control me, Fletch. Do not make that mistake."

"It is not a mistake, Talia. It is me keeping you safe from harm whether you like it or not. I will go into the brothels. I will find Louise."

Her scowl jerked off his face, her look landing on the window.

Just when Fletch thought the matter settled and his wife was adhering to his wishes, her mouth opened, her voice calm.

"Let it never be said that I have been dishonest with you, Fletch."

He eyed her, suspicion settling heavy into his belly. "What is that supposed to mean?"

"Ask me what I am going to do when we get home, Fletch."

Fletch paused, the air dangerously thick between them before words hissed out of his tight lips. "What are you going to do when we get home, Talia?"

She looked at him, her hazel eyes skewering, but her voice serene. "I am going to darken my hair. I am going to bind my chest. I am going to steal a maid's uniform. And I am going to one of those brothels the moment you leave the townhouse to search for my sister."

"You would not."

"I would. Do not doubt it. She is my sister and I will stop at nothing."

His fingers balled into fists as he looked away from her. How he needed to hit something—pound anything at the moment. Openly defiant to his wishes. Once more, she thought she could do a better job at finding her sister than he could. How in the bloody hell had he let this woman into his life? This maddening, irrational, fool woman that would not listen to reason.

She wouldn't listen to reason. So Fletch was going to have to keep her safe in a much more dangerous way.

They rode in silence for five blocks, Talia avoiding his stare as Fletch debated his plan.

"Then I am coming as well, Talia."

She jumped at his words, her eyes whipping to him. "You cannot."

"Ask me what I am going to do the moment after you escape from the townhouse in your maid's costume."

She sighed. "What are you going to do, Fletch?"

"Follow you. You will not even know I am behind you until you see me in whichever brothel you find yourself in. I can hover about a whorehouse as well as the next man. And I can keep you safe. Heaven knows you need it."

"Or maybe I just need you." She smiled sweetly—far too sweetly.

Fletch knew instantly Talia had just manipulated him to get her way.

He heaved a sigh.

She would be the death of him—if he wasn't already on his way there.

~ ~ ~

"Here." Fletch walked into Talia's chambers and flipped a dagger into the air, softly catching the blade end of it. He held out the handle to her, dark green jade entwined with wraps of thin silver cords.

She stared at it, her nose wrinkling as she twisted her darkened hair about her head, sticking in pins to hold strands in place. "What is this?"

"If I am going to allow you to go into this brothel, then I want you to have a blade on your person as well. I want you to be able to defend yourself—at least until I can reach you."

"Fletch, I do not know how to use a blade." Sighing, Talia set the handful of pins on the dresser below the silver-encased mirror, even though her hair was only half pinned up. She turned to Fletch, noting he had changed his clothes. Not quite rags, but not his usual impeccably tailored clothing. Rumpled in the down-on-his-coin look of a foxed dandy. "I am much more likely to cut myself than to cut someone attacking me."

"Then I will teach you." He waved the handle to her. "Take it, Talia."

"Look at me, Fletch." She pointed to her head, the darkened hair wet down so it looked greasy and unkempt, then to her face where she had splotched a mixture of dirt and charcoal. "I am gloriously unattractive right now. I look like a ragamuffin twelve-year-old boy in a dress. No one will pay me any mind. I do not need the blade."

He stepped toward her. "All I see is you, Talia. And you—unfortunate for where you are determined to put yourself—are beautiful."

She couldn't hide a smile, even though she recognized he was still trying to sway her not to go with obvious pandering. "You are looking beyond the dirt, Fletch—and you already know exactly what is under my chest bindings."

He licked his lips. "I do. And I mean to protect all of that."

He picked up her hand, wrapping it around the hilt of the blade. "Do this not for yourself, then. Do it for me. Do it because I am asking my wife for this one small request."

She sighed, her fingers folding around the handle. The feel, the weight of it was awkward. She had never held a dagger before. Cutting knives, yes. But never a blade such as this—one meant to harm. "Fine. But you will need to teach me what to do with it."

Fletch smirked. "I will go retrieve a blunt-tipped blade for instruction."

She looked down at the shine of the sharp blade. "And I will alter my sleeve so I can conceal this."

"It cannot go about your waist—under your apron?" He lifted the side of her apron, bending to the side to see behind it. "It will be easier to hide in here."

"No. Too many patrons brush by my waist—or grab me there. I do not want to arouse any suspicion, and a lowly maid slopping chamber pots does not carry a fine dagger such as this."

Fletch's jaw tightened. His mouth opened, but then he clamped it shut, turning to silently walk out the adjoining door to his chambers.

Talia stared at the closed door.

Maybe she shouldn't have mentioned the handsy patrons to Fletch.

But better that he know what was coming, so he could keep a proper distance from her in the brothel. That was imperative.

He couldn't overreact at the first hand to slap her backside.

Talia turned back to the mirror, picking up the pins.

As much as she wanted the protection of Fletch within reach, she prayed he wouldn't interfere in finding Louise.

She had already failed her sister for too long.

{ CHAPTER 10 }

The Oak's Pleasure was the smallest of the three brothels and the furthest from the docks. Talia wanted to start in that establishment, partly because she hoped its size and proximity meant it was the least depraved of the three, and partly because she still held out hope that Louise was not in the nastiest of nasty places.

Once darkness had fallen, begging for a job from the barkeep had gone well in the back alley, especially at the ridiculously low price she had named for her services. Five hours into hauling chamber pots and scrubbing ancient spit from the ragged front wood of the bar, Talia bent down to the floor behind the chair Fletch sat in to clean up a glass that had shattered. Shattered by her husband, for just that very purpose, she guessed. Setting the chamber pot she had been carrying onto the floor by her black skirts, she started picking up the shards of glass, angling her head to be close to the curved wooden slats along the back of Fletch's chair.

"Anything?" Fletch asked, his mouth hidden behind a tankard of ale.

"Nothing," Talia whispered loudly enough for him to hear with the off-key pianoforte clanging out a tune across the room. "And I have seen all the rooms except for the ones on the third floor above."

"We only have an hour left, maybe less. It is getting too raucous in here, and I will drag you away if I have to."

Talia stifled a sigh, tossing glass into the pot. She dragged her forearm across her face, hiding her mouth. "I am attempting to make my way up there now."

Fletch gave a slight nod, setting the tankard in front of him on the small square table. He raised his hand to a barmaid, waving her over.

Talia dropped the last few shards of glass into the chamber pot, happy she only cut her fingers twice. Wiping the two lines of blood on her apron, she picked up the chamber pot and began to snake her way through the small, closely bunched tables to the back door.

Two tables away from Fletch, a drunkard tossed his arm out, capturing Talia around the waist. She spun, sending liquid from the pot splashing onto his arm. It made no difference to the louse. The weight of his arm went heavy on her belly, dragging her down onto his lap.

She shoved at his arm, trying to twist away while not sending the contents of the entire pot onto her clothes. Blast it. The drunk was already waving his hand at the main procurer.

Talia had identified the brothel's procurer early in the night. Smartly dressed with a keen eye on the room, he was the one that made the deals, completed the transactions for the prostitutes working the floor. And if the drunk clamping her down, grinding her into his lap was waving at the procurer, it only meant one thing.

She squirmed harder, trying to escape the drunk before the procurer made his way across the wide room. Five tables away. Three tables away. One table away.

"Three shillings. She be gross—a wretch smelly and dirty 'er be, but it be all I got," the drunk clutching her to his lap shouted out past her shoulder.

A hideous blast of his breath, straight past his three black teeth, sent her head spinning.

Talia attempted to not be offended by the cur calling her gross—that was what she had intended with her appearance—but the man's own level of disgustingness gave him little right to judge.

The procurer stopped at the edge of the table just as Fletch stepped in front of him, blocking Talia from his view.

Fletch leaned forward, talking into the procurer's ear. The procurer leaned to the side, looking Talia up and down, and then quizzical, he looked back to Fletch.

Fletch nodded, then leaned forward to say something else Talia couldn't hear.

With a shrug, the procurer stepped around Fletch, grabbing Talia's arm and wrenching her away from the drunkard and to her feet. "You're to go with this one, wench."

"But oye—oye—oye be clean'r, sir. No more. No more." Talia dropped her words into her thickest gutter accent, clutching the chamber pot to her chest in feigned fright.

"She will do." With a nod, Fletch handed the procurer a sack of clinking coins.

Tucking the coins into an inside pocket, the procurer grabbed the edge of the pot Talia held, ripping it from her as he shoved her toward Fletch. Talia sprawled into Fletch with a terrified squeal, clawing at his clothes to catch herself before she fell.

"Room fourteen, third floor," the procurer said.

Fletch gripped Talia's upper arm, forcibly pushing her out in front of him as he weaved them through the maze of tables. She squirmed and twisted, making a show of wanting to escape his grasp.

They made it past the door that led to the stairs and Fletch loosened his grip on her. He wrapped his arm about her shoulders, drawing her into him as he ushered them up the skinny flights of stairs.

"You could have acted faster." Her accent dropped with her harsh whisper as she glared up at him.

"I wanted you to fully understand what an asset having your husband accompany you to a brothel would be."

She smacked his chest. "That was a lesson? You ogre. You saw how that drunk was manhandling me, and you just let it happen."

"You were in no danger." He squeezed her shoulder. "And he got most of that pot spilled onto him, which was well done by you. You knew what you were doing, and I knew what I was doing."

"You are an arse." She stomped up the next three steps next to him and then glanced up at him. "But thank you. What now?"

Fletch shrugged. "We go upstairs and have sex, I suppose."

Her eyes flew wide. "No."

Fletch didn't curb his smirk.

Moments later, they slipped into room fourteen. A bed, neatly made with a shiny, blood-red coverlet commandeered the middle of the room. In front of the bed sat a backless bench, half the width of the bed, upholstered in red and black stripes with the sides swooping upward into Grecian scrolls. Draperies matching the blood-red coverlet lined the far wall.

Talia glanced up. A large mirror was attached to the ceiling. She had seen it in many of the brothel rooms, yet still wondered at it.

Fletch freed her shoulders from his arm.

"This room is much nicer than the ones below," Talia said. "Cleaner, as well."

He moved to face her, leaning in, his mouth next to her ear as he dropped his voice to a whisper. "Speak softly. There are always holes in rooms like these." He stood straight, his voice normal. "When one pays for the whole night, one gets better treatment."

Her look flew around the room, looking for holes. She went to her tiptoes to reach his ear. "All night? How long is it expected that we stay in here?"

Fletch slid his hands down around her waist, burying his face in her neck. "I imagine for at least a few minutes. I look virile, after all." His nose rubbed the handkerchief that wrapped over her ear. "I hate this blasted wrap on your head."

His fingers moved up and started to slide under the edge of it, but she caught his wrist. "Leave it. I still have to check the rooms on this floor."

He dropped his hand back down to her buttock, squeezing it.

She smiled into the side of his face. "You can take it off when we get back to your house. And you can unwrap my bindings as well."

"You liked how I did that the other night?"

She nodded into the heat of his neck, her lips grazing the dark stubble lining his neck. "I did. You did it so slowly, your fingers slipping along my skin. I both wanted and did not want you to be the gentleman you were."

"Do not tempt me with visions of your naked body, Talia, or I will strip you down right now and take what I paid for."

She pulled slightly away from his neck. "You don't think to actually—"

"They have peepholes everywhere, Talia." Both of his hands slid down, tightening his hold on the curve of her backside. "We have to make this look real."

She looked around the room. "The bed?"

"No. You are mine, Talia. I am not about to let a lecher see you. Not about to let the slightest bit of your skin show." Fletch moved backward, lifting her slightly and dragging her on her toes along with him.

For all she didn't care for Fletch's constant manhandling, she couldn't deny the way her chest tightened when he staked claim to her. Raw and male. A primeval lust awakened in her core, teasing to the surface.

Reaching the scrolled bench at the foot of the bed, he sat. "Here. Straddle my lap. Your skirts will cover you and we can mock the motions."

His hands still clutching her backside, he drew Talia forward and split her legs, making sure her skirts still covered her legs down to her tall boots. She dropped to sit on Fletch's lap, the heat of her nestled onto the bulge in his pants.

His hand came up, fingers slipping under the back of the handkerchief covering her head, and he pulled her down to him, his lips meeting hers. They were creating a farce, but the kiss was the furthest thing from false. Fletch plied her lips, his teeth running along the swell of her bottom lip. His tongue plunging up, seeking to taste her deeply.

Her hips started moving on their own volition. Circling, gyrating slowly on his hard shaft as his tongue swept long strokes into her mouth.

What had been contained when she sat on Fletch's lap was quickly spinning out of control. Her core throbbed as she grew to despise the flap of fabric on Fletch's trouser that kept their bodies apart. Kept him from entering her.

If she had learned anything about herself in the past few days, it was that she was wanton, through and through, and she wanted Fletch deep inside of her at any opportunity.

His lips left her mouth, his hand shifting her head to the side as he traced kisses down her neck. Talia leaned into it, her eyes closing as her body demanded more. Her knees went wide, bracing on the bench to leverage herself harder onto him.

Her hips swung with force against the fabric of his trousers, his cock granite against the pulsating swell of her folds.

"Why do you do this to me?" Her voice came out in a raspy whisper, foreign to her own ears. "Make me want this, make me feel this when all I want to do is concentrate on finding Louise."

His lips did not leave her skin with his words. "I do this to distract you, Talia."

Her hips stopped circling and her eyes opened to look down at him. "Distract me from finding my sister?"

He held her in place with his left hand on her backside, his right hand dropping from her neck to dive between them and under her skirts. Invading the heat of her, his fingers found her pulsating core and he twisted his forefinger around it. Talia jerked from the sensation ripping through her—both fighting and wanting to succumb to his manipulation.

He nipped her neck, then ringed the spot with his tongue. "To distract you from your worry. It is destroying you, and there is nothing else we can be doing at the moment than this very thing."

His fingers flicked through her folds, and Talia curled onto him, clutching the back of his neck.

She dropped her head, her words in his ear. "This is too much, Fletch. I am throbbing. I need you in me."

His fingers stopped. "Damn, Talia. No."

"Yes. My skirts will hide everything." She reached down, pulling her skirts higher up to hide his abdomen before her fingers worked fast along the line of buttons on the front flap of his trousers.

His lips never left her neck. Denied her nothing.

His shaft free, jutting up, Talia went up onto her knees on either side of him, lifting herself and then guiding him into her depths as she descended. He filled her, massive, stretching her, but her slickness was her ally as he slid up into her, reaching so deeply within that she wondered at the ability of her body to accommodate him.

Her arms went wide to grab the tops of the side scrolls on the bench as Fletch gripped her hips, his thumbs digging into the flesh around her hip bones.

He lifted her slightly, rocking her in circles as he let her slowly descend. Torture. Her body met his and a scream escaped, catching in her throat as she buckled, burying herself tighter to him. He let her gyrate for a breath before lifting her again, taking the same cruel path downward with her body.

Her fingers nearly cracked the wood of the bench when he landed her fully onto him. He swiveled under her, the pressure on her core too much as her body ripped away from her conscious thought, the eruption gripping her every nerve, contorting her body as she ground wave after wave into him.

Gasping for breath, the rolling sparks of climax still seizing her body, she felt herself being lifted, losing his shaft from her body as he dropped her onto his thighs. A growl into her chest, and she could feel Fletch's body shudder violently under her, wetness suddenly smearing onto her thighs under her skirts.

Her mind only half aware, she realized he had just climaxed not inside of her. But outside.

She froze in place, her arms still wide, her chin curled over the top of his head, trying to comprehend what he had just done. Again.

A repeat of every time they had been together.

He didn't want to ejaculate into her.

Fletch had not done it once—always pulling free at the last moment.

Maybe she didn't understand something about sex. Even after all she had seen in the brothels. Maybe that was how he enjoyed it. Maybe he needed air, to not be constricted to come.

Maybe.

But the harsh truth of the only reason he wouldn't want to do so squirmed into her mind and began eating away at her thoughts.

He didn't want his seed in her body.

She wasn't good enough for it.

Wasn't good enough for him.

His body still twitched under her, but Talia could not take another instant of touching him.

She jerked backward, yanking her skirts with her and jumping to her feet. It left him bared to the world, but she didn't care.

Before Fletch could react, she grabbed the chamber pot from under the table by the bed and rushed toward the door. "I need to check the other rooms on this floor. And then we can be done with this place."

She sped out the doorway, escaping into the hallway and closing the door with held breath.

She stopped, gasping for air as she leaned against the door.

Fletch had married her. But he didn't want her. Not truly. She was beneath him after she had been ruined by her circumstances.

That much was evident.

She allowed herself one more gasp. The whimpered gargle of it spiked her ire, pride straightening her shoulders.

Giving herself a shake, she hurried down the hall, knocking on the first door she came to.

She had rooms to check.

~ ~ ~

"We will go to the Pink Filly tomorrow night. I am sorry your sister was not at the Oak's Pleasure."

Talia jumped, looking across to Fletch in the low lantern light of the carriage.

After she had checked the last rooms on the third floor, they had said very little as she had disappeared out the back of the brothel, and he had followed her, ushering her through the shadows to the carriage a block away.

She shifted on the carriage bench, nodding quickly, her gaze dropping to the dark blue cushion next to his right leg.

"What is amiss, Talia? It is more than your sister—you left me in that room with hardly a word and now you are avoiding me. You are not one to usually do so."

Her eyes stayed on the cushion, replaying in her mind the scene in the brothel room with Fletch. Maybe she misunderstood all of it. Maybe he had other reasons.

Or maybe she was very right about his opinion of her.

"Talia?"

Her gaze skittered up to him. "Why do you pull away—out of me? The first few times I did not think on it. I thought that was how you liked to…finish." Talia could feel her cheeks starting to burn, a hot flush blanketing her neck. "But I know. I have seen it in the brothels. That is what they do to avoid becoming with child—have the men finish outside of the women."

Fletch straightened on his bench. "Talia, you are making assumptions."

She shook her head. "I thought you wanted to satisfy your aunt with our union."

"I did."

"Yet you do not want me to be with child?"

His fingers ran through his hair, mussing it wild. He sighed. "No."

"No? But why?"

Fletch's jaw clamped shut, and he looked away from her, staring at an upper corner of the carriage.

Talia's gut sank. "Is it because of where I have been? What I done? What I have witnessed? I have ruined myself and I am beneath you."

She stared at him, stared at his eyes, waiting for the slightest twitch, the slightest blink to tell her she was wrong. Tell her she was imagining all of her worries.

He said nothing, his eyes trained on the dark corner.

The silent rejection blasted her, struck her deep in her chest, a brick of humiliation that threatened the very air she breathed.

Her chin dropped, her look landing on her lap as she tried to control her breathing, tried to control the panic threatening to seize her body.

What had she done? Married a man that thought so little of her, he could not taint himself with her blood?

The panic snaked around her belly, squeezing. It moved to her chest, cutting her breath. No. Not now. Her hands clamped together in her lap, fighting the fear gripping her. She could not break. Not now. Not in front of him.

He would see how his rejection affected her, and she could not allow that.

If he did not think she was worthy of him, then she sure as hell would not let him have the satisfaction of seeing her falter at the news.

Talia parted her lips slightly, trying to draw an even breath. It only came in ragged, halting.

She needed to stop thinking of Fletch. Stop considering him as part of her life now.

She gulped another breath. It brought air into her lungs. Not a lot, but enough to hold at bay the panic attempting to seize her.

He had said one year.

Maybe it was time to convince him a much shorter time period would be convenient for both of them.

CHAPTER 11

Talia knocked on the study door. No answer.

She stopped, staring at the grain of the dark wood panel as she debated.

She knew Fletch was in his study. They had not spoken since the carriage ride home in the earliest hours of the morning, but Talia had thought of nothing but their conversation since then.

Even in her tousled sleep, she had dreamt of his words, or rather, the lack of his words. She had awoken to find Fletch had sequestered himself away in his study. The day had passed, and he had not left the room.

But now that darkness had settled, the time for her to get ready to go to the next brothel was quickly approaching. She needed to talk to Fletch. Needed to settle her mind before they went out looking for Louise again.

Without another knock, she turned the door handle and stepped into the room.

Fletch sat in one of his wide leather chairs that he had moved to the large window overlooking the gardens. The only light in the study was the flicker from the fireplace. It cast long shadows across the room, only a sliver of Fletch illuminated. He sat with his right bare foot propped atop his left knee, wearing only dark trousers and a white linen shirt open partway down his chest.

Asleep. Or so she assumed. Talia started to back quietly out of the room.

"Is it time to leave for the Pink Filly?"

Talia moved into the room, her silk slippers soft on the floorboards. She came to a stop next to the arm of Fletch's chair, looking down at him. Dark circles sat under his eyes—or was that merely the shadows? She noted the half-empty brandy glass in his left hand, balanced on the opposite chair arm. Had he slept at all?

"It is not yet time, but soon," she said. "I was about to go darken my hair and pull myself into the uniform."

He nodded, taking a sip of the brandy. His look didn't veer from the window.

Talia drew a deep breath. "Fletch, I know you said one year and I would be free to move about as I wish. I propose that after we find my sister, I excuse myself from London with her to help her recover."

His gaze snapped up to her. "That was not our agreement, Talia."

"No. But I did not realize how little…esteem you had for me. I was mistaken because you were kind with me. I understand now that all of this has been solely for your aunt's benefit. Do not worry. I will attend any functions you deem necessary to continue the facade. I wish your aunt to know the truth no more than you do, as I do admire her."

His head tilted down slightly, but his look stayed riveted on her. "Why are you even suggesting this, Talia?"

She shrugged, her voice taking on a defensive tone she didn't care for, but couldn't curb. "While I am grateful, above all, for your assistance in finding Louise, your opinion is such that I am beneath you, Fletch. Not worthy of you. And as much as you are entitled to your viewpoint, I would prefer to not be held under the thumb of a man that does not respect me, that holds me in disdain."

"Holds you in disdain? Talia—"

Her hands clasped in front of her, twisting together as her voice pitched higher. "Please, Fletch, please, I just want to find my sister and escape this city that has torn me into a thousand pieces."

Setting his brandy glass down, he stood, facing her. "Talia, you clearly are mad if this is what you think."

"Mad?" Her face crumpled, her head trembling. He thought her beneath him, but she hadn't expected him to be cruel. "What? You have not humiliated me enough, Fletch? Now you would like to remind me of how insane I am as well?" She spun from him, looking out the window at the dormant plants filling the rows of neat, square plots. "You made me…made me…" Her voice petered out.

He moved next to her, his chest touching her shoulder. "I made you what, Talia?"

Her head shook violently. "It does not matter. I have been a fool since I arrived in London. I intend to stop that from continuing to be the state of my life."

She turned and strode to the door.

Fletch intercepted her, jumping in front of her a step before she reached the entrance. He grabbed her shoulders, halting her motion as his grey eyes pierced her. "You are not beneath me, Talia. You are so far above me, it is laughable."

"I am not laughing, Fletch."

His grip on her shoulders tightened, jerking her body slowly with his low words. "I am going to die, Talia. Die."

Her hand flew to her belly, stunned. Stunned and not believing his words. She staggered backward, ripping herself from his hands as her voice shrank to a scared whisper. "Wh—what?"

"I am going to die, Talia. Soon."

"What—when—no—how do you know this? Are you sick? Is someone trying to kill you?"

"No."

"Then what? This cannot be." Her head shook furiously.

"It is, Talia."

She looked up at him, her eyes going wide. "No. No. No. You promised me you would not die, Fletch. Before I agreed to…to marry you…you promised…you swore you would not give me footing and then rip it away from me."

She ran past him to the door.

He snatched her around the waist before she could get her hand on the knob. "No, Talia, let me explain."

"No, you bastard." She spun, hitting his chest. Her hands clamped into tight fists, ramming his chest, pummeling him. "You bloody bastard. You swore to me this would not happen and I trusted you. I trusted you and you used me. You bloody well lied to me and used me. You swore, you bastard, you swore."

He grabbed her wrists, forcing them down to her sides. "I did not want to tell you now. I never was going to tell you, Talia. I thought we would have more time before you knew."

"So you were just going to bloody well die on me one day?" She twisted her arms, trying to break free from his hold. "Out of nowhere? Just happy one day and dead the next?"

"I thought it would be kinder this way, Talia—you not knowing what was to happen. I was not going to tell you, but I cannot have you believing I would ever reject you. Ever. I would never think you less than me."

"How is that kind, Fletch? How is this kind? You know what happened to me—you know what happened when my father died. How we lost everything in that moment. How could you do this to me?" She looked up at him, her eyes to slits as she yanked at her arms. "This...this is nothing but cruelty."

He lifted her wrists above her head, shoving her back onto the door and clamping her arms to the wood. "Dammit, Talia, listen to me. I never meant this to be cruel. But what happened last night—it was even crueler. I will never not want you, Talia. Never." His head dropped before her, his breath hot on her face, his grey eyes only an inch from hers. His voice went low, rough. "Of all the words I have spoken to you, Talia, none has been truer. I want you. This, you must not doubt."

The ferocity in his look stopped her struggle. Stopped her from fighting to leave.

Her eyes closed to him, her mind still unable to comprehend what he was telling her. "But why—why do this to me? Marry me when you..."

"I just wanted normal, Talia. For the time I have left. I wanted you. Normal. I was selfish. But I wanted—needed something real. And you appeared and you are real, Talia. Real. Genuine. Owning every second of your life, no matter where it has taken you."

Her head dropped, tears she could not control slipping off her cheeks to fall into the space between them. Slowly, her head lifted, her eyes opening to him, her words trembling. "But why? There is no reason—why do you have to die, Fletch? Why?"

"It is destined, Talia."

"Destined? No, that is insanity. How could that be?"

"My brother, father, grandfather, great-grandfather, and five before him—all of them died by the time they were thirty-three. Every single man in my lineage."

"But you are…"

"Thirty-two and three quarters."

Her knees gave out. Only Fletch's hold on her wrists above her head kept her upright.

"But why? How? Not you, Fletch."

"Yes, me. Everyone has tried to escape the curse, and all have failed. I have accepted it, Talia, and you need to do the same."

"No. This is ridiculous. A curse cannot kill you. There must be some explanation."

"There is none. The curse is real, Talia. Real and it is coming for me soon."

Her head swung from side to side until she buried her face in her upper arm, refusing to hear his words, refusing to look at him.

"My death—this ends with me, Talia. The Lockston line. This curse. I refuse to condemn an innocent child to early death. It is why I pull from you before I climax. My actions have not a thing to do with you."

She pulled her face free from her burrow, looking at him. "You do not want an heir?"

"No, and that was why I wanted to marry you." He loosened his hold on her wrist, letting her arms drop. "Aside from my aunt, who is not long for this earth, there is no one to inherit the fortune. My brother died years ago without an heir and my sister died in childbirth. There is no one of the line left aside from me."

His hands went to her cheeks, cupping her face. "You are my chance to do something meaningful, Talia. The estates, the wealth, I want all of it, every bit of it I can control, to go to you, your family. You are the most good—the most deserving—person I have ever encountered. And also the most wronged—what you have endured at the hands of what we like to label gentle society has been atrocious. There is nothing gentle about this world we live in."

"You married me in pity?"

"I married you because I want the estate to go to you. Because you are worthy of it. Because you are strong. Because you are smart and will know how to use it best. Because you see so much more of the world than I can. Because I want to leave a legacy through you. Pity has not a thing to do with it."

Her fingers went up, wrapping around his wrists. "But you have the possibility for a child, Fletch. With me. You could have a girl. She would not be cursed."

"I will not chance it, Talia. This is the way it needs to be. I am the last in the line. A line that needs to end with me. I made that decision years ago. But you—wanting normal with you—I did not plan upon."

"No."

His hands dropped from her face as he jerked away. "No?"

"No. You have a chance to leave a true legacy, Fletch, your own flesh and blood, and you are not choosing to fight for that. You look at me and you want normal—well, this is normal, Fletch. Wanting a life, wanting children with you. If you are asking me to deny that, then everything we do in this marriage is only a performance—furthering the farce it started out as."

"Talia—"

Her hands went onto his chest, pressing into him. "No, Fletch. You wanted real—this is real. Me. Me wanting to bear your children is a real desire. I want a real family. Not a life where I am waiting for death to come and rip me to shreds again. I cannot live like that."

He looked up to the coffered ceiling, his head shaking. His gaze dropped to her, his fingers clasping over the back of her hands on his chest. "You do not understand what life is like, Talia, knowing when you will die. Knowing the year. I have known my whole life."

He paused, taking a deep breath, his chest trembling under her hands. "I harbored the smallest hope, for some time, that my brother would survive, and I would be free of the curse as well. But he did not. Three days before he turned thirty-three, he died. It came on sudden, and he was dead within hours."

Talia's fingers curled on his chest, her heart splitting at the agony pulsating in his grey eyes.

But she could not conjure words to help ease his pain.

She had suffered loss as well, but her father's death had been a blow, a shocking occurrence that had dismantled every piece of her life in its wake. Fletch's loss was very different—something she could only barely begin to imagine. He had lived with loss his whole life—a suffocating, always impending cloud of pain that never parted to let true light shine upon his life.

Yet for everything she didn't understand in the moment, could not yet comprehend, she knew one thing— she could not promise him anything she honestly wasn't about concede to.

And she already knew, deep in her gut, she would not concede to accepting his death.

Not as he had clearly done.

Her hands slid down his chest from under his grip.

"I…I cannot…I have to get ready for the brothel, Fletch." Her voice came out a mere whisper, her chest allowing no air to her words.

Fletch nodded, leaning past her to open the door for her.

Talia stepped past him, her feet in a flurry until she reached her chambers and collapsed into the chair before her dressing table.

She looked at herself in the mirror, noting her red-rimmed eyes.

She stared at herself a long time, truly coming to terms with all that had happened to her since leaving Norfolk. Arriving in London. Searching for her sister. The things she had had to sink to. Approaching Fletch. Every moment they had spent together. Becoming his wife. How incredibly important that man in the study below had become to her.

She was not the woman that had left that tiny village in Norfolk to bring her sister home. And she never would be again.

She now knew she would battle to the depths of hell to save someone she loved.

And she was not about to allow Fletch to die on her.

Not without a fight.

{Chapter 12 }

Talia stared up at the hulking man. Hulking with the round cherub face of a sweet baby. She wasn't sure if she should be slowly backing away or smiling up at him and pinching his cheeks.

"What of ye?" the barkeep asked from one of the two back doors at the Pink Filly brothel as he tossed the contents of a metal pot into the alley.

Talia cowered appropriately, glancing with a side look up to him as she slipped into her harsh accent. "Oye be lookin fer work—'em pots o' filth aye cin empty. Oye 'ave no problems 'bout 'em and will empty 'em, 'n scrub 'em right good. Not but a sixpence."

The barkeep tilted his head toward the door with a sigh, his thick hand pushing it open. "Come with ye, then. If ye cin last the night, ye cin get paid."

Talia bowed her head, scurrying past him. She saw the shadow of Fletch move from the end of the alley as she disappeared inside.

The barkeep sent Talia upstairs almost immediately to service the rooms above. This brothel was larger than the last, but much more intimate, the décor catering to a more well-heeled customer than in the previous brothels where she had searched for Louise.

But it was all cut from the same cloth—the blood-red curtains in these rooms were the same as in the room she and Fletch had found themselves in the night before.

She emptied pots, going up and down the stairs for two hours and passing each time by the table Fletch had staked out in the corner of the main room.

The brothel as a whole was classier—the ladies working through the tables in the main room had bodices on their dresses that actually covered their bosoms. Cleavage was still plunging, but at least the nipples were covered.

Talia gave slight thanks for that minor token, as she had to watch her husband ogle and pander to the many women that approached his table.

Working her way up to the fourth floor in the building, Talia's hope for the evening was waning. She looked down the hall on the last floor, noting she only had six more rooms to check in. At least they could leave the place soon.

She stepped around the burly man that stood guard at the end of the hall. Curious, as there were no guards on the levels below, only at the bottom of the stairs.

She knocked on the door closest to the stairs and the guard. With no answer, she opened the door.

Inside, a woman sat alone on a bed, her back to the door. Talia could tell the bright turquoise dress the woman wore was similar to the ones the other prostitutes modeled, cut low all around the torso—showing everything but the nipples. The woman's shoulders were softly shaking.

"Fer the pot, miss?" Talia kept her voice soft so as to not startle the woman.

The woman turned on the bed, and Talia almost dropped to the floor.

Louise.

Louise turned away from Talia. "Take it and go."

Frozen, it was a full minute before Talia realized Louise didn't recognize her.

Talia shuffled forward, grabbing the chamber pot underneath the foot of the bed. Striking the insane need to run to her sister and grab her and drag her down the stairs, instead, Talia backed out the entrance and closed the door, forcing herself not to say a word.

She spun to the stairs, her chin on her chest as she went past the guard to reach the stairs. Chamber pot clutching her belly, Talia veered to the inside wall of the main area and made her path to the back door. It sent her behind Fletch's chair, and she flung out her pinky, scratching his neck as she passed him and continued to the alley.

Calm, he didn't even twitch at the scrape. But he did set down his drink with haste.

Within moments, he joined her in the back alley, pretending to relieve himself against the brick wall next to the cesspit.

Talia had already dumped the chamber pot, but stayed bent over, shaking the pot, her back to Fletch as she whispered. "She's inside. Top floor, first door on the right. Closest to the guard by the stairs."

"Do nothing, Talia. I will get her out," Fletch hissed.

"I will meet you in her room."

"Tal—"

The door next to the bar opened and another patron stepped into the alley. Fletch coughed.

A very pointed cough, but Talia refused to acknowledge the warning. She kicked the cover over the cesspit closed and tucked the pot under her arm.

She scampered up the four flights of stairs as quickly as she could without drawing any attention to herself.

Passing the guard, she moved back into the room. Louise still sat on the bed, silent to the movement behind her.

Perfect.

Talia lifted high the chamber pot and smashed it as hard as she could onto the floor. The porcelain shattered, sending jagged pieces far and wide on the floor of the room. Talia dropped to her knees.

The door to the room opened almost instantly. The guard glared down at Talia. "Bloody id'it, ye fool wench."

"Oye slipped, sir." She looked up at him, tears in her eyes. "Please don't tell yer barkeep. I slipped."

"That'll be all yer wages, wench. Clean it."

Talia nodded, her hands flying along the floor, trying to scrape the pieces into a pile.

With a grunt, the guard closed the door.

Talia looked up to the bed only to see Louise looking down at her with tears streaming down her face.

"Ta...Tally?"

A huge smile broke through the crusted muck on Talia's face as she got to her feet, running over to clutch Louise.

Holding Louise to her chest, she bent to her sister's ear. "Do not say a word. There is no time to talk. No time for anything except for us to change clothes."

Louise nodded.

Within two minutes, both sisters had stripped out of their dresses. Naked save for her boots, shift, and the binding around her breasts, Talia slipped the black maid's dress up her sister's body and tied the apron as quickly as she could around Louise's waist.

The door opened, sending Talia's pounding heart into a frenzy as she jumped in front of Louise, her arms flying backward to keep her sister behind her.

Fletch was in the doorway, glare unmistakable at the scene.

But she saw the flash of understanding flicker across his face.

His scowl deepened. He realized instantly what Talia intended. And he didn't care for it one bit.

He leaned backward out the door, a wide smile on his face as he looked down the hall in the direction of the guard. "This one. This one I'll take."

Louise whimpered behind her, but Talia could only offer a squeeze on her arm to soothe her. Fletch stepped into the room, closing the door behind him, and Talia dropped Louise's arm and quickly untied the handkerchief wrapped around her head.

He went to Talia, grabbing her shoulders. Barely bridled anger threatened to pitch his voice loud. "Absolutely not, Talia."

Talia twisted out of his grip and spun to her sister. "It is already done. Louise is going to walk out of here and you are going to get her to safety." She started wrapping the handkerchief around her sister's head.

"No."

Tucking escaping strands of Louise's blond hair under the cloth, Talia glared over her shoulder at Fletch. "Yes. You are getting her to safety and then you are coming back for me."

She looked to her sister. "To your knees, Louise, hold out your apron."

Louise dropped to the floor, and Talia started scooping pieces of the broken pot into the apron. Fletch bent next to her, helping her to shovel pieces into the apron.

The apron full, Talia grabbed Louise's face. "You are going to walk out of the room with your head down. Go to the left, past the guard, and down the stairs. Do not look up at anyone. This is Fletch. You will trust him. He will follow you, catch you on the stairs, and guide you out. Keep your head down. Do not look up for anything. Do you understand?"

Louise nodded.

Talia looked to Fletch, her eyes pleading. He had to do this. She recognized how infuriated he was, and she would have to deal with that later. Right now, getting Louise out of this hellhole was the most important thing.

He sighed, his lips drawn tight, but he nodded. "Get the bloody dress on, Talia."

Talia grabbed her sister's arm, pulling her to her feet and pushing her to the door. Before fear overcame her sister, Talia shoved her out the door.

Fletch moved past Talia, stepping into the hall. He looked toward the guard, pointing back over his shoulder as he closed the door. "No pot in there, I'll be back up after a piss."

Talia set her ear on the door, listening. No sound, no scuffle.

Fletch had to succeed. He had to.

~ ~ ~

Where was he?

How long did it take to squirrel away one frightened girl from the East End?

Unless something had happened. Something bad.

Sitting on the bed, Talia stared down at the silver strands wrapping the dark green jade on the handle of the blade in her hand. She had pulled it free from the sheath in her maid's dress before putting Louise in the garment, and was now praying she wouldn't have to use it. Yet every second that ticked by, she was getting closer and closer to that very possibility.

Her thumb moved over the silver, counting the bumps, attempting to speed up time.

It had been too long. Something happened to Fletch. She trusted him to get Louise out, but something had to have happened to him on the way back to her. It had been far too long.

Or maybe it just seemed long.

Or maybe he wasn't coming back for her. Maybe she had demanded too much of him. Defied him for the last time. Did not offer up what he needed.

Maybe he was abandoning her.

Her fingers tightened around the blade of the handle. Stop. She needed to stop her imagination. Fletch was coming for her. He was.

But when?

The door opened in a fast swing, and Talia froze, unable to turn around to her fate. Her eyes closed, her breath held, she sat on the bed in Louise's cheap gown, her back to the door.

It was either Fletch or it wasn't. If it wasn't, she prayed the person didn't recognize the fact that Louise had blond hair and now the person sitting in the room had greasy black tinted hair.

"Wot the bloody 'ell?"

Heaven help her.

Boot steps came rushing at her and Talia fumbled with the blade in her hand, nearly dropping it before she got her grip on it, and spun. But she spun too late, just as the guard snatched her by the hair and yanked her off the bed.

She swung wide with the dagger, her thumb and forefinger pushed up against the guard of the blade, slicing into his arm.

Her wrist crumbled with the force of steel hitting flesh. She wasn't holding the blade like Fletch had shown her— instead pointing it straight out along her arm—weak—it was weak and now she knew why.

The guard yelped, swearing, but his hand stayed tangled in her hair and he ripped at her scalp, swinging her to the side. Her feet flying from under her, Talia hit the wall, her head feeling as if it were being torn in two.

Scrambling for footing, only the wood floor in her vision as she hung from his hand, Talia swung the blade, frantic. She didn't hit flesh, and her flailing didn't cut short his vicious chuckle. He caught her wrist with his free hand and slammed it onto the wall. The blade dropped from her hand.

More boot steps. Something splintering above her.

She fell to the floor, free from his grip. She got to her hands and knees only to see the brute tackling Fletch. They fell hard, two unyielding bodies crashing into a chair that crumbled under the mass. Fletch was on the bottom.

It only took a second for Fletch to shove the man off of him, and he was to his feet in an instant. The brute staggered to one foot and one knee, but Fletch was quicker, his boot flying up, kicking the man in the face before he could stand straight.

The blow sent the guard down. Unconscious at Talia's feet.

Fletch stepped past his legs and grabbed the dagger from the floor at the same time he snatched Talia's hand.

"We have to run."

She nodded, jumping over the brute's legs.

Out the door and down the stairs, they shoved past the bottom guard and could hear yelling behind them as Fletch slammed the door to the alley closed. They ran, Fletch dragging Talia down the alley, along a street, and into an alleyway cutting to the next street over.

Eight blocks they ran—a haphazard path through mazes of alleys—before Talia could breathe no more.

"Fletch—Fletch—" Her words were cut off by her lack of air. She yanked on his hand gripping hers.

His feet slowed, but kept moving as he looked over his shoulder to her. "We have to keep the pace, Talia."

His fingers tightened around her left hand, his steps quickening. She grabbed his wrist with her right hand, digging her heels into the ground. The cold air was hitting her now, even with the blood pounding through her body from the run, it hit her hard in Louise's low-cut, bare-threaded gown. Every breath a shock to her lungs. Her ears stinging from the cold.

"Fletch, slow."

He looked at her again, looked at her face, at her panting. His gait tempered. "We cannot be here, Talia." He glanced around, searching the surrounding buildings. A horse and cart passed, and he quickly dragged her across the street, ducking into an alley.

He propped her against the wall, and Talia's hands went to her sides, trying to squeeze out the sharp pains that had started to cut viciously across her innards below her ribs.

Fletch stood in front of her, staring at her with his stance wide, shielding her against anyone passing by. "Our exit was supposed to be quieter than this, Talia. And now we're thick into the exact area we should not be in."

"Louise?"

"She is safe. The carriage should be nearing—or even at our house already."

Nodding, Talia pulled one hand from her side, gripping his left upper arm as she tried to suck in breath that would not fill her lungs.

He instantly flinched away.

"Your arm?" Talia asked.

"It is nothing. It took the blow from landing on the chair—all my weight, all his weight."

"Can you move it?"

"Yes." He lifted his elbow, giving the limb a quick shake to prove it. "It is nothing, Talia. Can you breathe now? We need to move onward."

The dark forms had moved in silently around them in the alley. Small forms, but a number of them. Silent in their stealth. It wasn't until the voice came out of the dark that Talia realized they were surrounded.

"We be tak'n yer purse, now, guv." A growl, it was meant to intimidate, even if it had the high pitch of a young man.

Talia's look ran along the shadowy group surrounding them in a half-circle against the wall. Fletch spun, drawing the dagger from the waistband of his trousers.

Reckless.

He was going to fight ten? Half of them not even fifteen years old. Two women. Three were tall, but thin and lanky. All of them looked desperate. Rabid. Foaming at the mouth at the rich threads that had just appeared in their alley.

Fletch flashed the blade in a wide arc, defending the last of their space.

Bloody reckless. Reckless when they could get out of there without anyone getting hurt. Talia had seen this countless times on these streets. This hodgepodge gang wanted a fight no more than she did.

Talia went to her toes, hissing into the back of his ear. "Fletch, give them all the coin you have."

His hand jutted out behind him, pushing her to the wall. "Stay behind me, Talia. This was what I was meant to do."

She stared at the back of his head in the shadows. What he was meant to do? Meant to do?

Dammit. The idiot was being utterly reckless—reckless because he was waiting for death. Ready to die saving her.

Her hands went onto his shoulders, fingernails digging in with her whisper. "Fletch, do not dare to think now is the time to be a bloody hero."

"Stay the hell behind me, Talia."

The tall, thin boy to the right took a jabbing step inward. Fletch swung the blade in his direction as he pushed her harder against the wall.

She pulled herself up to his ear, her voice a wicked whisper. "You are not going to die in some imbecilic grand gesture of saving me, Fletch. No. You do not go down like that. Not because of me." In one quick motion, she ducked under his right arm and ripped the blade from his hand as she jumped in front of him.

She grabbed the dagger correctly this time, her thumb tucking over forefinger on the handle, the silver blade cutting out in a right angle to her fist. She could slice like this. Slice without her wrist crumpling from the force.

Strong.

She manifested her lowest guttural accent as she slowly flashed the knife in a half-circle at the group, finding each face. She was dressed as a whore, and she could very well speak like one. "Ye bloody rabble, 'e be mine, I cornered 'im fair—and I be cuttin' each and every one of ye, if'n ye be takin' a step."

The tall boy shuffled a step closer. "There be plent' o' 'im, ducky."

She whipped the blade in his direction. "No, ye bleatin' scrap dog. Ye want to put me—Redrock's best whore in the gutter, and 'e be comin' after the lot of ye—ye know 'e will. Now be gone with ye all, fer I cut ye just fer pleasure. This cull be mine."

Talia met each of the eyes she could see in the dark shadows, the blade high in front of her, moving slowly, with intent, in front of their faces.

It took long seconds before a few along the edges started to shuffle off, grumbling. The rest followed suit within moments.

Talia's knees nearly gave out the instant they disappeared fully into the darkness from where they had crept. Fletch's steel grip clamped onto her upper arms, holding her upright as he shoved her from the alley.

He ripped the dagger from her hand, yanking her down the street, his voice sinking to a low, furious tirade. "Reckless, Talia. Foolish recklessness. You don't know how close you were to having your fool head bashed in. Beyond reckless."

Each word was punctuated with a jerk on her arm.

She would have none of it. She kept up with his pace just to refuse him the satisfaction of manhandling her. "And you were not reckless, Fletch? I'm not going to trade my life for yours—no matter how you think fate wants this to play out. Death is not coming for you, Fletch. Not while I can stop it."

He growled, his feet speeding. He was back to dragging her. Dragging her to safety.

Talia ran, attempting to keep up with his long strides. Staring at the back of his dark jacket, she wondered if he was truly mad at her.

Or mad because he had just dodged death—dodged fate.

～～～

Fletch rubbed the bare flesh of his left triceps, turning the muscle to the light of the fire to look at it. The bruise was deep to the bone and already starting to discolor his skin.

He had been ready tonight. Ready for the end in that dark alley. And the end hadn't come.

He wasn't sure if he could be mad at Talia for what she had done. He had used brawn to get them out of the brothel, and she had used her brain to get them out of the alley. Both tactics had their place, whether or not his ego wanted to admit to it.

With a sigh, he forewent putting his shirt back on and instead grabbed the brandy he had set on the mantel and sipped it, staring at the door connecting his room to Talia's.

As if on cue, a soft knock floated from the door to him.

"Come in." He took a step away from the fire, stopping as Talia cracked the door and moved into his chambers.

Freshly bathed, she glowed like the goddess Amphitrite slipping from the gently rolling waves of the sea. Her wet hair hung over her right shoulder, back to its normal red-blond color, her fingers still working through a few rogue tangles as she smiled at him.

Had he been debating about being irate with her? Looking at her in clean innocence, he couldn't quite conjure the reason she had vexed him.

"Louise is settled?" Fletch asked.

"She is asleep. She was rabid when I went into her room. She thought she had only imagined me and that she had been sold again."

"I feared that, sending her alone in the carriage, but I had to come back for you."

"I know." Talia walked slowly across the room, stopping in front of him. "The physician and the nurse you sent in helped tremendously. Thank you, for that."

"Did she have any injuries?"

Talia shook her head, twisting her hair over her shoulder. "No. At least none that are physical. Her mind is in a precarious state, though."

Fletch watched as three fat drops of water fell from the tip of her twisted hair onto her cream robe, wetting the soft silk. Her skin showed through the fabric, the dark pink of her nipples making obvious her lack of a chemise beneath the robe.

Fletch took a sip of brandy, attempting to calm the instant twinge beneath his trousers. One look at a half-revealed nipple, and his mind was consumed with picking up his wife, parting her legs, and sliding her down onto him—instead of where it should be, which was easing her worry over her sister. Ass.

He offered a grim nod to Talia. "Her state of mind is as expected. She has been through an extreme trauma. I did send a carriage up to Norfolk to retrieve your mother. She should arrive within days if the roads allow it."

Talia's eyes widened. "You did not tell me you sent for my mother."

"I did not want to add to your worry. I sent for her the day we were married, but I did not want you to be concerned over what would happen if she arrived and we had yet to find your sister."

She offered one nod, a distinct frown settling on her lips.

"You are not pleased?"

Fletch could see her attempt to ease her frown. She failed. "I love my mother."

"Yet?"

"It is just that we have a difficult relationship. Finding Louise was my concern, and I hadn't begun to think about my mother."

"Why difficult?" Fletch took a sip of his brandy.

"It wasn't always so. Not until after we lost everything. But she stood by me when it was most needed."

That piqued Fletch's curiosity and his eyes lifted from drifting down to her nipple again. Again, an ass. "When was that?"

"There was one thing I didn't tell you before about how Cousin Arnold removed us from Rosevin." Her fingers twisting her hair tightened, pulling the red-blond strands. "Cousin Arnold wanted to marry me. But he is twenty years my senior. A hideous, vile man. I could not fathom it. Papa had just died, and he had already come in and taken over everything. And then he demanded I marry him— threatened us if I did not." A shiver visibly ran through her body. "Had I married him…"

"The three of you never would have lost everything. You could have stayed at Rosevin."

Talia nodded. "But I could not marry him. And mother supported me. Stood up to him. She told him she would not prostitute her daughter for her own comfort." She heaved a heavy breath. "And the next day we were removed from Rosevin."

Fletch swallowed back his rising rage at Talia's story. The current Earl of Roserton needed to be ruined in every way possible, and now that they had finally found Louise, he planned to get to that very task on the morrow.

But not at that moment. At that moment, he had his wife half naked in front of him, and for the first time, the constant worry in her hazel eyes had finally eased.

"Fletch, do not look murderous. All of that happened years ago, and we all eventually accepted the consequences—we had little choice but to do that very thing." Her fingers fell from her hair. "And my mother never broke, never asked me to reconsider marrying him. He waited, watched and ensured our descent, and then sent numerous offers for my hand—offering us back everything we had lost. But she did not falter. So as complicated as she is for me, I will always respect her for that. Love her for that."

"I am sorry I did not ask you if I should send for her," Fletch said. "I assumed you would want her here posthaste."

"I do. It just caught me off guard." Talia smiled. "But you doing that for me…it was too kind, Fletch."

Her head cocked to the side as she looked up at him, the blue in her hazel eyes dancing with the light of the fire. "You are an uncommon man, Fletch. Very uncommon."

He smirked. "You are only realizing that now?"

"Maybe." She shrugged. "I realized you were uncommon from the start, but the depth of your kindness. I don't think I understood it at first. From the very thoughtful little things—making sure I eat enough—to the fact that you have righted all of the wrongs in my life in an amazingly short amount of time. I do not know how you have managed to do so. Or why I have been so fortunate."

"I look at you, Talia, and I wonder the very same thing." He turned from her, setting his glass on the mantel.

She followed his movement, slipping between him and the fire, her right hand sliding around his bare waist just above his trousers. "Fletch, I do not want you to think I accepted anything you said to me earlier."

"When?"

"Before we left for the brothel."

He stiffened. "Talia—"

"No—hear me out." She squeezed his side as she cut him off. "You gave me all of this—a home, a life, security, my sister, my mother. It was a future I never could have imagined—comprehended a month ago."

"Yet here you are."

"Exactly. Here I am." Her left hand slipped around him as well, her fingers touching in the middle of his back, playing with the ridge along the base of his spine. "It proves that one cannot see the future, Fletch. No one can—you do not know that death will be your fate."

He inhaled, his jaw tightening as he tried to take a step backward. Talia's fingers instantly clasped behind him, holding her body to his. He shook his head. "I know, Talia. I also have proof. I have a dead brother. A dead father. Generations of dead grandfathers. I know."

"I refuse to accept that. Refuse to accept that you have come into my life to give me footing, and that death will rip you away. I refuse to accept that you will not give me all of you."

His head jerked back. "You speak of my seed?"

"I cannot accept that you will refuse me this." Her hands tightened around him. "Refuse me this essential part of you."

His chest expanded in a heavy breath as he cupped her face. "Everything—land, homes, money—not obliged to the crown will be left to you, Talia. You will always be taken care of. I swore that to you, and the estate is already in place. You do not need to bear my child, an heir, to ensure that."

"I don't care about the bloody estate, Fletch." Fire flashed into her eyes. "I care about you. I refuse to let you believe you are done for this earth within a year—within months. I refuse to let you keep this one thing from me—keep you from me."

Her fingers unclenched from his waist, her left hand untying the belt holding her robe tight, her right hand dropping to his trousers, grabbing him fully through the cloth, massaging.

Fletch nearly jumped away.

Move. Move away from her before actions became regrets.

But for the life of him, Fletch could not move from his spot.

Talia's robe fell open, the full of her, naked. The firelight sent glowing shadows along the lean lines of her body.

"What are you doing, Talia?"

Her left hand joined her right, moving along the buttons on the flap of his trousers. "Proving to you that you are worth this. That I want you—all of you—without hesitation, without fear of a future you have no way of knowing. That I need you right now."

He grabbed her wrists. "I do not want a child only to curse him, Talia."

She looked up at him, her eyes blazing. "It is not a curse, Fletch. You are not a curse. This is you, all of you I am demanding."

"Are you prepared to watch me die, Talia? Are you prepared to watch our child die before you thirty-three years from now?"

"I do not accept that will happen."

"It is reality, Talia."

His hold on her wrists did not stop her fingers from moving, from drawing his shaft full, straining to escape the last buttons that held him captive.

"And I do not accept your death, Fletch." She managed to flick the last two buttons free, his trousers falling as his cock stretched free. Her eyes not leaving his, she grabbed him fully in her hand, stroking the length of him. "I need all of you. Every last piece of you, because you are not cursed, and you do not know the future, and you are not going to leave me."

She stared up at him, the will in her eyes an undeniable force. "All of you, Fletch. All of you."

He wanted to believe her.

Hell, he did believe her.

In that moment, the vehemence, the unshakeable belief in her eyes made him believe it.

Growling, he lifted her. Sliding her onto his cock in one motion.

Hot, slick, he drove deep into her until her legs stretched wide, wrapping around his backside. Her hips swiveled on him, torture with every loop.

Fletch spun the two of them, moving them to the wall next to the hearth, his lips meeting hers in hunger.

Fletch thought he was gentle, but a slight grunt escaped Talia as her back hit the wall. He pulled free, searching her face, but she just wedged a hand up, grabbing the back of his head and forcing his mouth back to her.

Her appetite for him was no less ravenous than his own. Her hips shifted, and Fletch took control, supporting her backside as he slid out of her. To the edge, sending him to shaking, he drove himself into her at the very moment his last defense crumbled.

Twelve times, methodical, he remained in control, until control was lost. He slammed up into her, his fears of her pain overshadowed by the scratches down his back, the guttural hum in every breath she took. She only wanted more.

And then she said the word.

"Harder."

Fletch needed no other encouragement, and he sank into her, possessing her with every part of his body.

"Harder."

A growl, and he crashed into her.

"Harder."

He plunged, lifting her higher, reaching her deepest core. She screamed, her body shattering against him. The cracking sound blasted into his soul, and Fletch could take no more, his mind and body splintering as he came into her. Gripping her as the very life that could deliver him from death.

He stood, Talia pinned against the wall, as he pulsated into her, his body shuddering against the trembles of her flesh. Her mouth opened on his shoulder, her teeth resting into his skin, clamping with each wave racking her body.

He had never lost such restraint—or come so brutally. Reckless.

It hit him cruelly, stealing the last remnants of the only true, glorious freedom he had ever felt in his life. His gut instinct that only moments before had believed in escaping the curse, reminded him that his death was inevitable.

He couldn't renounce that one truth he had spent thirty years believing in.

Yet even as his seed continued to flow up into Talia, he could not force himself to draw from her. Could not force himself to deny her what she needed of him.

The regret came hard, swift.

Regret he had no one to blame for but himself.

He had lived his whole life without a weakness—easy to do, when death loomed over him with every step.

But one weakness had sneaked into his life without his even realizing it—his wife.

And he had just done the one thing he swore he never would.

{ CHAPTER 13 }

"Mother, no." Talia stepped into her sister's room, her look immediately going to Louise's face.

Near tears, her sister swayed, trying to keep her feet as three seamstresses scurried about her, sticking pins in the fine silk draped over her body.

Talia spun to her mother. "No, Mother. Louise has not recovered—it has only been days and you think to make a pin cushion out of her."

"Nonsense, Natalia." Talia's mother gave an airy smile, her fingers waggling in the air as she stood by the armoire, her eyes not moving from the seamstresses. "Louise is as docile as a plump kitten. She did not argue with me in the slightest. She is not doing anything she does not want to."

Talia moved to her mother's side, her voice low. "She didn't argue with you because she can barely speak, Mother. Or did that escape your notice?"

Talia stepped in front of her mother, facing the seamstresses, and clapped her hands. "That will be all for now. I can see you have enough measurements to move forth. Thank you all so much for your work today." She looked over her shoulder, glaring at her mother. "My mother will be happy to walk you down to the drawing room, where you can discuss further whatever it is that is being concocted."

Waiting until they undraped Louise, Talia ushered the seamstresses out the door and into the hallway. Her mother paused, not following until Talia cleared her throat pointedly, trying to keep the edge out of her voice. "You do not need Louise for another second, Mother—you can finish what you started with the seamstresses below."

"Do not take that tone with me, Natalia. You are still my daughter and you will treat me with the respect I am due." Her mother strode past her, her aristocratic chin high.

Talia inhaled as her mother passed, biting her tongue on the word "due." Her mother was due a lot of things.

Before their father died, before they lost everything, Talia knew her mother to be the best parent she could have asked for. But the ensuing years had shed light on all of their faults—faults that had always been concealed under the veil of wealth and power.

It wasn't until their lives were destroyed that she realized how little perseverance her mother possessed. Or how embarrassingly useless her mother was at taking care of herself.

The perfect mother she had once known was now just another thing lost to the past.

Talia closed the door, turning back to Louise. Her sister still stood in the middle of the room, her eyes on the floor, her shift the only thing to keep her warm. Her slight frame drooped, her right hand gripping her left elbow. Louise had withered during her time being held. The bones along her shoulders cut sharply out of her skin, the sight sending a lump into Talia's throat.

If only she had been faster. Found Louise sooner.

"Don't fight her. Please, Talia," Louise said, her voice quivering.

"Get back into bed. Get warm." Talia wasn't going to promise her sister anything as ridiculous as that. She stepped aside Louise, slipping a hand on her lower back to prod her to the bed. "Did you eat the soup earlier?"

Her sister shook her head as she crawled into the bed.

"Are you still nauseous?"

Louise nodded, her head settling on the pillows.

"I will get the physician. And I will have some fresh soup and tea brought up. You can try again."

Louise was asleep before Talia left the room. Closing the door, she leaned against the wood panel, her hands over her eyes as exhaustion tried to entice her to go to bed and crumple, even though it was only late afternoon.

She needed Fletch.

He would have ideas about how to help Louise. How to manage her mother.

He would also make her eat. Make her sleep. All things she hadn't done in days. He was good at those things— taking care of her.

But he was gone.

He had been absent for three days—absent since she had awoken in his bed to be greeted by cold sheets where his body had been.

Gone, and he followed it with complete avoidance.

The first day it happened, Talia had told herself Fletch was being kind, giving her space to spend time with her sister to help her readjust after the horrors she had endured.

But on day two when her mother had arrived, it had become evident that he was avoiding Talia.

Avoiding her at all costs.

After her mother had settled in, Talia had been consumed with intervening between her and Louise. Their mother wanted Louise up and out of bed, ready to pay

calls about town. She wanted to pretend nothing at all had
happened to Louise. While Louise only wanted to stay in
her room, buried deep within the bed covers.

Talia couldn't blame Louise—she would want to hide
from the world just the same. A fact their mother could not
seem to understand.

She could clearly see Louise was deeply damaged
from her ordeal. The only bright spot in the past few days
were the visits from the physician Fletch had hired, Mr.
Flemstone. He was kind and funny and did not mind that
Louise couldn't always conjure a laugh at his oddball jokes.
But Louise did brighten around him—or at least she sat up
in bed and attempted to carry on conversation.

It gave Talia hope. She liked the man, even if she was
nervous about the laudanum he was giving Louise to calm
her. But Talia was comforted by the fact that he worked
at Lord Wotherfeld's research hospital, which meant,
unlike most physicians, he had a combination of the best
traditional and surgical medical training.

The whole of it combined—curtailing her mother,
worry on her sister, and Fletch's avoidance—had turned her
days into exhaustion. All Talia wanted was to curl up with
Fletch at night. To be held warm in his thick arms.

His avoidance had become almost unbearable, mostly
because Talia didn't know why Fletch had disappeared. She
had thought what they had done—what she had made him
do, finish deep within her—would prove to him how much
she wanted him—curse be damned. She knew he wasn't
going to die on her. And there had been no other way she
could have shown him—she had needed him to feel how
much he meant to her.

But something had undeniably shifted in that moment. He had removed himself from her life, from the townhouse, and Talia had begun to question every moment they had been together. He was avoiding her for a reason. Had she pushed him too far? Did he decide he did not care for her now that her sister was found—an obligation satisfied? Or was he so determined to meet death soon that he was hastening the event along?

Talia worried on it for days, worried on it every moment she wasn't worried on her sister.

Her hand dropped from her face, and she stepped from her sister's door only to have her head spin. She fell back against the door, taking deep breaths. Her dizziness was not helped by the fact that she could barely eat for the worry in her stomach, and her head had begun to spin far too often.

She apparently needed to eat some soup as well.

Walking down the stairs, she made her way quietly past the drawing room so her mother didn't call her in, moving to the rear of the house to talk to Cook.

She paused at Fletch's study to look in, unable to bridle her fool's hope that he would be behind his desk and look up to see her. And he would smile. His warm, off-kilter smile that he reserved for her alone, as if she was a wonderment he was trying to decipher. That very smile had sparked a glow deep in her chest from the very first, and she never would have imagined how much she missed it.

No Fletch. Just cool air inside. Only a few stray coals glowed in the fireplace, nothing to heat the room. Fletch was gone during the day, gone during the evening. The staff had made little note of his absence, the household running the same without his presence.

Talia thought she had heard him once, late at night in his chambers. But he did not enter her rooms. And before she got out of her bed to investigate, she realized she had probably just dreamed the noise.

Talia turned from the study, aching for anything she could do to make him appear. But she didn't even know where he was.

She stopped. What if it hadn't been a dream? What if he had been in his rooms, and she had missed him?

Hope brewing, Talia realized she had been far too passive.

If her husband was going to appear, she was going to make sure she didn't miss him.

~ ~ ~

Deep into the fifth night of Fletch's absence, Talia woke from the rustle of the bed, the coverlet lifting and cool air invading the warmth of her cocoon.

She popped up, squinting in the glow of the low coals in the fireplace to see Fletch jumping back out of the bed.

"Fletch."

"Blast it, Talia, I didn't see you in there." He jerked on his robe, hiding his bare skin. "Get a damn shift on."

Surprised, Talia glanced down to see her naked breasts above the coverlet—she had forgotten she had decided naked in his bed would be best. She scampered out of his bed, following his path. "No. Fletch, stop."

He spun from her, walking toward the door.

She grabbed his forearm, trying to stop his exit. "I need to talk to you, Fletch."

He paused for a second, looking over his shoulder at her. "Is something amiss? Your sister?"

"No. Not Louise." Talia tugged on his arm. "You. Where have you been sleeping?"

He exhaled a long sigh, turning to her. "It is late, Talia. Let us not do this now."

"This is the only way I have cornered you, Fletch, so yes, now." She could feel the muscles on his arm flex at her demand. She didn't care. "Where have you been sleeping?"

His grey eyes settled on her, his gaze guarded. "The club."

"You have been avoiding me, Fletch."

"Have I?"

"Yes, dammit." Her grip on his arm stiffened. "And I want to know why. Did I do something?"

"You did, Talia."

"What?"

"You made me believe in what is not possible." His look turned cool in the scant light. "Belief I cannot afford. Belief you cannot afford."

He was protecting her.

The realization swirled in her mind. A fool, she had not considered that very thing. Why wouldn't Fletch try to protect her from what he believed was his impending death—he had spent the entire time they had been together protecting her at every turn.

She grabbed his other arm, looking up at him. "You did not marry a weak woman, Fletch. I want all of you, for as long as I have you. You think that will be a short time, but I think it will be a very long time."

She drew a long breath, searching for words as her fingernails dug into his muscles through his robe. "But I cannot have you if you are not here. And you are wrong—this belief I have—I can afford it because I know, to the bottom of my soul, you are going to be at my side until we are old and wrinkled and grandchildren are crowding our feet."

"And if your soul is wrong?"

His grey eyes pierced her.

She suddenly felt every wisp of the cool air on her naked skin, making her vulnerable, wishing she had put on her robe. She steadied herself against his look, pulling her spine straight. She was not weak. She had said it, and now she had to mean it.

She met his stare. "Then my soul will take solace in the fact that every single day we had together I gave you everything of me, and you gave me everything of you. That we did not waste a moment that we were destined to be together."

His glare did not falter. "What if there is a babe?"

"That babe will be loved just the same, every single day of his or her life."

His jawline tightened as his head gave a slight shake.

He was not about to concede this battle.

Neither was she.

Her chest heaved as her hands moved up, gripping his upper arms. Fletch had never had a day of hope in his whole life. He had been given this death sentence the day he was born. He didn't even know what hope was.

She wasn't just fighting him. She was fighting decades of cruel fate. Generations that believed they were cursed because it was the only explanation. She needed to move him from a lifetime of that one constant. She couldn't lose him.

She closed the distance between them, her breasts touching his chest. He looked to the side, refusing to watch her.

"Fletch, I believed for years that only bad things were destined to happen for me. But it didn't start that way—even leaving Rosevin, I had boundless hope. But then day after day, I lost a little piece of it, until one day, I had no hope left. None."

She shook his arms. "Ask me what happened."

His tongue jutted into the side of his cheek as he exhaled, still refusing to look at her.

Silence pounded in the heavy heartbeats between them, neither moving.

Fletch opened his mouth. "What happened?"

"Your feet. Your boots appeared before me, buried in dung behind that brothel." She reached up, grabbing his jaw in her hands and forcing him to look down at her. "Everything changed in that one moment, Fletch. Everything. You gave me hope. Let me do the same for you."

"Hope will not change the future, Talia."

"Dammit, Fletch." Her voice spiked. "Then you leave me my hope—you do not get to tear that away from me. But I want you. I want you now. Here, while you are alive, and it is not fair that you remove yourself from me."

"Why is that not fair, Talia? It is what you will live with the rest of your life after I die, so what does it matter if I hasten my absence along?"

She slapped him, the sting still vibrating through her palm as she captured his face between her hands in her next motion, her voice cracking. "You are alive, that is why. Here and now. You may not want your life to mean anything, Fletch, but you cannot ask me to deny how very much you mean to me. That you are alive. That your life, that you, are important to me. You mean something. Do not dare to insist that I deny that."

She went to her toes, dragging his face down to hers, kissing him. Her lips met his with brutal force—anger, frustration, need—driving her mouth on his, forging through his resistance and drawing him open to her.

For a long moment, he could not refuse her.

Then he growled, ripping himself away.

He yanked her hands from his face.

Turning, he left. The door slammed behind him.

Talia stood, naked, staring at the door, her lips still pulsating from the kiss. Slowly, her arms curled around her stomach, holding in the waves of nausea starting to twist her belly.

She hadn't given him hope.

Nothing of the sort.

She had only driven him away.

Further.

{CHAPTER 14 }

Talia woke up with one thought in her mind.

One thought that did not falter even as she noticed the neatly folded letter on the pillow next to her. One thought that did not falter even as she realized what would be inside the letter.

One thought.

She was in love with her husband.

She had spent the night pacing her room, tossing and turning in bed, trying to talk herself out of that very fact. But it was no use. She was in love with Fletch, and his leaving had only made that fact painfully clear to her.

Her husband had made her fall in love with him.

And now he intended to die.

Without lifting her head from the pillow, Talia reached out, ignoring how her fingers trembled as she opened the note. She rolled onto her back, holding the crisp vellum above her face.

Talia,

I cannot do this to you. Cannot let us go further. Hope is not the salvation you think it is. Hope, in this instance, is only cruel. I refuse to encourage it.

So I must leave. This home, all of my homes and land that will not return to the crown, are now yours. You can visit my solicitor, Mr. Gleeson, for details, as he is steward of all the holdings.

Know that, above all, I wish I could offer you all of the things you want from me, Talia. A child. Hope. A lifetime together.

But I cannot give you those things. While at the very same time, I have discovered that I cannot deny you, Talia. So I must remove myself from you. There is not another option. We cannot move forth in ways one, or both of us, will regret. I cannot do that to you—create more pain in your life only to appease my own selfish desires.

I wish you nothing but a long life filled with happiness, Talia.

—Fletch

Tears slid down her face, rivers along her temples that pooled in her ears. Damn him. She had known exactly what she would read in the note, but the reality of the words written in Fletch's own hand stung her chest, constricted her air.

She loved him. Yet he was gone.

She crumpled the note, pride hardening her. Bastard. He was not going to let her love him. No matter what she wanted.

Pride sent her spine straight, stretching in her bed.

She needed to break from this as well. Not love him.

He was going to die soon, be lost to her forever. Maybe he was right. Maybe it was better for them to part ways before the pain would become too unbearable at his passing.

Except what if he didn't pass? What if his death wasn't imminent? What if the curse was just a string of unfortunate accidents that spanned generations? What if they both lived until eighty, bitter and alone for decades because of this very moment?

Her hope could not be squelched.

Fletch had shown her how to live with hope again, and she was finding it very hard to now curb the hope he had kindled.

But he had rejected her.

And he would again. And again. And again.

The raw humiliation of that one moment—naked, the door slamming in her face—swept her, curdling her stomach. Her pride could not stomach that again.

Wiping the wetness from her face, she sat up and smoothed the note to flatness on the bed next to her. She didn't care for the crumples she had put in his words. Words she would have to read again and again in order to believe the truth of them.

Fletch wished her happiness.

Now she just needed to find out how to achieve that without him.

~ ~ ~

Four days later, Talia walked in the front door of the townhouse only to be greeted by a din escaping from the very active lower drawing room off the foyer. Without stopping to remove her cloak, she rushed forward, her heart speeding, palpitating out of control before she turned the corner into the drawing room.

A blur of faces turned to her. Chattering stopped.

"Talia, come in." Her mother stood, waving Talia into the room. "Had I known you were stepping out, I would have set the time for our guests to be later."

Talia's eyes swung about the room. Six—seven of her mother's old acquaintances sat around the room. Friends— friends that had denied them help years ago. Cut her mother when they had been in the position to help. Friends that had deemed her mother tainted with poverty. Deemed Talia and Louise unmarriageable.

No. Not in her home.

Her breathing sped, her chest hurting with the pounding of her heart. Talia gulped air through clenched lips—air that refused to stay in her lungs, every quick exhale forcing the next gasp.

Just when Talia was about to spin to run from the room, she spied Louise sitting on a side chair, partly hidden behind two plump ladies that had angled their chairs right in front of her.

In the richest dress Talia had seen in the past five years, Louise shook, her face ashen as tears brimmed in her eyes. The dress could withstand the busybodies. Louise could not.

Talia's panic twisted, spiraling into rage. Across the room in an instant, she wedged herself between the two ladies that held Louise captive and grabbed her sister's wrist, pulling her to her feet.

Without a word, she dragged Louise out of the drawing room, not stopping until she had her sister up the stairs and into her room. She sent a passing maid to fetch the nurse and Mr. Flemstone.

The door closing, Louise crumpled onto her bed, her tears streaming. Talia rushed across the room, drew her into her arms, holding her sister as Louise both shook in sobs and tried to jerk from Talia's touch.

"She made me go down and I could not fight her, Talia." Hiccups sent Louise's words wobbling as she stopped trying to escape and leaned into Talia. "I could not be in there and I did not know what to do or say and I just sat there and tried not to cry. I could not speak and Mama is so mad."

"Shhhh. Do not think on that. Mother should not have put you in that situation below." Talia stroked her back, noting the elaborate upsweep in her sister's hair that must have taken an hour to concoct. A fresh wave of fury scurried down her spine at how long her sister had been forced to sit, preparing for the event below. "Come. Let us strip you out of this dress and get you into bed."

Louise had only just pulled the bed covers over her legs when the door flung open, their mother bursting into the room with the rabid anger of a bull defending its territory.

"Unacceptable, Natalia. Completely unacceptable." Her mother went straight to Talia, hand waving hysterically. "Do you know how much cajoling and begging I had to do to get the lot of those ladies gathered down below? It has been impossible and you have ruined it beyond compare. Right now they are teetering with gossip."

Talia returned her mother's glare with full force. "I do not care in the slightest what those women down below think on me. Or you."

"You need to change your attitude, Natalia."

"I cannot believe you would have the gall to invite these women into Fletch's home, Mother." Talia's voice hissed. "Women who turned their backs upon us the instant we were tossed from Rosevin. Have you no pride?"

"No. I cannot afford pride, daughter. Pride disappeared as an option for me long ago. Pride rarely delivers results. Pride has no place when happiness is at stake. Pride does not find a suitable husband for my youngest daughter. So do not dare to be high-handed about the matter, Natalia." Her mother's hands went to her hips. "You may not care about yourself, or me, but you do need to care about what those women below think of your sister, Natalia. She is unmarried and she has already lost precious years in the marriage mart. We have no time to waste if she is to find a suitable husband."

Momentarily dumbstruck by her mother's unapologetic gall, Talia's eyes went to slits as she stepped to her. "Does it matter if Louise is married? Does it matter to anyone but you? Do you hear yourself Mother? This is madness. Louise is not in a position right now to be courted. To be married. To be with society. It has only been days—"

"Do not say it." Both of her mother's hands flew up, stopping Talia's words. "Do not even utter it, Natalia. We will speak of what happened no more."

"Yet it happened, Mother."

"No, it did not." Her mother glanced over to Louise in the bed. Tears still streamed down her face. "It did not happen if Louise is to make a proper match. Move on with her life. Move on with a husband."

Talia's voice dropped low, and she turned slightly away from Louise. "You are assuming she can move on with her life. There are certain things Louise will never be able to hide from a husband."

"She will. I will school her on what she will need to do."

Talia's head shook. "Louise jumps every time someone touches her, Mother. This is far too soon to force her into society. What sort of match do you expect her to make?"

"She will improve at this, Natalia. We need only work at it." Her mother's arm swung in a wide arc. "We do not have time to waste. We have to keep up appearances, now that fortunes have changed for us. We need to salvage what we can of Louise's prospects for marriage—if only she could have entered the marriage mart years ago. As it is now, we do not have the luxury of time, and every single one of those ladies below is crucial to that end—to Louise making a match."

Growling, Talia rubbed her forehead. "Mother—"

A sharp knock on the door cut Talia's words. She went to open it.

"Mr. Flemstone." Talia stepped aside to let the doctor and the nurse into the room before closing the door. "Thank you for coming so quickly."

Mr. Flemstone was already to the side of the bed, looking down at Louise with worried eyes.

Talia looked to her mother, her voice shaking, just barely under control. "Mother, please, you need to go below and finish whatever it is you are trying to accomplish with those ladies, and then rid them from this house."

Her final glare evident, her mother moved past Talia without a word, anger in every step. Talia opened the door for her, and she exited Louise's chamber.

Closing the door, Talia ducked her head as she took a deep sigh, attempting to control her right hand that wanted to grab the vase within reach on the bureau and heave it across the room.

She looked up only to see Mr. Flemstone reach down and gently pick up Louise's hand. Her sister didn't jump. Didn't cower.

Louise jerked away when anyone—even Talia—tried to touch her. But with Mr. Flemstone, nothing. Louise was as solid as a rock.

Her tears, in fact, had dried.

Talia looked from her sister to Mr. Flemstone, curiosity squinting her eyes. He continued to whisper to Louise in a low rumble, his look never veering from Louise's eyes.

And then it happened. The slightest curl to Louise's lips. A smile. Tiny. But it was a smile. Talia had thought to never see her sister smile again.

She approached the bed, stepping behind the physician. "What did you give her?"

His hand not releasing Louise's fingers, he glanced over his shoulder at Talia. "Actually, nothing. I weaned her off of the laudanum days ago."

"You did?" Panic clutched Talia's heart. "But that was the only thing calming her—that is cruel."

Talia recognized the instant look Mr. Flemstone gave her as patience for the ignorant.

"It would be crueler to keep her on it, Lady Lockston. I do not intend to have her harmed, and I have seen too many become harshly dependent upon the substance." He looked back to Louise. "I am not about to allow that to happen to your sister."

Talia shook her head slowly, staring at the profile of the physician. "No, I do not suppose you are, Mr. Flemstone."

She looked down to her sister, recognizing for the first time the obvious adoration—but more importantly, trust—in Louise's eyes as she looked up at the doctor.

Talia backed away from the bed, nodding at the nurse by the door as she passed her. Talia left the room.

Thoughts firing, saturating her mind, Talia's feet moved down the hall and stairs on their own accord.

When she looked up, Talia realized her feet had brought her to the center of the rear gardens. She stood in the middle of the neat rows of the dormant gardens, her boots crunching the cold gravel of the path.

Having never taken off her cloak, she tightened the heavy wool around her waist. The cool air wrapped around her head, chilling her flushed cheeks.

She stood for minutes, unable to lift her feet from that spot.

Glancing upward, she found her sister's window in the back of the townhouse. The peach curtains were drawn, an extra layer against the chill.

A deep inhale and the cold air went sharp into her nostrils, stinging. She exhaled, her eyes not veering from the window.

All of her problems were solved. Louise saved. Her mother already working to rebuild their social status—whether Talia wanted it or not. A beautiful house to live in. Food more than plentiful. More money than she could ever imagine spending in five lifetimes.

Every single thing wrong had been righted.

Everything.

Yet here she stood, lost, in the middle of long-dead plants. Hollow.

A hollow hole gaping in her chest that only grew larger each day.

She had tried to ignore it. Hoped it would ease. But it remained, casting a shadow over everything she had thought she needed.

Maybe her mother was right. Pride had no place when happiness was at stake.

She did not want this life.

She wanted Fletch.

And she wanted him alive.

CHAPTER 15

Shifting on the hard settee, Talia pulled her shoulders as far back as she could strain them. She had feared her anxiety would flare on the carriage ride to Aunt Penelope's home, but now, sitting inside her warm drawing room, Talia felt at ease for the first time in a social situation since her father had died.

"Tell me, dear, what has prompted this unexpected call?" Ensconced in a wingback chair that hugged her perfectly, Aunt Penelope donned a short silver turban that matched her silver day dress. The color brought sparkle to her grey eyes. Shrewd eyes that settled on Talia.

An exquisitely translucent Spode teacup and saucer had been thrust into Talia's hands by a maid immediately upon seating, and it afforded her an elongated moment of silence as she carefully took a sip and then set down the cup and saucer onto the low table in front of her. Her hands folded on her lap as she met Aunt Penelope's look, attempting to keep the creep of humiliation from flushing her neck. Talia had hoped for a few minutes of inane chatter, but she should have known not to expect it from Fletch's aunt.

"Do you know where Fletch went to—currently is?"

"I do, dear." Aunt Penelope didn't flinch with the question, but her head tilted slightly to the side. "Why is it that you need to ask me?"

"He left. Left me."

"Why?"

Talia's bottom lip drew inward, at a loss. Why did he leave her? She wanted to bear his child? She wanted him? She wanted the exact thing a wife would want from a husband?

"He finally told you of the curse?" Aunt Penelope asked, her eyebrows rising into her wrinkled forehead.

"He did."

"You did not react well?"

"I do not know how I reacted." Talia shrugged. "It was not right, whatever I did. I thought…I want him, Aunt Penelope. I told him as much. I do not believe in this curse, but even if it is true…I want him."

"I told that fool boy he needed to tell you before you were married." Her cane hit hard on the floor, the area in front of her chair a battered mess of bruised and torn wood. "Selfish of him, but I let it slide. He deserves happiness—at least for the next months."

Talia's breath caught. "So you believe he will die as well?"

"I have witnessed the death of every male in my family by the age of thirty-three, my dear." Her fingers tightened over the gilded pigeon on the top of her cane. "So yes. I have no choice but to believe in the curse."

Talia nodded, trying not to let Aunt Penelope's obvious acceptance of Fletch's upcoming death dishearten her own hope.

"I can see the hope in your eyes, child. Hope is dangerous. Hope will destroy everything." She waved her cane in the air at Talia. "For that fact alone, I will not tell you where he is. If Fletcher desires to be alone, I must respect that. He left you for a reason, dear."

"No." Talia scooted to the edge of the settee, leaning forward. "Please, you must tell me. I am denying every shred of pride I have just to come to you, Aunt Penelope. Please."

"Pride is a tricky thing, dear. It too easily manipulates one's objectives. Yet pride does not deliver results."

A chuckle burst past Talia's lips.

"Dear?"

Talia's fingers flew in front of her mouth. "I apologize. My mother said very much the same thing not but two hours ago."

"She did?" The cane tapped lightly on the floor. "I shall have to reacquaint myself with your mother."

Talia nodded, attempting to keep the dryness from her voice. "I am positive my mother will make that happen very soon."

"Good."

"But what of Fletch, Aunt Penelope? Please tell me where he is. For whatever I did, I know I asked too much of him, and I need to make it right."

Aunt Penelope leaned forward, her hands clasping on the top of her cane. Her eyes went to slits, burrowing into Talia. "I have one question for you, dear."

"Whatever it is, I will tell you."

"How do you love someone that you know will die at any moment?"

Talia's gaze met the steel in her grey eyes. Unflinching, her answer was immediate, her words shaking with vehemence. "As hard as I possibly can. Within every single second, enough for a lifetime. That is how."

Aunt Penelope stared at Talia for long seconds, weighing her words. With a pleased grunt, she sat back, letting the chair wrap her once more as she nodded. "Good, girl. He is in Surrey, staying with his friend, the Duke of Wellfork, at Wellfork Castle two hours south of London."

A pent-up exhale whistled past Talia's teeth, her chest tightening. "Thank you."

"But you cannot travel alone, dear. I will ask Lord Reggard, Rachel's widower, to accompany you. He is family, and he still does my bidding. Rachel made a wise choice with that one."

Talia nodded, her mind already planning.

She would get to Fletch. And she would make him listen to her. Make him see that, curse or not, he belonged in only one place. With her.

~ ~ ~

Her back so ramrod straight it ached, Talia had forgotten how much maintaining the proper posture at all times could hurt. Her face angled to the carriage window, her eyes slipped to the left to steal another glance at Lord Reggard.

He was a titan of a man with the surly disposition to fit. His large frame swallowed the bench across from her in the carriage—he was not only tall, but wide. Talia could tell by the lines of his finely tailored jacket dropping inward toward his waist, that his girth came from muscle instead of fat.

He had said little more than five words to Talia since he had picked her up from her townhouse, the line of his mouth never veering from the bottom lip that insistently pushed upward, forcing a constant frown. True to Aunt Penelope's declaration, he still did her bidding, but that didn't mean he enjoyed being called upon.

They had left early in the morning and were now already outside of the last sprawl of London, fields lining the road.

Talia turned toward him, a smile forced onto her face. "I do apologize, Lord Reggard, that I have taken you away from your…" Her voice trailed off. She had no idea what this man did to fill his days.

"It is no bother. When Aunt Penelope barks, I jump. I always have. Rachel always enjoyed watching me squirm under her aunt's unnerving eye."

Talia expelled a nervous giggle, her body relaxing slightly. "I am not the only one, then? I do imagine she has half of London jumping at the slightest twitch of her pinky."

Half of his mouth curled up, close to erasing the surly lines along his eyes. Several stubborn lines of discontent lingered, but Talia was happy with the slight progress.

"I do not doubt it," he said. "I only hope when I am her age, I will wield my cane just as splendidly. She does not even need that thing for walking."

"She doesn't?" Talia's head cocked to the side. "I wondered at that. She can be unusually spry when she desires to be so."

"I heard she was rather quick to follow you and Lockston into the Vauxhall Gardens."

"You heard that? She is a canny one." A flush tickled Talia's neck. She didn't want to have to revisit the embarrassment of her and Fletch getting caught in the gardens. She forced her voice light. "But still, you must have much better things to do than to accompany me in a chase after my wayward husband."

He brushed an invisible spec from his black trousers. "I wondered if you would admit to that."

"The wayward husband part?"

"Yes."

"I have already swallowed my pride on the matter, so I will not attempt to cover my reason for this trip to Wellfork Castle," Talia said. "I do not intend to make Fletch's escape from me easy."

His eyes narrowed at her. "It is three months until his thirty-third birthday. Aunt Penelope told me you are aware of what that means?"

Talia's eyes went to the ceiling of the carriage, a cold inhale taking hold of her chest. "That fool curse Fletch believes in? Yes, he told me. It is why I am after him."

"To try to convince him he will live?"

"To convince him that a curse—whether or not it is real—should have no bearing on the present."

Lord Reggard nodded, the blue in his eyes darkening as he looked at her. The center of his bottom lip lifted, returning his mouth to a frown. "Can I tell you a story?"

Talia felt her own mouth go to a grim line, reflecting the somberness in Lord Reggard's eyes. She nodded.

He looked out the window, pausing as he gathered his words. "When I was five, I had the grandest dog that ever lived. A Spaniel, the best hunter in the shire, Goldie." A soft smile touched his lips and he looked at Talia. "I loved that dog more than anything, and I still don't think I loved her more than she loved me. Goldie slept at the foot of my bed every night. Would jump up the second I arose, licking my leg. Until I was nine. I woke one day, stepping out of bed, and there were no licks. Goldie was not there."

Talia's heart sank, her breath held.

"At first I thought she had snuck down to the kitchens. Or that a new housemaid had shooed her out of my room. I looked everywhere. But she was gone from the castle— nowhere to be found. I was frantic. My father knew what was happening, but he went out into the countryside with me anyway, searching for her."

Reggard's hand went to the back of his neck, scuffing the short hairs as his gaze went back out the window. "I found her under a bush, not too far into the woods. She was wheezing, hacking. Fighting for every breath. I reached for her, but she would not have it. She nipped at me. Me. She was my shadow for four years. I was her world. I tried again to grab her. She bit me. Bit me hard. And then she took her last breath."

Talia couldn't help the instant tears welling in her eyes.

His head shook. "I couldn't believe she had left my side in order to die alone—she knew I was the one that loved her the most in the world, but she did not want to die with me. Alone. She wanted alone. My father said it was innate— Goldie knew she was dying and left because she didn't want to weaken the pack."

He took a deep breath, his wide chest expanding, taking up even more of the bench he already nearly filled. His gaze meandered back to Talia, lazy, but when it landed on her, Talia could see the heartbreak, still, in his eyes. "But I never believed my father—I believe Goldie did it as a kindness to me, so that I would not see her suffer. Would not have to witness her last breaths. To the end, she tried to force me away, tried to protect me from it."

The hairs on the back of her neck spiking, Talia shook her head. She knew exactly what he was insinuating, and she would not have it. "But that is not dignity—dying alone under some random bush. That is selfish and insulting to all that loved it."

Lord Reggard pursed his lips, nodding. "Possibly. I think it depends on one's perspective."

Her eyes narrowed. "So you are defending Fletch's actions? Defending his abandonment of me?"

"I cannot defend something I know nothing of." His hand lifted, palm outward to Talia to calm. "I do not know what has happened between the two of you. But I know that you are willing to go after him, and I also know the curse he has lived with his whole life. How it has shaped his perspective. So between what I can imagine, and what Aunt Penelope has said to me, I can see there is a bond between the two of you that Lockston does not know how to handle. I doubt he knows what to do with himself in his current married state."

Talia sighed, calming her pounding heart. Lord Reggard was not her adversary. Nor was she sure he was her ally. "You have known Fletch for some time?"

"I have known Lockston for a very long time. Lockston, and I, and the Earl of Newdale were inseparable for many years—since childhood."

"The three of you are friends?"

"The most loyal of friends once." Lord Reggard's eyes dropped, darkening with the words.

"But not now?"

"No."

"Why not?"

He looked at her. "I fell in love with Lockston's sister. Rachel was the end of our friendship."

"But I would think Fletch would have been happy—relieved at the very least—to have his sister marry one of his best friends."

"She died in childbirth."

"Fletch told me that. I am so sorry for your loss." The pit of her stomach hardened, and Talia was glad she hadn't had a chance to eat before they had left. Food in her flipping stomach would do her no good. "But Fletch was there for you as a friend to see you through, I imagine?"

Lord Reggard stiffened. "No. You do not know?"

"Know what?"

"Lockston blamed me."

Talia's eyebrows drew together. "Fletch blamed you for her death? What could possibly have made him do so?"

"The babe was too big for her body. Rachel was slight. My babe was not."

A lump formed in Talia's throat at the tone of pain in just those few words from Lord Reggard. The air thickened in the coach. Lord Reggard had obviously loved Fletch's sister deeply, and was still wounded by her death.

She scratched for some flimsy hope in the story. "But you still count the Earl of Newdale as your friend?"

Lord Reggard shrugged. "I have avoided him as well since Rachel's death."

"Surely he did not blame you as Fletch did?"

"No, he did not." Lord Reggard looked out the window of the carriage, his face going blank, resigned. "But I blame me. Lockston warned me, fought me on it until we were married, but I did not listen. He knew what would happen to Rachel. But I…I never expected it. Never imagined— refused to imagine."

Talia inhaled, dragging air deep into her lungs, the pain of her own father's death slicing unexpectedly across her chest. Lord Reggard had had everything—the world—and then lost it. That, Talia understood.

"Lord Reggard, I know how a sudden death can tear a life apart. In a thousand unexpected ways. How one can be so happy one day, and then the next…everything is ripped away in seconds. How one is left searching—wondering what it was they did wrong to deserve such a fate. I have been that way since my father died."

His gaze on the passing fields, Lord Reggard did not look to her, but the flicker in his eyes told Talia he knew exactly what she was talking about.

Her hands clasped in front of her belly, pressing into the plum fabric of her carriage dress to hold against the churning in her gut. "Frankly, it has left me slightly insane."

He looked at her, eyebrows raised. "How so?"

"I cannot be in social situations very well—I panic."

His fingers flicked toward her. "You appear fine at the moment."

"Kind, but you are family to Fletch and Aunt Penelope—and it is just you. Larger gatherings resemble too closely the happiness of the past for me, before my father died, and then I can only fear the loss. It closes in

upon me and I lose all sense of speech and moving and even breathing properly."

"Overwhelming?"

She nodded. "Yes, and I am aware that it is not at all proper for a marchioness. Fletch must have been a little mad himself to have chosen me to marry."

"Why do you think Fletch was drawn to you in the first, Lady Lockston?"

Talia's cheeks flamed. Fletch wanted her body—while he had always been a gentleman, he had never made any secret of that fact. But she wasn't about to discuss their guttural attraction with Lord Reggard.

"Can I make a guess?" he asked.

She nodded.

"You are a survivor, Lady Lockston. You did not let death defeat you when your father died. Aunt Penelope has told me of the poverty you experienced after his passing. My guess is that Fletch knows you can survive him. Make sure a part of him lives beyond his death."

Her forehead crinkled. "You think he chose me as a legacy?"

"I think he chose you for your spirit."

"My spirit?"

Lord Reggard shifted on his seat, his long leg bumping into her calf as he worked to find space to stretch. Talia wondered how he rode anywhere in a coach for any length of time with his size.

He leaned forward, his forearms balancing on his thighs as he looked at her. "Tell me, with your father, would it have been worse to know his death was approaching—to have had time to prepare?"

Talia pondered the question for a long moment, only to find herself without an answer she could stand behind. She met Lord Reggard's look. "I honestly do not know."

"Now imagine not even having that choice. Fletch was handed a death sentence thirty-two years ago."

Talia's lips drew inward, her heart constricting.

"Fletch has always known it—death is coming for him. The year he would not live beyond. Can you imagine how that has shaped every single day of his life? How that would make most things pointless?"

"I can."

"So I think he chose you for your spirit—for your grit—to make his last days mean something, to not be pointless."

"Did he ever not believe he was cursed?"

Lord Reggard's lips drew in sharply. It took long seconds for him to exhale. "I think he did. Before Rachel died. He adored her." He shook his head, his eyes landing squarely on Talia. "Lockston would have fought to live for Rachel. She would have made him. She was so delicate, soft—but with him, she was nothing but steel. Iron that would not bend."

"So I make him fight?"

"That is what his sister would have done." He sighed, sitting back against the cushions. "And, quite frankly, why I am delivering you to him. He is still my friend, will never be anything less, whether he wants it or not."

Talia nodded, her heart heavy. Lord Reggard didn't speak it, but Talia could see it wasn't just friendship in his eyes that drove his actions, it was atonement as well.

{ CHAPTER 16 }

Looking down from the minstrels' gallery, the balcony afforded Talia the perfect view of the great hall—a stone-walled relic from the years of maces and knights. Its evenly spaced Gothic arches lined long walls that soared into a delicately vaulted ceiling. Portraits, tapestries, large windows, and the flames from the largest fireplace she had ever seen lightened the hall, but she could still feel the weight of hundreds of years in the cold stone.

She shivered as her eyes swept to the far end of the great hall and she scanned the ten round tables set up near a long sideboard laden with breakfast dishes.

Too many people.

She took a gulp of air, searching the many bodies moving about, several of them balancing plates of food as they moved to open chairs, footmen scurrying to fill glasses. Too many men and women sat in their morning splendor chatting with ease and gaiety.

She had been prepared for an intimate gathering, ten, fifteen people at most. Fletch being one of them. Not this.

She took another gulp of air. Her eyes skittered from face to face.

At the second table on the left—Fletch. She barely caught his profile as he looked to the woman on his right before smiling. His head turned to the other two at the table, one man and one other woman. They were all laughing.

The woman to his right touched his arm, drawing Fletch's attention back to her. She was in mourning, if her black dress—low-cut that it was—was any indication. But that didn't stop her smirk as she talked, drawing the table into laughter again.

Even across the cavernous hall, Talia could hear the rumble of Fletch's low laugh, but she couldn't see his face. She could, however, see quite clearly that the woman intent on garnering his attention was beautiful. Dark hair. Almost exotic for how she had twisted her locks into an intricate upsweep. Maybe she wasn't in mourning. Maybe she just thought dark colors were proper in the morning because they framed her beauty perfectly.

Fletch's table burst into another round of laughter. Dizziness seized Talia's head and she grabbed onto the stone balustrade before her.

She hoped it was lack of food and not panic seizing her head. She could not have an episode at the moment. She could not. She would not.

"May I accompany you down?" Lord Reggard pointed in Fletch's general direction.

She gave Lord Reggard a weak smile, grateful that he gave her a very distinct task to undertake. Get down the stairs. First goal to accomplish.

Taking his arm as they moved to the staircase to the right of the balcony, her other hand went to the smooth stone railing that snaked along the ancient stairs. Her fingers dug harshly into Lord Reggard's thick muscles, but he did not appear to notice as they started down. Again, a wave of silent gratitude passed over her. She needed all the support she could get at the moment to make it down the steps without passing out.

Why had she not considered there would be a sizable party here? But it was too late now to excuse herself back to the coach and London. She set her eyes on Fletch, walking down the curved stairs and toward him. Lord Reggard's gait kept her steady, and as long as her look didn't slip off of Fletch, she would be fine.

It wasn't until they were close, only three steps away from Fletch, that the other man at Fletch's table pointed at Lord Reggard and leaned forward with low words to Fletch.

Fletch spun in his chair, his eyes finding Lord Reggard. "Reggard, what the—"

Fletch froze as his grey eyes gave a courtesy flicker to the woman attached to Lord Reggard.

"Talia?" Fletch jumped to his feet, stepping to Talia in one long stride, and he grabbed her upper arm, jerking her away from Lord Reggard.

Not aware she was about to be manhandled, Talia's fingers on Lord Reggard didn't loosen, and she dragged him for a moment before losing her balance.

Fletch didn't right her from her stumble, instead using her momentum to haul her to the side of the hall, moving them out under the nearest pointed archway that led to a door.

His strides long, his grip on her arm a vise, Fletch didn't stop until they were two hallways removed from the great hall. In the middle of a long, empty corridor of portraits, he halted, spinning on his heel, his grey eyes blazing as he glared down at her.

Talia's look veered past his head, only to be greeted by an immense wall of oil paintings—golden, gilt-framed ancient eyes looming down upon her. Judging her.

Her breath sped, dizziness grabbing a hold of her again.

Fletch grabbed her other arm, giving her a slight shake. "Get control of yourself, Talia."

The long hall shifted, leaning, until her feet felt like they were slipping. Was that the floor or was that her moving? Talia ripped her left arm out of Fletch's hand and bent over at the waist, gulping mouthfuls of air. It took minutes before she could stand and look at him without the room spinning around her.

His forehead pulsating red, the few minutes had only enraged him further and his grip tightened on her right arm. "Of all people to show up here with, Talia? That one? Reggard? The bastard that killed my sister, and you just stroll right into the middle of the blasted hall on his arm?"

Her hand went to her forehead, attempting to still the remnants of dizziness. "Cease your ranting, Fletch."

"No. No, Talia." He flicked his fingers free from her arm, turning and stomping several feet from her, his hands flailing in the air. "You do not appear with that man on your arm and tell me to cease my ranting. My damn ranting is the only reason my fists are not in Reggard's face right now. The bastard knew exactly what he was doing walking in there with you—he already took my sister and now he thinks to take my damn wife from me before I am bloody well in the ground."

"Fletch." Talia had to nearly screech his name to interrupt his flying words. "Lord Reggard is family— nothing more. Aunt Penelope sent him to accompany me. I was the one that wanted to come here."

He spun back to her. "Aunt Penelope did this?"

"Yes. And Lord Reggard was kind enough to escort me."

Fletch growled, both of his hands going to his face and furiously rubbing his eyes. "The blasted old bat. Of course she did."

"Fletch, have you gone bloody mad?"

"She wanted to ensure I didn't ignore you—she knew where I was and then she not only told you when she had no right to, but she went a step farther and sent the bloody bastard with you, the manipulative old bat."

Talia stepped to him. "Fletch, stop calling her an old bat."

"She could have sent you with anyone but him. You didn't know—but she did, she knew exactly what she was doing."

"Fletch, stop. Just one moment. Please. You were dear friends with Lord Reggard. I did not come with him here to anger you. But I don't understand why…" Her hands spun in circles in the air. "Why this reaction?"

His fingers clenched into fists, his glare left Talia as his eyes ran up the tall wall before them. He stared at the portrait right above them, five children in various poses around a whimsically upholstered Louis XV chair, two hounds weaved amongst their feet.

He exhaled, shaking his head. "Reggard was always too large for Rachel—too large by far. A monster compared to Rachel's delicate frame. I never should have allowed the marriage—I almost didn't."

"Yet you did."

His eyes closed, his head dropping. "She was in love—I feared what would happen—fears that came true."

A sigh lifted his chest, and he opened his eyes, looking to Talia. "What are you doing here, Talia?"

"I needed to talk to you."

"The note I left expressed all I have to say."

She took one more step to him, her chin having to tilt upward to look at him as she invaded his space. "Yes, you had your say. But what about my say?"

"Your say is what I am attempting to avoid, Talia." The air around him palpitated with unspent rage. Rage that was morphing into voracious salacity as his eyes swept down her body and back to her face.

Talia edged a small step backward, realizing her mistake in setting herself so close to him. The instant manic flutter that manifested between her thighs at his look was taking all wits of reason from her mind. Wits she needed to keep about her if she was to tell him what she needed to.

She filled her lungs, steadying herself from his stare. "Fletch, in the days that you have been gone, I realized something."

His eyebrow arched. Not exactly encouraging her, but neither did he turn and walk away.

"My mother has already immersed herself into regaining the life she once led. Hosting her friends, days filled with calls. She is attempting quite desperately to make life as it was before Papa died."

"Has she been successful?"

"No. And that is what I realized. Nothing can ever be what it once was. You gave me everything in my life back— my sister, the home, the estate, security. But it is not the same—it cannot be when I have been irrevocably changed."

She ventured a slight step forward, her eyes intent on his. "I have been changed by you, Fletch. And I cannot live in the past as my mother wishes to do. Nor can I wait, worrying about living in a future I cannot even fathom. All I want is today. Living with what is in front of me on this day, this second."

"What are you saying, Talia?"

"You are today, Fletch." She swallowed hard, her chest constricting. Her hand lifted, trembling as she set it flat on his chest. The distinct thud of his heartbeat reached her fingers. Unable to look into his eyes, she stared at her knuckles as her forefinger slipped under the dark lapel of his jacket. "Today you are alive. Today I want you. Today I want you in your home, in your bed, with me. And I do not care what it takes to make it so. I will do anything. Whatever you need of—"

His lips slammed onto her mouth, cutting her words as his hands wrapped around her waist, pushing her back against the wall. The kiss held fury twisting with ecstasy, his hands frenzied along the sides of her body.

Just as suddenly, he yanked himself away from her. "Dammit, Talia."

She sprung after him, her hands wrapping around his neck. "No—no 'dammit.' No leaving me."

Her left hand dropped, wrapping around his backside to pull his hips hard into her, refusing to let his body escape her again. He tried to avoid her eyes, and she dug her nails into his neck, forcing him to look at her.

"I was wrong, Fletch. I was trying to make you into what I wanted. What I thought I needed. And I gave no respect to what you needed." She swallowed, shaking her head. "But what I need is you, Fletch. For as long as I can have you, I need you. I will not ask you to come in me. I will not try to entice you to do so. But I need you—with whatever part of you that you are willing to give me, Fletch. I love you and I am begging you, without pride, without demands—"

He kissed her, cutting her words once more. He drove her backward again, her back hitting the wall, his shaft jutting into her belly, demanding release. He could no further control himself than she could, his mouth ravaging her lips, seeking truth to her words.

She fought for air, angling her mouth to grasp a breath enough to speak. "Yes?"

"Yes." It spilled into her mouth as more growl than word, but Talia heard it perfectly.

His mouth closed on hers, his tongue plunging, freeing all of her needs from the past days to his command.

A purr rumbled through her throat and Fletch dropped, his lips trailing to her neck, his hand cupping her breast, teasing the hardened nipple through the layers of her plum-hued dress. She arched into him, near to losing herself completely in his ruthless onslaught.

Yet there was one more thing. One more request she needed to make before she lost all ability to think straight.

"I only have one thing to ask of you, Fletch." The words tumbled rough, breathless from her lips.

He did not pull away from her neck. "What?"

"That when the time comes, you fight."

"Fight what?" His voice was muffled on her skin.

"Death. You will fight it for me."

His head lifted, his hands clasping the sides of her face.

His forehead fell onto hers, his eyes closed.

Breath ragged, his chest heaved, but no words fell from his mouth.

His eyes of steel cracked to her, his tortured soul clear. "Talia…I would fight a thousand hells for you. But my death, it is not a fight I can win. I accepted that long ago."

"Or maybe you've always accepted death because you never truly wanted to fight for life."

"Talia—"

Her fingers went to the back of his head, digging into his hair. "I am asking you, Fletch, right now. Fight for it. Fight for us. Fight for the life we deserve to have together. Fight for it when the time comes."

His eyes closed. "I cannot fight what I cannot change, Talia."

For a moment, the world stilled.

Stilled until her next breath. In that breath, devastation rolled up from her toes, stealing all feeling, crumpling her body.

He would not fight for her.

Did he want death?

The possibility struck her, shattering her air, a thousand tiny blades attacking her chest.

Her hands dropped from him, her vision muddied by a wall of tears that would not leave her eyes. She stumbled from his grasp, staggering down the long hall. Blinded, she disappeared into the bowels of the castle.

Run.

It was all she could do.

Run away from the possibility that Fletch wanted death.

Run from what she could not accept.

~ ~ ~

It was minutes—eons in what had become Talia's garbled mind—before she found the great hall in all the corridors she had immediately gotten lost in. Around every corner she had had to stop and listen, peek around the stone walls, and pray Fletch was not in her path.

She couldn't face him again. Not now.

She had asked for nothing, except for the very thing that meant the most—that he would want to live—and he had denied her.

She loved him. But if he could not do that one thing for her—fight death—she wasn't sure if she could look at him and not be crushed every single time she touched him.

All she wanted was hope.

All she wanted was for him to try and live.

Stumbling into the great hall, she realized too late what a walking mess she was, tears streaming, her gait not solid. More than fifty pairs of eyes turned to her, snide curiosity obvious. Perfect fodder for the gossips.

She considered turning and disappearing back into the corridor she had just exited at the exact moment she saw Lord Reggard.

Standing by the sideboard, chatting with two men, he looked past the tops of their heads, seeing her almost immediately. He was to her side before she could commit to skulking back the way she had come.

Grabbing her hand, he set it in the crook of his elbow as he steered her across the length of the long hall, blocking her from the many gaping eyes of people at the tables. He leaned down, his voice low. "That did not go well?"

Talia had to swallow three lumps before she could manage words. "No. I would like to leave."

"Of course. It will take a few minutes to prepare the horses on the carriage." He pointed to the balcony at the top of the curved staircase along the end of the hall. "There is a drawing room we passed on the way inward that appeared to be empty earlier. Perhaps you would like to wait in there."

Talia nodded.

They made their way up the stairs, walking past the minstrels' gallery they had surveyed the room from earlier. A footman passed them, and Lord Reggard halted, stepping aside to request the carriage be readied. Talia turned to the edge of the balcony, looking down at the far tables.

Whatever scene she had just created, it had already passed, as not a person looked up in her direction, the throng of them going about their conversations and concocting plans for the day.

Aside from a few men at the sideboard filling plates, only one lady moved through the tables, the widow, the dark-haired beauty that had been seated earlier with Fletch.

Talia looked over her shoulder to Lord Reggard, silently encouraging him to hurry with his conversation. She needed to be rid of this place. Needed to remove herself from Fletch's vicinity before she did the very thing he feared. Agreed to something she would only regret.

And watching Fletch die without a fight was a regret she wasn't willing to live with.

She looked back down the hall, her fingers tapping on the grey stone railing of the balustrade.

The swish of the widow's black skirts drew Talia's attention to the arched entrance the woman walked through. It was the same corridor Fletch had steered Talia through earlier when they left the hall.

Talia's fingers froze in mid-tap above the railing. The beauty had stopped in front of someone. From her angle, Talia couldn't see the other person until the beauty moved to the side.

Fletch. She was chatting with Fletch.

Reaching up, the beauty wrapped her hand behind his neck, and she went to her toes, setting her mouth on his, her dark head tilting and blocking Talia's view of her husband.

Talia's knees went to jelly. For a breath, she thought she would sink. Become a puddle right under the vaulted ceiling. Instead, her mind went blank as her legs sent her spinning, running down the hallway.

"Lady Lockston? Talia?" Lord Reggard yelled after her. "Talia?"

She didn't stop. Didn't slow her feet.

She wasn't about to wait another second.

She was leaving this place.

~ ~

"What just happened?" Reggard looked to the footman. "Where is Lady Lockston going?"

The man looked just as puzzled. "I do not know, m'lord. I just heard the gasp and then she ran. Mayhap she is sick?"

Reggard looked down the empty hallway, Talia already out of view. He glanced down into the great hall. "Bloody hell."

Reggard was down the stairs and to the far end of the hall in seconds, his large frame a force of fury. He snatched Fletch's arm, ripping him from the woman who still had her talons wrapped around his neck. "Bloody blasted hell, you bastard."

Fletch yanked his arm free from Reggard's grasp. "What of you, Reggard?"

"You just did that." Reggard flew a finger in the general direction of the dark-haired widow. "In front of your wife."

"I what?" Fletch wiped the spit from the woman off his lips. "I was just walking into the hall when…" His eyes narrowed, swinging to Lady Canton.

"You are a blasted fool, Lockston." Reggard's fists ground into his sides. "And you are twisted. You cannot have life, so you want to destroy everyone around you. You bloody well did it with me—I lost Rachel, and then you made sure to take everything else from my life—and I was left with no one. No one. And you have everything—friends, family, a wife—and ass that you are you're throwing it away."

Reggard shook his head, snarl curling his lip. "We were friends once, Lockston. No more. You have gone too far. I always thought you would redeem yourself before the end. Rachel always believed that you had that in you. But now your bloody selfishness and petty cravings are ensuring you are to leave this earth a worthless human being."

"Shut your vile mouth, Reggard." Fletch took a step toward his brother-in-law.

"You shut yours, Lockston. Did you not hear me? Do you not realize what you just did? Talia saw you kissing that tart from the balcony, you fool."

Fletch looked up through the great hall to the far balcony.

"She saw your repulsive display and she ran. She is the best damn thing that has ever happened to you, Lockston, and you just threw her away."

Fletch couldn't tear his eyes off the empty balcony, his voice still seething. "Why do you even care, Reggard?"

"I don't. But I do for Rachel," Reggard said. "She would not have wanted to see your despicable ass leave the earth in this way."

"Rachel's dead, Reggard. So you can leave me the hell alone."

"I should leave. It's what you deserve after the way you dismantled my life after Rachel's death." Reggard rounded Fletch, blocking his view of the balcony. "I should leave you in the sniveling shell you are determined to rot in."

"So leave." Fletch's lip curled, the words vicious.

"I will. Do not worry on that, Lockston. There is nothing I would rather do in this moment." Reggard unclenched his fists, heaving a sigh. "But unlike you, I loved my wife. So I care about your life because of her. Because she would have demanded it of me."

"You know nothing of what I feel for Talia."

"No. You're right. I know nothing because I never would have treated my wife—or any woman—like you just did." Reggard's eyes narrowed at Fletch. His voice notched downward. "Do you know, Lockston, that even before your sister, I always believed that if anyone could break the curse, it would be you. But now I am beginning to wonder if the curse is exactly what you are meant for. Had your sister just seen what you did, I think she would think the same."

"Bloody well stop throwing my sister in my face, Reggard. She is dead."

"So you have forgotten Rachel? What she wanted for you?" His head shook in disgust. "Damn, Fletch, she believed far too much in you."

Fletch's mouth twisted. "Yes, well, she always was misguided when it came to the men she loved."

Reggard refused to acknowledge the insult, not allowing so much as a twitch. His finger swung in the air, pointing again at the far balcony. "That woman—Talia. Talia is what Rachel wanted for you. Not this." Reggard's look swung to the dark-haired widow that had backed to the wall, making herself small. "Not this wretched harlot."

"Watch yourself, Reggard."

"No, you watch yourself, Lockston. You need to make a choice, friend. Life—life with meaning. Or whatever sorry state this is." Reggard's eyes pointedly ran up and down the widow. He crossed his thick arms over his wide chest, glaring at Fletch. "Now am I going to have to go after your wife, or are you?"

Fletch's mouth opened, then he stopped and his lips clamped shut.

With a shake of his head, he pushed past Reggard, sprinting across the great hall.

{ CHAPTER 17 }

Talia paused at a wooden pillar along the entrance to the mews. Dizziness had attacked her three times on her push back to London, and just as she had descended from the mare she had borrowed from Wellfork Castle, another wave had overtaken her.

Gripping the pillar, she closed her eyes, her chin down until the tilting of the gardens in front of her subsided. Then the fury in her gut propelled her forth.

Entering the townhouse through the rear, Talia considered for a moment going to the kitchen for food, then realized she wouldn't be able to choke down anything in her current state. She walked down the hallway, trying to keep her feet from stomping. It had only taken an hour of hard riding to get into London, and then another fifteen minutes of picking her way through London streets to get to the townhouse. Not nearly long enough to quell the rage still ripping through her veins.

Passing the lower drawing room, she heard voices and glanced in. She skidded to a stop in the open doorway.

No.

Not him.

Not in her house.

Not Cousin Arnold.

Her mother flittered about the room, nervous with the glass of port she held in shaking hands. But Talia barely noticed her. She could only stare, stunned, at the man sitting in her drawing room, in her house. Her mother handed the glass of port to the current Earl of Roserton.

It was him.

There was no mistaking the stringy grey hair tied into a ponytail off the back of his bald head. The nose that twisted on the end. The beady eyes looking up at her mother. The jowls.

The bastard sat in the middle of her drawing room, his feet propped on the low rosewood table in front of him, scuffing the gloss. Owning the place.

Talia's rage erupted.

"Get out of my home, Cousin Arnold." Her words thundered into the room before her feet could get her in front of the bastard.

She stopped, heaving in front of him. Her arm flew up, shaking as she pointed to the doorway. "Get the hell out of my home, Cousin Arnold."

He looked up at her coolly, a slight sneer lifting the left side of his mouth. Still the same. Same sneer. Same greasy grey locks of long hair falling about his face from his ponytail. Same jowls—one, two, three deep down his neck. Same portliness.

"Cousin Natalia," Arnold said. "You truly should address me as Lord Roserton. You were mannered, once in time. I think you can be so again."

Talia stepped closer, shoving her knee into his shin to knock his foot off the table. "And you would do well to address me as Lady Lockston."

He looked down pointedly at her knee, his sneer deepening. "Ah, yes, your marriage. I was disheartened to realize I somehow was neglected to be invited to the nuptials."

"Yet you did not take that as the direct cut it was, and instead, you have egregiously erred in inviting yourself into my home." Talia's arm did not lower from its point to the door. "Again, I ask that you leave at once. You are not welcome in this home, Cousin."

Talia's mother grabbed Talia's outstretched arm, pushing downward on it, her voice frantic. "Lord Roserton wishes to marry Louise now that you are married, Talia."

Talia's jaw dropped, her eyes whipping first to her mother, and then falling to skewer her cousin. "What? What lunacy is this?"

"Your sister is now of marriageable age, and as you are now married, there is nothing unseemly about our union."

"Nothing unseemly?" Talia's stomach flipped, bile threatening upward. "No. Absolutely not."

Cousin Arnold's sneer turned into a smile. "Yes. I would like to marry her in four weeks' time."

"No." Talia's head shook. "She will never marry you, Cousin."

Her mother moved closer to Talia, flanking her side. "We were just preparing Louise for the upcoming season, Lord Roserton."

Talia bit her tongue. One battle at a time. And she needed her mother at her side on this one.

The sneer overtook the smile on Cousin Arnold's thin lips. "Do not tell me you honestly think to put a girl such as Louise on the marriage mart."

"What do you mean, a girl such as Louise?" Talia's eyebrows furrowed, and she looked to her mother.

"I mean one that has already been on the open market," he said.

Talia's gaze snapped to him. "What are you speaking of?"

His head tilted to the side, his sneer deepening. "Perhaps I should be more specific—a girl that has been *purchased* on the open market."

Hand flying to her throat, Talia's mother gasped and stumbled backward, falling to sit on a side chair.

Talia took another step closer to Cousin Arnold, staring down at him, her words seething through clenched teeth. "Just what exactly are you insinuating, Cousin?"

"Your face has turned quite dire, Lady Lockston. Interesting." Cousin Arnold shrugged. "I was merely referencing a conversation I had at my club with a gentleman that has the most peculiar tastes in young females. Not my sort of thing, but he went to great lengths to explain some of the girls he has recently taken a…liking to. One with an unusual birthmark of a six-pointed star on her left shoulder."

Hell.

He knew. How he knew of Louise's very specific birthmark, she didn't want to imagine. But he knew of it. And he knew Louise had been in a brothel, sold for her innocence. Ruined.

Talia's hands curled into fists, aching to pound the sneer from his face, consequences be damned. Yet she forced herself a step backward. "Get out of my house, Cousin Arnold."

"I would hate for any untoward gossip to taint Lady Louise," Cousin Arnold said as he stood. "I would prefer she not become my bride with a wave of scandal upon her tail."

Talia's arm swung up again, pointing to the door, her voice vicious. "Out of my house this instant, Cousin Arnold."

He gave a slight bow of his head. "You are right, Lady Lockston, it is time for you and your mother to think upon consequences again. Perhaps you will take greater care in consideration this time, than you did the last time we were at this juncture."

He stepped past Talia's arm and exited the drawing room.

Talia's shaking arm fell slowly to her side, the true horror of the situation sinking into her mind.

"You cannot let this happen, Talia," her mother said from the side chair, her fingers rubbing her brow. "I would not let you marry that odious man, and I will not allow Louise to either. You need to fix this, Talia."

Talia's palms swung up to the ceiling. "I do not know how to, Mother."

Her mother gained her feet, moving to stand in front of Talia. "You must figure out a way. Louise has been through far too much. You cannot let him ruin her, nor let him force her into marriage. You need to fix this, Talia."

Talia spun from her mother, her throat clenching.

Fix this. Fix this. Fix this.

Words that she had heard repeated again and again during the past four years.

Talia stared out the front window at Cousin Arnold heaving his lumbering form into his carriage. The Roserton carriage. Her family's carriage.

She shook her head, failed plan after failed plan flashing through her frantic mind. Each and every plan she contemplated ended in her sister's utter ruin.

Talia knew she herself could weather any scandal, but Louise was still in much too delicate of a place to even fathom putting her within striking distance of Cousin Arnold's threats. She needed to protect Louise. There was nothing more important. And Cousin Arnold's demand of four weeks' time was far too short a span to work within.

Time. She needed more time than four weeks.

If only…

With a gasp, Talia sprinted from the townhouse, not stopping for a cloak. Down the front stairs, she searched the street to see Cousin Arnold's carriage turning at the end of the block. She ran, attempting to not slip on the splotches of ice that lined the sidewalk.

Three blocks of racing after the carriage, and Talia was within yelling distance.

"Arnold—Lord Roserton—Cousin Arnold," she screamed at the black coach. "Lord Roserton, stop. Stop. Cousin Arnold."

The carriage slowed.

Talia caught up to it, her chest burning with every breath. She reached the carriage door before the footman alighted from the back of the coach.

Flinging the door open, she forced breathless words. "I will do it."

Lips pursed, Cousin Arnold looked down at her. "Do what?"

Talia gasped for air, one hand clutching her side. "I will do it. I will marry you."

His eyebrow cocked at her. "Need I remind you that you are already married, Lady Lockston?"

Talia reached down and yanked out the metal carriage step, jumping up onto it and leaning into the carriage, her voice low. "My husband. Lord Lockston. You have heard of the curse of his family?"

"Curse?" His curved nose wrinkled. "I do not put stock in curses, Lady Lockston. Leave me. Close the door. You are letting a draft in here."

She leaned in further. "The curse, Cousin Arnold. No man in my husband's family has ever lived past the age of thirty-two."

"What does this have to do with marrying your sister, Lady Lockston?"

"My husband is three months shy of his thirty-third birthday." Her stomach flipped at her own words, and she had to take a quick breath to gather her spine with her next utterance. "I will be a free woman very soon, Cousin Arnold. I will marry you."

"You?" He shook his head. "I can have your younger, even more delectable sister, Lady Lockston. Why would I not take her over you?"

Talia made her lips curve into a smile. "You always wanted me, Cousin Arnold. You still do. I saw it in your eyes when I entered the drawing room just now." She leaned forward, taking a deep breath to push her breasts out as her voice dropped to a whisper. "Louise is broken. And I do not think you want a broken wife, Cousin Arnold." Her eyes narrowed as her words slowed. "No, I think you want a wife you can break."

Bile slipped up into Talia's throat as he stiffened and then reached down to adjust himself through his trousers.

As gruesome as they were, her words had the effect they needed to.

He cleared his throat. "You say three months?"

"I do."

"You understand what will happen if you betray your word? It is your sister that will be sacrificed." He adjusted himself through his trousers again.

"I understand."

"Then get yourself off of my carriage. You're of no use to me now." He kicked his foot out, the ball of his boot landing on her ribcage and shoving her from the carriage step.

Talia slipped backward off the metal step, flailing. She hit the cobblestone street hard, her left wrist snapping under all her weight. Brutal pain sparked up her arm, wrapping around her.

Gasping at the stabbing agony, she dropped her head, fighting for breath.

She couldn't let him see.

Toes scrambling on the rounded stones of the street, she found her feet but refused to look up. The carriage door slammed shut and it rolled away.

Clutching her mangled wrist to her belly, vicious pangs rolled up her arm. Talia started to walk, wobbling.

The spasms collected in her gut before running to her head, wooziness setting thick into her mind. Talia searched in front of her.

Park. Bench. Sit.

She stumbled across the street and a horse brushed her backside. She staggered. Yelling. Lots of yelling.

At her?

The park. The bench. She forced her feet forward. Step. Step. Another step. Then blackness fought into her vision, even as she tried to blink it away. The park started to slide sideways in front of her.

A tree. She could reach that tree. Catch it. A tree could hold her upright.

Her fingertips went forward, far, far from her face. She touched bark. The bark slipped away into darkness.

She dropped.

~ ~ ~

It was only the smallest fold of her plum-colored skirt trimmed in gold cording. That Fletch saw the tiny swatch of fabric in itself was a miracle.

But there it was, a splash of gold and plum flopping out past the feet of a group of men huddled around a tree, looking downward. One of the seven riffraff had a hatchet propped over his shoulder.

His heart sank.

He had missed Talia at the townhouse by only minutes, her mother had said. So frantic she could barely get words out, she had sent Fletch out the direction Talia had disappeared.

One of the men by the tree shifted, stepping on the edge of the skirt, digging it into the cold dirt.

It was that slip of cloth, the gold cord grinding into the ground that turned him savage. That sent a raw rage so brutal through his limbs that he transformed into a warrior of old.

He was across the park in seconds, ripping the closest man to him from the group and throwing him to the ground.

"Get the hell away from my wife, you bastards." Fletch's roar echoed around the trees of the empty park.

"Pardon, sir." The man directly across from him standing by Talia's head threw his hands up. "The lady was bumped by our horse."

Fletch pushed his way to the man by her head, shoving each of the men near Talia a step back on his way. He stopped in front of the man that spoke, his hands shaking to choke the bastard. "Your bloody horse hit her?"

"T'was just a nudge, sir, honest." The man's palms stayed up, attempting to calm. Fletch would have none it. Talia was lying in the dirt.

"Sir, honest, we all seen it. Her eyes be closed when she ran in front of us and then the rump o' the beast sweeped 'er back. She stepped away a ducky, but then she staggered along, fell by this tree."

Fletch's head whipped around, looking at the crowd of men. Through the blinding red in his eyes, he could see all of them were nodding.

"Truly, sir, we seen she be a lady, and we stopped to help her. Good thing ye came. Cause we ain't know what to do with 'er."

"Do with her?" Fletch's look snapped back to the man.

"She fainted—she still be in blackness—look at 'er. We think it be 'er wrist."

For the first time, Fletch truly looked down at Talia. He hadn't wanted to do it for fear of what he would find.

His stomach curdled. Talia's eyes were closed, dead to the world.

His look travelled down her body.

Her left arm was awkwardly splayed onto her belly. Her hand flopped over to the side, grotesque, the angle of it unnatural in every sense. Fletch could see raw bone poking rough just below her skin.

"Oh, shit." His grunt came out flat. He turned from the man, dropping to his knees at Talia's side.

"Can we help with 'er, sir?"

Fletch shook his head, staring at Talia's closed eyelids. "No. No. I will bring her home."

"Do you need help carrying 'er?"

"No. I can bloody well carry my own wife."

"As you say, sir." The group of men backed away, the lot of them going to the wagon that they had been riding in.

Fletch glanced up to the departing group, offering up a weak, "Thank you."

A few nods and a wave came in his direction.

He turned back to Talia, a rock settling into his gut. "Dammit, Talia, what did you do?"

Slipping his arms under her knees and back, he lifted her, trying to curl her body into him so her head wasn't completely limp, dangling off his arm.

He walked through the park before he realized her left arm was starting to slip from her belly.

Fletch shifted Talia, getting her rebalanced in his arms. Her wrist bumped into his chest.

Damn.

Her eyes jarred open, terrorized with a gasp. Then she saw his face and instantly calmed, but the pain remained evident in the crinkle in her forehead. "Fletch?"

Relief swept him, his arms almost turning to jelly. Her eyes were clear. Pained, but clear. Whole—a wicked crack in her wrist—but she was whole. He gave her a half smile. "Sorry. I didn't want to move your wrist, but I bumped it."

She gasped against the pain, her eyes squeezing shut. After a long breath, she opened her eyes. "Fletch, you're carrying me."

"Yes."

She paused, looking up at him, confusion plain on her face. It took several steps before she looked from his face to her wrist resting on her belly. Her face blanched as the confusion drained away and she identified where her pain came from.

Her eyes stayed on her crooked wrist. "Fletch, I can walk."

"Not at the moment, you cannot."

"I can. I got dizzy and I fell. I did not eat. That is all."

"That is all? Is that how you broke your wrist?"

She looked up at him. "I broke it?"

"You did look at it, didn't you? That is what a break looks like, Talia."

Her gaze dropped down to her wrist once more, a soft groan floating up to him.

His earlier savage rage not fully dissipated from his veins, Fletch glared down at the top of her head. "Dammit, Talia, what were you doing? You nearly sent me to my grave seeing you unconscious under that tree."

Her look flew up to him, her hazel eyes skewering him. "Do not utter such blasphemies as your grave, Fletch. Never. Not in front of me. You do not get to do that. Be mad at me, but you will not speak of your grave in front of me. Save it for your whores."

Fletch had to hide an instant smile. She was furious at him—and rightfully so—but he didn't care. The harsh edge in her voice told him that she was fine—her fire was already back about her—and that was all that he cared about at the moment.

"And you need to save your ire, Talia. You are going to need all your strength about you for the next hour."

Her eyebrows furrowed. "Why?"

"I'm going to have to call the bonesetter."

She swallowed hard. "A bonesetter?"

Fletch nodded. "Yes. He is going to have to reset that bone. And it is going to hurt like hell."

{ CHAPTER 18 }

Fletch afforded himself a quick look out the back window of his chambers. He had watched nothing but Talia's face contorting in pain for the last half hour, and he could take no more.

He could take no more of the bonesetter's rough hands on his wife's delicate skin. Of his chest crushing with every whimper that escaped through Talia's tightly drawn lips. Of her hazel eyes, huge, filled with tears, begging him silently for the pain to stop. Of her body convulsing against his chest as he held her while the bonesetter stretched the contracted muscles in her arm.

He almost wished she hadn't woken up on the way back to the townhouse. He would have much preferred she suffered this in unconsciousness, her pain hidden from him.

The bonesetter was fast in assessing how the bone had broken. But not nearly fast enough for Fletch. He wanted his wife out of pain, and he wanted it with haste.

Talia screamed, but before Fletch could look from the window down at her, she had cut herself off, swallowing the sound.

The bonesetter yanked her left arm, grunting. Fletch had to tighten his grip around the front of Talia's waist and chest, holding her steady as he propped her upright in front of him on his bed. Another yank. The wide span of her back shook against his chest as she gasped for breath and Fletch had to hold down his left foot from kicking the bonesetter away from his wife's body.

"Done." Splints in place, the bonesetter quickly wrapped Talia's arm in a long, tight bandage.

Yet Talia was still quivering, wave after wave of pain rolling through her body.

Fletch felt every single tremble as his own.

The bonesetter stood, collecting his belongings.

Fletch gave him a nod, not moving from his clasp on his wife. "My man will pay you downstairs."

The bonesetter disappeared out the door, leaving them alone, and Fletch remained still, holding Talia against the shudders of her pain.

His lips dropped to the crown of her head. "You could have screamed. It would have helped."

"I could—" She had to swallow back the shake in her voice. "I could not. I could not have Louise hear. She would worry. And she is already in such a state."

"She would understand. You cannot make everything in the world always right for her, Talia."

Talia stiffened under his arms, twisting on the bed and wedging her right hand in between them to push him away. "I can try. For every moment I failed her by not finding her in time, I can try."

Fletch released his arms from her body, his head cocking to the side at her sudden vehemence. She moved gingerly away from him on the bed, collapsing against a stack of pillows by the headboard.

Fletch eyed her. "How did that happen? Where were you going, Talia? Your mother could not get three words out of her mouth—just enough to send me after you."

She winced, and Fletch wasn't sure if it was from pain or his questions.

Closing her eyes, she shook her head. "It does not matter, Fletch. I got dizzy because I have not eaten, and I fell. And then you were there."

His jaw slid to the side, but he did not press her for details. "You left Wellfork Castle."

She exhaled, the blue in her hazel irises sparking as she opened her eyes to glare at him. "I was not about to stay there and watch you fornicate with that woman. I went there for you—begging—and that—"

Her left elbow twitched, and she closed her eyes, a rush of pain clearly overtaking her words.

Fletch waited until her face slightly relaxed. "You came back to London on your own, Talia. You didn't wait for a carriage. You didn't wait for Reggard. It was not a safe thing to do."

"I have done it before." Her eyes opened, but she refused to look at him and tilted her face to the grey canopy above the bed. "I needed to leave and I thought it would be quickest to do so on a horse."

"But not on the Duke of Wellfork's prized mare."

Her look dropped to him. "That is his prized mare?"

"Yes."

She shrugged, her gaze returning to the canopy. "Then I shall send a groveling apology when I have the mare returned."

"You never should have left the castle alone, Talia."

Her eyes centered on him. "I denied every spec of pride I have to go there for you, Fletch. And then for you to… to…" Her head started to sway, her eyelids dropping as dizziness cut her words. Her mouth kept moving, words

slow as they struggled against the faintness overtaking her. "For you to—"

His hand clamped over her mouth. "Stop. We are talking no more until you eat."

~ ~ ~

Two hours later, they were alone together once more in his bedroom, and Fletch sat in a chair by the bed, watching his wife in silence.

Propped against the headboard of the bed, she had eaten—mostly picked at her beef, potatoes, and beets. But her eyes were no longer slipping into random glassiness, and the color had returned to her cheeks.

Most important to him, though, was that her body had—except for the occasional spasm—stopped twitching in pain.

Between her shift and the top of the bandaging that ended at her elbow, Fletch stared at the stretch of bare skin along her upper arm. That was the swath where he could clearly see the pain twinge up her arm, and he was busy willing it into nonexistence.

"What were you doing with that woman?"

Talia's sudden question made him jump. His gaze flickered to her eyes. "What? Who?"

"That woman in black—a widow—the dark-haired beauty at Wellfork Castle."

Fletch sighed, leaning back in his chair. "So you did see that. Reggard said you did."

"Yes."

"What you saw was absolutely nothing, Talia. The woman, Lady Canton, intercepted me in the hall—she surprised me more than anyone. That woman has a host of her own games she was concocting there at Wellfork Castle. Games that I was not a part of until you appeared. And then she attacked me out of nowhere. Unprovoked. Unwanted. I imagine she knew you were within sight."

"It did not look like an attack."

Fletch shifted forward, his hand slipping past her knee to squeeze her thigh through the coverlet. "Believe me, it was. I was searching for you. I would not do that to you, Talia, betray you with another—try to hurt you like that." A wry smile fought through the frown on his lips. "I think it has already been proven I cannot deny you anything, my wife."

"But you were having fun with Lady Canton, I saw you laughing with her at your table when I arrived at Wellfork Castle."

"Fun?" A dry, caustic chuckle from deep in his chest cut into the air. "I have spent my whole life masking what I feel, Talia. What you saw at Wellfork Castle was exactly how I lived my life before you dropped into my world and took it over." He stopped, looking up at the bed canopy with a shake of his head. "I am a good guest. A witty conversationalist. A pleasure to be around. Polished. But there is no real feeling behind it."

"Not real?" The ire had eased from her voice.

"No." His look dropped to her. He shifted from the chair to the bed, setting himself next to her, his hand wrapping along her far thigh. "Not like I am with you, Talia. Real feeling. Real desire."

He leaned in, twisting back a red-blond lock of her hair so he could set his mouth next to her ear. "You are the one that makes me feel, Talia. You."

His head dropped, his lips finding the strong line of her neck. "With you I am a man with purpose, Talia. With you I am genuine. I am real."

"And complicated. Aggravating. Stubborn. Vexing. Hard. Amazing. Brave. Strong. Kind. Generous." Her words went soft as her head tilted, giving him access to her neck. "And sending me to my knees."

He took full advantage of her body's invitation, his lips dragging across her skin, his tongue moving in slow circles, just enjoying the way her flesh sparked under his taste, the way she stretched, opening herself even more fully to him. "As long as I am under you, I like you on your knees, Talia."

She grabbed his face with her right hand, her fingers hard on his cheekbone, her thumb digging along his jawline as she pushed him from her neck. Her eyes met his, the blue flecks, vibrating, alive, in the hazel of her eyes. "Don't leave me again, Fletch. Don't."

His look dropped from her, heavy. "I do not want to, Talia. Never. But I also do not want you to ever have to watch what I just witnessed. I do not want you to suffer that."

"You are planning on breaking your wrist?"

He looked up at her, a small smile surfacing before his face went tense, his voice grim. "You were in pain. You still are. I do not want to watch it."

"I am fine, Fletch. My arm hurts, yes, but it will heal. You yourself said that bonesetter is the best in London."

He grabbed her right hand, enveloping it between his palms. "It is not just that…it was just hard, Talia."

"Why?"

"Because I have been selfish. I have been so consumed by my own death that I never considered I would have to watch something like that—that I would have to watch someone I love in pain—that you could die." His head shook as his eyelids fell shut for a long breath. "You cannot imagine how my heart stopped when I saw you on the ground—saw your eyes closed. Gone from the world. You could have been dead. It is that moment I do not want you to have to endure. To bear a scene such as that. It is not fair. Not fair to make you suffer that."

She pulled her hand from his grasp, lifting it to gently cup the line of his jaw. "You love me?"

"Yes." His reply was immediate, the one word a force.

A small smile lifted the corners of her mouth. "Then you must know this one fact about me—that I can endure anything. That I will bear whatever is necessary for those I love. And I love you, Fletch."

His look dropped to her lap, her words seeping into his chest, twisting it, devouring it with a rawness so brutal he lost his breath.

"Tell me you don't want to die, Fletch."

He froze, unwilling to breathe, unwilling to lift his gaze to her.

Talia waited in silence.

It took a full minute before he gathered himself enough to open his mouth, his eyes remaining lowered, shuttered. His words were quiet, a low whisper not truly meant for the world. "If I admit to it, Talia, acceptance of my fate is gone." He stopped, swallowing hard. "If I don't have acceptance…all I am left with is…fear."

"And love." Her fingers curled under his jaw, lifting his face. "You are left with love."

His closed eyelids crinkled hard, a tear escaping to roll down his right cheek. Without breath in his lungs, without the fortitude that had carried him through the last thirty-two years, his lips parted, his voice cracking. "I want to live, Talia."

He opened his eyes to find tears brimming on his wife's lower lashes. He had to say it again. Say it so it was true. Real. "I want to live."

Her whole body lifted in a deep breath, and her hand slipped down to his neck, her fingers insistent as they clutched the back of his head. "Then you need to fight. Don't leave me, Fletch."

Watching his wife, it took long, painful breaths before he could speak. "As long as it is in my power, I swear I will not leave you, Talia."

"Good." A smile cut through the tears streaming down her cheeks. "Because I need you today, Fletch. I want you tomorrow, I want you when we are old, but I need you today. This moment."

The right side of his face lifted, a half-smile curling his lips. "I love you, Talia, and fate willing, we are going to be old together."

Hope beamed behind the tears in her eyes. "And you will fight to stay with me?"

"I will fight." He gave a solemn nod. "When the time comes, I swear I will fight."

{ CHAPTER 19 }

"I need you today."

His wife rolled over on top of him, her naked flesh pushing aside the sheet his legs had been tangled in.

Every day for the last six weeks, Fletch had been woken up in this exact manner. The huskiness of Talia's just-risen voice pulling him with gentle demand into the daylight.

If heaven on earth existed, this was it. Heaven waking him, day after day.

She spoke those words to him every morning. And every day she meant them. Every day she had a purpose for him. Take her riding out to the countryside. Accompany her and her sister to Bond Street. Hold her steady in front of the visitors her mother continued to entertain. Help her to untangle threads for her needlepoint—a stretch of the word "need," though she insisted her healing wrist demanded his assistance.

She had a million tasks for him, and every day, she made it quite clear she needed him.

Every day, Fletch didn't mind in the slightest.

He had even begun to look forward to what she would concoct overnight to surprise him with in the morning.

She had been true to her word—never asked him for more than the moment, never talked of the future past the day ahead. He had continued to refuse to let his seed touch her body, yet she never mentioned or even hinted at her displeasure on it. Of course, he made sure her body was shattering, ecstasy throbbing through her veins when he withdrew. He imagined that helped.

Her cold nose nuzzled into the warmth of his neck.

"What do you have planned for me?" Smile on his face, Fletch stared at the grey silk of the canopy above as he grabbed her waist and shifted his hips under her, enticing. Not that there was any way she could have missed his rock hard shaft, ready and waiting for her.

She giggled into his neck, her breath warm on his skin. "That first, of course. I always need you for that. But after that I must monopolize you for the entire day. You cannot even imagine the many ways in which I will need you today."

"Preparations for the dinner this eve?"

"Yes."

"What is the final count?"

"Thirty-six. But I believe it will expand to more than fifty by this eve, if mother has her way. I still cannot believe I let her convince us to host this dinner."

Fletch's hands slipped down her tailbone, rounding along her backside. "Well, your sister's sudden engagement to Mr. Flemstone did put a damper on your mother's plans for the upcoming season. She had grand designs for parading Louise about. You saw her face when she found out about the engagement."

Talia gave a grunt into his neck. "One would have thought we just stole the crown jewels away from her." She scooted down slightly on him to set her chin on his chest. "I am just so happy Louise and Mr. Flemstone have made a match of it."

Her wiggling sent his cock straining even harder for her, and Fletch attempted to clamp down on the need, moving to lift her left arm up to distract himself. His thumb ran down the line of bone along her forearm to her wrist, noting the straightness. Aside from lingering tenderness, Talia had healed quickly and the tight bandages had been removed a few days prior. "So you approve of the physician?"

"Yes, I do. Mr. Flemstone has been immensely helpful in so many ways. Indispensable, truly." She nodded, her chin rubbing on his chest. "Especially because he is privy to all of what happened to Louise, and he adores her aside from it all. She will never have to hide her past from him."

"Indeed. And I think the dinner to celebrate the engagement is a perfectly acceptable appeasement to your mother in this situation—can you imagine how many soirees you would have had to attend if your sister had been plopped into the marriage mart next season?"

Talia shuddered. "Do not even say such things. I don't even want to imagine."

Fletch grabbed her hips, shifting his wife to the exact spot he wanted her on top of him, his cock slipping up between her legs. His lips went to her shoulder, his tongue slipping out to taste the sweetness of her skin. "Then let me take your imagination elsewhere, my wife."

An exhausting sixteen hours later, the last of the guests were lingering in Fletch's upper drawing room. Ignoring the conversation with the two men in front of him, Fletch looked across the room at his wife escorting Lord and Lady Fantling out the door, and he could not help but beam.

She had managed to make it through the evening with no true panic—she had had to reach him only twice, placing herself under his arm with her heart beating so hard he could feel the pulsating along her neck. But then it had only taken a few minutes of the security of his body before her heartbeat would slow, her gasping breaths recovering, and then she would leave his side to mingle with the guests again.

Every inch his beautiful, charming marchioness.

Fifteen minutes passed before he accompanied the last guests to the front entrance. The door closing against the cold air, he spun in the foyer, realizing he hadn't seen Talia since she had left the upper drawing room with the Fantlings.

After a quick glance in the lower drawing room, he looked to Horace. "Did Lady Lockston retire?"

"No, my lord. She is speaking with one of your guests in the study."

Fletch ran through the list of people attending the party. He had believed all of the guests had departed. He moved down the hall to the study, only to find the door closed.

"You know what I can do." A man's voice, his volume uncurbed, came through the door.

"And you know what you will gain." Talia's words came softer, desperate, muffled through the heavy oak door.

Fletch shoved the door open, swinging it hard.

Talia and the one man stood in the middle of the study. Fletch assessed the man in a quick glance. A stranger. Portly—slovenly, even. At least twenty years his senior. His eyes landed on his wife. "Talia?"

She had jumped, spinning around at his intrusion, and now her face went white. "Fletch...this..." Her eyes darted over her shoulder to the older man before she looked back to him. "This is Cousin Arnold—the current Earl of Roserton."

"So you are the one that is not dead yet." The earl stepped around Talia, looking Fletch up and down before Fletch could say a word. "It would be unfortunate if your death was hurried along, as I understand your wife is quite attached to you. As it is, it should only be a few weeks now."

Fletch stilled, instantly on guard.

He looked the man up and down again, reassessing the threat. And he knew without a doubt the man was a threat. Not only because he had once tossed Talia and her family into poverty—but because Talia did not blanch white at minor irritations. "Talia, leave the room."

"Fletch—"

"Leave, Talia. I will have your obedience on this matter."

She opened her mouth to argue, and Fletch skewered her with a look. Her jaw closed and she silently slipped out past him, closing the door behind her.

Fletch squared his look on Talia's bastard cousin, but held his feet in place. No need to pummel the man straight away. He wanted information first. "Lord Roserton, I shudder to think on the sheer amount of pomposity it has taken for you to enter my home. Yet as it is that you are here, I will ask you what exactly is it that you think you know of my demise?"

Roserton shrugged. "I know you will die soon, Lord Lockston. Promised it, actually."

"Who told you that?"

A sneer lifted the left side of Roserton's face. "Your wife."

The words were a gut-punch that Fletch hoped he imperceptibly absorbed. Yet he could not keep the scowl from his mouth. "Why is this your business, Roserton?"

The earl's sneer widened. "I am merely an interested party."

Fists clenched, Fletch allowed himself one small step toward Roserton. "It is far past time you exit my house, Lord Roserton."

Roserton looked around the study slowly, assessing his surroundings. His beady eyes landed back on Fletch. "Not to worry. I can wait. I will enjoy these luxuries in the future."

Fletch lost all semblance of propriety and rushed Roserton, grabbing his arm and twisting it behind his back in one furious motion. Shoving him toward and through the door, he manhandled Roserton along the hall, his voice a growl. "I would normally relinquish this particular pleasure onto my man, but in your case, Lord Roserton, I will make an exception."

Horace was a step ahead of Fletch in the foyer, flinging the front door open wide.

Fletch shoved Roserton out the door, sending him stumbling down the front stairs.

Horace closed the door. "Well done, my lord."

A quick nod to Horace, and Fletch turned around. The foyer was empty except for Louise standing at the bottom of the stairs, visibly shaken. She looked to Fletch. "Thank you.

Thank you for removing him. We could not do that last time."

"Last time?"

Louise blinked hard, confusion mixed with worry. "Talia did not tell you?"

He advanced on Talia's sister. "No." He lorded over her, not softening the fact he was about to get answers from her. "When was he here?"

Her eyes darted about the foyer. "He was here more than a month ago—the day you came back from the countryside."

"What did he want?"

Louise's body began to tremble, her head shaking. Fletch had no patience for it.

"Tell me, Louise. Right now. What did he want?"

"To marry me. Mother told me. Talia came in and put a stop to it."

"Put a stop to it how?"

"I do not know. He was in the drawing room with mother and she could not get him to leave. Talia went in, and he left and has not been back." Louise's hands started wringing as she strung together more words than Fletch had ever heard from her. "Talia—she went after him after he stomped out. When she came back with you and her wrist was broken, I wondered what happened, but I didn't ask— I've been too afraid. You were with her so I thought all was well. She said she would rid him from my life. And he hasn't been mentioned since, nor has he called, so I just assumed she took care of him…"

Fletch pushed past Louise, charging up the stairs three at a time.

"Talia." He thundered her name as he stomped down the hallway. "Talia."

He opened the door to her chambers. Silent and still. "Talia."

He moved on, stalking into his chambers.

At the side window of the room, craning her neck so she could see the front street, Talia jumped when the door swung open, twisting around.

"Talia, I just shoved the devil out of my home and you have some explaining to do."

She didn't move from the window, her nervous eyes looking over her shoulder out the window once more.

"He broke your wrist, didn't he?"

Her gaze whipped to him, then to the floor. "He pushed. I slipped."

Fletch crossed the room in two strides. "And you promised that bastard I would die?"

"What? I…I…" She slid backward, her hands gripping the windowsill behind her.

Fletch closed the distance she gained. "What the hell did you do, Talia?"

She cringed. "I told him I would marry him."

"You what?" Fletch slammed his hands onto the window frame on either side of Talia's head. "You told the bastard you would marry him?"

"I…I needed to gain time. He knows what happened to Louise, and he wanted to marry her—he threatened to ruin her with her past if we didn't agree." Her tongue flew fast, words tumbling in a rush. "I couldn't let him ruin Louise's life—she has already lost so much. So I just wanted to gain time and I told him about the curse because it was convenient and he would believe that I would marry him."

"Dammit, Talia, you should have let me handle him."

"*You* were not here. You were at Wellfork Castle. It was all I could think to do in the moment—gain enough time for Louise to find a good, kind husband. One that would be loyal to her and protect her, no matter the circumstances. One that would keep her safe from Cousin Arnold's tentacles. I needed time for that, and that is what I got."

"By wrapping yourself up in his tentacles?" His palm slammed again on the frame, shaking the glass. "Blast it to hell, Talia. What would possess you to whore yourself out like that?"

Her look snapped up to him, her voice vehement. "I don't plan on ever having to marry the man because I am your wife, Fletch. I don't plan on you dying. Or have you not noticed that?"

"So instead you refuse the possibility of my death and put yourself in danger—within the bastard's clutches? Idiocy. That is madness, Talia." He grabbed her shoulders, shaking her. Shaking sense into her. "You have to prepare yourself, dammit. Prepare for when I am not here."

"Prepare myself?" Her hands flew up, shoving his chest. "You swore you would fight, Fletch."

His fingers snapped away from her body and he whipped from her, his chest heaving.

"You swore it to me." The words flew at his back, and he could hear the shake in her voice.

Fletch refused to turn back to her, his gaze landing on the tall flames licking high in the fireplace. "Do you not even consider my death a possibility, Talia?"

"I do not."

"You are lying. You do. I do not know how you could not." His head shaking, his look lifted from the fireplace to the door. He needed to leave.

Silent in her quickness, she appeared in front of him, her eyes searching his face. Her hand went onto his chest as her eyes narrowed. "Stop. Whatever you are thinking, right now, Fletch, you need to stop it."

"You don't know what I'm thinking, Talia."

Her jaw set hard. "You will not leave me. You will not pull away from me. I can see you wavering—wavering from us."

"I do not want you to have to suffer the pain of loss again, Talia." He bit the inside of his cheek as he looked to the ceiling. "I would give anything for that pain to never mar your soul. Do you not see you have to prepare yourself? And if you won't do so, I need to make you do so."

Her eyebrows went high. "So you are going to walk out on me? That will prepare me?"

His gaze dropped to her. "If it will lessen the pain, then yes."

"Fine, Fletch. Fine." She turned slowly from him, moving to the fireplace. Her hands gripped the arm of the wide leather chair, her shoulders slumping.

Fletch stared at her back, at the slight shake in her shoulders with every breath. All fire had left his wife, the shell of her, vulnerable, trembling. He had thought to make her finally face the real possibility of his death, but not this. Not defeat. Not defeat from the one person that unequivocally believed he would cheat death.

"You don't think I've thought about it, Fletch? Thought about losing you?" She curled forward into herself, words spilling softly, so softly he had to take a step forward to hear her. "I have thought about nothing else since you told me. If you are gone—"

She gasped a breath, a swallowed sob cutting her words. Her fingernails dug into the leather of the chair. "If you are gone. How my fingers will reach for you without thinking and they will only grasp air. How I will roll over in bed, and instead of the warmth of you, it will only be cold. Cold sheets. That I will have something funny to share and I will immediately want to turn to you to tell you. And you won't be there. That I will walk by your study, and not see you behind your desk. Not see your indulgent smile when I interrupt you with the most inane request. I won't watch you bend over to tug your boots on like I like to. I won't have your arm to lean into. None of it. It will only be a memory. Fading. That I will visit your grave. Tend to your flowers. That I will sit by your gravestone, in the dirt, talking to a slab of granite that I am supposed to be comforted by. That I will have to imagine you below ground, in a box—" Her voice choked off.

Three sobs shook her body. Shook it so violently Fletch thought she would collapse.

She swallowed, a garbled moan sending a tremble through her body as she shoved herself from the chair, turning to him. Tears stained her face, but her eyes were clear as they looked at him. Met his gaze with everything in her soul raw, bared to him. "So, yes. Yes, I have thought on it, Fletch. Dwelled on it. But it does not stop me from waking up every morning and needing you. Needing you today. Dreaming of how I will need you tomorrow."

She moved toward him, her fingers twisting behind her back, loosening her gown. Three steps and she stopped, her gown dropping off her body. She stepped over the wide puddle of silk, untying her stays. Four more steps, and her stays and shift were on the floor.

She stopped in front of him, naked, her nipples brushing the dark cut of his jacket. Staring up at him, her hands slipped under the lapels of his jacket, pushing it off his body. "Beyond that…beyond today, I do not care, Fletch. I cannot allow myself to care. I only want today. You. I need you now in this moment."

Transfixed, he watched his waistcoat and shirt disappear under her soft fingers, his trousers slipping to the floor as she shuffled him in a circle and then backward. His calves hit the ottoman, and Talia shoved him down to sit, then bent to pull off his boots.

Her hazel eyes didn't leave his face as she yanked on the leather. "I choose to believe I will never have to suffer any of those things. I choose to not let a future no one can predict get in the way of my happiness in this moment."

She paused, climbing onto his lap, straddling him as she wrapped her hands alongside his face. "I choose to live in today. I choose to love you with every possible spec of my being. That is how I prepare. I prepare by having no regrets on today."

She slid onto his shaft slowly, descending, letting him fill her with tortured reserve until he was aching, throbbing to drive fully into her. But he held back. Denying her nothing. And she wanted control.

A groan rumbled from her chest as she reached his hilt, swiveling her hips. Her hands slid down to grip his upper arms, digging into the muscle.

Her body circled, playing with him, offering him depth, and then stealing it away. Sending his cock through her folds, making her growl, and then pulling free, only to slide him deep into her again.

The sheer carnality of her twisting body sent Fletch to an edge he could barely grasp onto. But before he lost all grip, he was determined to take her with him. He would demand no less. He wrapped his hands along her hips, lifting her, setting her down, grinding their bodies together, drawing trembles up and down her body, vibrations she could not control.

It turned her ravenous and her mouth went onto his neck, prodding him, her teeth running along the line of his shoulder, nipping at him when he slowed the pace. The spasms started pulsating in her core, he could feel them build, and none too soon. His last shred of control was splintering.

Shattering, her body jerked, the muscles all along her torso contracting, welling into a scream that vibrated into his neck.

It was all he needed.

He plunged upward, reaching a depth in her he hadn't fathomed existed.

He came. He came deep within her.

His seed so hard and fast from him, it belonged in no place but the center of his wife. His hands gripped her body tight to his as wave after wave ravaged every nerve, every muscle. Complete abandon.

Her body still shuddering, she pulled her head free from his neck to look into his face. Tears were streaming from her wide eyes.

"You are crying." Fletch licked the line of salty tears from her left cheek. "I would hope for a better reaction after my performance."

"You silly man." She laughed, swatting his back. "You came in me."

A smile slowly carved his face. A smile set so deep, it hurt his cheeks. "I did. I love you, Talia. And I am living for this day alone. The future will be what it will be."

She drew a deep breath, her smile not stopping the fresh flow of tears from escaping her wondrous hazel eyes. "You know this means more than anything?"

"I do, my love. I do."

He stretched up to catch her lips, dragging her down into a kiss. Devouring her very essence.

Not the slightest regret entered his mind.

Today was a fine day, indeed.

{ CHAPTER 20 }

Talia entered Fletch's room through the door to her chambers. His wife nearly floated, a silk concoction, primrose yellow and trimmed in a delicate lace of silver at the bodice and sleeves, flowed about her body, her face beaming. A vision. A vision that was his. He turned fully to her, buttoning his waistcoat. "Is your sister ready to get married?"

Talia's nose scrunched up. "She is currently in the bath, taking an inordinate amount of time. Mother is so frenzied, she set the maid to work on Louise's hair at the edge of the tub."

"So you are in here for escape?" Fletch smirked.

"Possibly." Her look turned worried. "Mr. Flemstone is not already here, is he? I will go and rush Louise if need be."

"No. He sent word he will be here in an hour. Several of our guests are already in the upper drawing room, though."

"Who? Do I need to rush?"

"Caine and Ara. Aunt Penelope. A few of your mother's friends." Fletch slid his arms into his dark jacket, pulling the sleeves taut. His valet would sigh at the sight of him already dressed, but it wouldn't be the first time Fletch had foregone the man's attentions. He looked to Talia. "But I understand your mother has moved below and already has the room well within her palm."

"We never should have reintroduced Aunt Penelope to her." Talia shook her head. "Those two are conspirators of the first order. I am not sure if mother is becoming one of Aunt Penelope's dragons, or it is the other way around."

Fletch moved to her, unable to resist wrapping his arms around her waist, wrinkles in her silk be damned. "Well, they were either going to love each other or hate each other. And this current state does make our lives much calmer." He kissed her forehead. "Though I do believe I will go down and rescue Caine from the room."

She poked his chest. "And leave Ara to the lot of them—shame on you."

Fletch chuckled. After Lord and Lady Newdale had come back into London weeks ago, Talia and Caine's wife had taken an extreme liking to each other, much to Fletch's satisfaction. He was managing to expand Talia's family of genuine, loyal people that she would always be able to depend upon. It eased the tremendous worry in his soul. "I am glad you now have a partner in the art of dodging social occasions. And as such, do not fear on Ara's fate. If I know her, she will find her way out of the drawing room soon enough."

A knock on the door cut their conversation.

"Yes?"

His valet poked his head into the room. "My lord, there is a slight disturbance."

"Disturbance?" Fletch dropped his arms from Talia, turning to his man.

"A Lord Roserton. He walked in behind Lord and Lady Evanton. Horace did not see him in time to not make a scene, and he thought it better to be handled quietly. Though Lord Roserton became quite belligerent when Horace would not allow him up the stairs to the upper drawing room. The man insists he has every right to give his cousin away in marriage."

Instant fury ran up Fletch's neck. "Where is Roserton now?"

"Horace has him in the lower drawing room, my lord, far from the other guests." His valet gave a slight cough. "He has mentioned several times the...wretched correspondence from you, my lord."

Fletch nodded. "Thank you. I will be down in moments."

His valet closed the door.

Talia grabbed Fletch's forearm. "Correspondence? What is that about, Fletch? He does not mean to ruin the wedding, does he?"

"I will allow no such interference from him, Talia. I will go down and speak with him."

Her grip didn't loosen on his arm and she walked across his room with him. "I am coming as well."

Fletch stopped, peeling Talia's fingers from his jacket. "No, you need to see to getting your sister ready. Mr. Flemstone and the clergyman will be here soon. That is the priority. Not the bastard down below. I will remove him from the house, Talia."

To his relief, Talia nodded, stepping away from him even as a deep frown set onto her face.

Fletch was down the stairs and into the lower drawing room within seconds. He slammed the door closed behind him.

Standing in the middle of the room, Roserton turned to Fletch. "Lord Lockston."

"Put my brandy down, Roserton." Fletch's fists instantly curled.

The man smirked, taking a slow swallow of the amber liquid in his glass. He smacked his tongue, exhaling. "So, my dear Cousin Natalia told you of our bargain."

"Yes."

Roserton took another sip of the brandy, and a sneer lifted the left side of his face. "I did not care for your letter, Lord Lockston. Although I can sympathize with your anger—a dying man knowing exactly who his wife will be sleeping with after his death is an annoyance to come to terms with. So I can understand your anger. Especially with your wife. Natalia is a specimen."

Every inch of Fletch's skin heated, threatening to explode. Yet he had a house full of guests gathered for a wedding to consider. He set his voice to an even level. "I thought my letter was extremely clear, Roserton, on what would happen to you if you so much as walked on the same block as my wife. Or her sister. Or her mother. Leave before I toss you from here once more. And this time, I will not be so gentle in my actions."

"That threat, along with every single one of the threats in your letter ring hollow, Lord Lockston. My presence alone should alert you to that fact. It is imperative I am here for this event. It does not do that I am not in attendance at the wedding of my future sister-in-law." His voice sneered high on the last five words.

"You will keep your bloody paws off my wife, you bastard." Fletch advanced on him.

"Or I can go upstairs and ruin Louise's life with one simple sentence. Would you rather that, Lockston?"

Fletch stopped an inch from his portly frame, heaving, his look skewering Roserton with all the fury twisting his skin—fury threatening to unleash and choke the very life from the pitiful creature.

Roserton looked up at Fletch, his sneer contorting his face into a grotesque gargoyle. "Here is what you have not considered, Lord Lockston—all of your threats—all of your demands—they all ring hollow. If you were alive, maybe I would take heed—but, ha—you will die, and there will be no one to protect Natalia. Not a soul to enforce what you think you can do to me."

He stepped away from Fletch and went to the sideboard, setting his glass down. Turning back to Fletch, his face twisted even more monstrous. "So I will take your wife, Lockston, long before it will even be proper of her to shed her widow's weeds. I will take her, right here on this floor." He pointed at the maroon threads of the Axminster carpet in front of Fletch's boots. "Right where you stand now. Because my feet will be master of this house soon enough. And there isn't a bloody thing you can do about it."

Fists rising, Fletch charged across the room.

"Fletch—no!" Talia slammed open the door of the room.

"Fletch!" Right behind Talia, Caine and Reggard both screamed his name in unison.

But he was already lunging. Red rage blinding his sight.

~ ~ ~

It was happening.

Time slowed. Seconds stretching into lifetimes.

The breath into his lungs stilled, his body swaying. Control of every muscle vanishing.

It was too soon. He still had weeks. A month. He had more time. He needed more time. He and Talia had only had months together. He needed more time. More time. More time with her. More time to protect her. More time.

His eyes swept the room. Chairs, fireplace, lamps. Caine rushing past him, punching Roserton. Reggard dragging the bastard from the room. Window, curtains, books, tables. Talia.

Her face. There she was. His look adhered onto her face.

He wanted nothing more than her in his vision.

She moved to him in the flurry. Where was the smile that was always on her lips when she looked at him?

She needed him today.

Today was the wedding.

She needed him.

Her mouth dropped, her hazel eyes panicked.

She needed him.

He took one step toward her. The world spun, dragging him down.

Talia's face. Find her face.

She yelled. He couldn't hear her, but he could see her mouth moving, screaming at her sister.

Down. Down. Down.

His body outstretched, he hit the floor—the thud not hurting, only a dull echo in his ears.

Talia's face. Where? Where did she go?

She appeared above him, hovering, gripping his head. Still screaming. Screaming at him now.

His eyes went to darkness.

One last word from her made it through the silence in his ears.

"Fight."

{ CHAPTER 21 }

The brutal hit sent his body jerking, folding, and then splaying out. Limp. Inert.

"Fletch." The word ripped from Talia's mouth, her hands shaking his head.

The next blow slammed down onto his chest. A flop. Nothing more. Her husband flaccid, leaving her. No.

She tore her eyes off of Fletch's face to the doctor. "You're killing him. Killing him."

Dr. Terrental glanced up at her, his eyes both commanding and calming. "He will be dead if I do nothing. This is what you wanted."

Mr. Flemstone's hands gripped onto her shoulders. "Dr. Terrental knows what he is doing, Talia."

Talia glanced at the white of Fletch's face, then looked up to Dr. Terrental, steeling herself. Whatever it took. She nodded. "Do what you must. Everything you need to."

The doctor clamped his hands together, bringing them down in another brutal blow to her husband's chest. His body flailed, then stilled.

She bent, setting her lips next to Fletch's ear. "Fletch. This is when you fight. It is right now. Fight."

Another hit. Another jerk.

"Dammit, Fletch, come back to me. You swore—you swore you would fight." Talia's head dropped, her hands gripping her husband, gripping him from death, gripping him from leaving her. He had been right all along. She could not take this. Not him leaving her. Not now. Time. She needed more time.

She glanced up as the doctor struck again. Fletch's body flopped.

Nothing. No breath.

Her mouth went to his ear, pleading through her tears. "Fletch, you get back to me right now. Fight. I am pregnant and I need you. Need you. Today. Tomorrow. Years from now. I need you. Our child needs his father, so you will come back to me this instant. This instant, Fletch. You will fight your way back to me. Now, Fletch."

She heard the blow to Fletch's chest, and his body jerked, folding in half, ripping from her hands.

A gasp.

A long, gargling gasp that sent Fletch's body doubling over on its side.

He gasped, again and again, his body convulsing against lack of air.

Dr. Terrental sat back onto his heels, his hands holding Fletch on his side, holding his body from violent spasms. He looked to Talia, disbelief plain on his face.

Talia scampered to where Fletch's head had landed, grabbing him again in her hands. "Fletch, Fletch, keep fighting. You are almost back."

Fletch's arm lifted, his hand landing on the back of her head. Squeezing it.

And then it fell limp onto the floor.

~ ~ ~

His eyes cracked open. Cracked open and found her face.

Not that there was anywhere else to look.

Talia scooted closer on the bed to Fletch's head, hovering above him, her nose almost touching his. Her fingers went to his brow, burying themselves into his hair. Touching him as she had been afraid to for the last nine hours.

She had only held his hand. Only his hand. Terrified to touch more. Terrified to upset the delicate balance his body was in.

He was breathing. It was enough. She would press for no more.

But now, now that his eyes had cracked, she would press for the world.

She dragged a breath into her lungs, exhaling it before she could find words. She leaned forward, her forehead touching his. "You fought for me."

A hard swallow went through his throat before his chest lifted as air filled his lungs. The darkest flecks in his grey eyes were bright. "I never could deny you, Talia."

She laughed, hard, her body shaking, her face unable to decide if she was smiling or crying. Both, she realized.

Lifting her head from his, she sat straight as she grabbed a handkerchief from the side table to wipe the wetness from her cheeks. She looked at Fletch. He was watching her as if she had gone half mad.

Her right hand slipped along the coverlet to wrap around the side of his belly. "Well, I am relieved we are done with that death business."

A smile cut onto his handsome face—handsome even if all the color hadn't returned to his cheeks. "Help me sit up?"

Talia nodded, helping him to lean up and grabbing pillows to prop him in the bed. She tucked the sheet around his bare chest and then grabbed water from the side table, holding it to his lips until he took several swallows.

Fletch situated, she sat on the side of the bed, her fingers tucked along his far hip, unwilling to let her hands leave his body.

His fingers lifted, rubbing his brow. "What happened? I went after Roserton and then blackness, and then…then there was a man?"

She nodded. "Dr. Terrental. He is still here. You need to properly meet him."

"Where did he come from?"

"I rented the townhouse at the end of the block and installed him in it. I even insisted he see his patients and do surgeries there. I wanted him close at all times."

"You what?" Fletch's dark eyebrows flew upward, incredulous.

"If something happened to you, I knew he would be the best person to help you. So I needed him readily available. I met him through Mr. Flemstone. He also works for the Wotherfeld Hospital, and you know they are focused on discovery—on the most advanced medical knowledge."

Fletch's eyebrows dropped to their normal position, yet his head tilted as his eyes narrowed at her. "I thought you said you didn't believe in this curse, Talia."

"I don't." She smirked. "You are alive, ergo, no curse."

Fletch cleared his throat.

She held his stare for a moment before breaking, her fingers tapping on his abdomen. "Yet, I was not about to leave such an important matter as your life up to fate alone. Even a curse can be nudged." She leaned forward, meeting his gaze. "But it was you that fought, Fletch. Fought for us. Fought to live. Dr. Terrental only gave you a path back. You did the rest."

Fletch took a deep breath, the air filling his chest, only to have the motion cut short with a sudden pained cough. His hand went flat onto his chest. "Just what was it that Dr. Terrental did to me? My chest feels like a horse kicked me."

"He beat your heart. Pounded it quite soundly. He said it had slowed to nothing, and it needed prodding." Her hand waved. "Well, not in those exact terms, his were much more medical. Mr. Flemstone translated for me."

"How did Dr. Terrental know what to do?"

"He didn't know for certain, but he thought he could help when I asked him months ago after Mr. Flemstone introduced me to him. It was why I had him move in only steps away, so he could be here in seconds." Talia shifted on the bed, tightening her hold along his hip. "I had been spending so much time with Mr. Flemstone in Louise's room, that I started asking him questions about what he thought could have contributed to the deaths of your brother and father and grandfathers.

"He found the mystery of the curse interesting—and not at all scientific—so I asked him to speak with Aunt Penelope, and with any and every one that witnessed your brother, father or grandfathers' deaths. Mr. Flemstone found enough commonality in their deaths that he introduced me to Dr. Terrental, a colleague of his at the Wotherfeld Hospital."

"Why?"

"Through his interviews, Mr. Flemstone believed your brother, father and grandfather all died of a weak heart. No curse. Just temperamental hearts. He thought there would be a chance to save you, and Dr. Terrental is the leading physician of research on the heart and how blood moves through the body. He has been collecting everything and anything of value from doctors, physicians, surgeons, apothecaries—methods, medicines, herbs, battlefront practices—he collects the research and synthesizes the information to determine best options for saving lives."

"Such as pulverizing my chest?"

She smiled. "Such as pulverizing your chest."

"You never truly believed in the curse, did you, Talia? I thought you had changed your mind after Wellfork Castle."

She shrugged. "I realized it didn't matter whether the curse was real or not, I was still going to do everything in my power to save you."

"And not tell me."

Her head tilted, scolding. "Not let you talk me out of Dr. Terrental's assistance. I was not about to lose you if I could alter the course of fate."

A soft knock came from the door.

"Yes?" Talia asked.

"It is Reggard. We heard voices."

"Come in," Talia said, staying on the bed next to Fletch but turning to the entrance.

Reggard stepped in, closing the door behind him. His look found Fletch, and he visibly exhaled, relief in his eyes.

"I apologize for the interruption, but I assumed you would want any additional worry eased, Talia, so I am to report your sister and Mr. Flemstone were married an hour ago, per your request."

Talia inhaled a long breath, relief filling her chest. "Thank you. That does ease my worry."

Reggard offered a slight smile. "I also know that Fletch will want to be assured that the other matter was taken care of."

Talia's eyes swung to Fletch.

He glanced from her to Reggard. "Roserton?"

Reggard nodded. "Caine and I dragged him off. It was made known to him—in no uncertain terms—that Talia will always be protected by the two of us as well. That every single threat you made to him would be executed, without mercy, should he decide to disregard your warning and so much as think about Talia and her family."

Talia's breath caught in her throat, gasping. She looked at Fletch, and then back to Reggard. "I—that you—"

Reggard offered a crooked smile. "We are family, Talia. Worry over a sniveling bastard like that never needs to be a part of your life again."

She nodded, her throat too welled up in gratitude to speak.

"Well done, man," Fletch said. "Thank you."

With a nod, Reggard turned to exit. He paused at the door, looking over his shoulder at them. "Oh, and you should know I broke his wrist."

"You what?" Talia's eyes went wide.

"That was retribution." Reggard shrugged. "The pinky I broke of his was just because he is an arse of the highest order."

Fletch chuckled. "Again. Well done, man."

Reggard slipped out of the room.

Talia turned her attention back to Fletch. "You told them of Roserton, what he did, what he threatened?"

"I did."

"But that is private, Fletch, what happened to Louise."

"I understand, but Reggard and Caine are trusted—they will keep the confidence to the grave."

She stared at him, her frown deepening.

Fletch sighed, his arm lifting to set his palm along her cheek. "I had to do it. You may not have wanted to imagine the possibility of me dying, Talia, but I had to consider it. What it would entail. I had to cover everything I could possibly think of to protect you, and that meant Caine and Reggard being privy to everything." His fingers dropped, sliding down alongside her neck. "It is my right to take care of you without you knowing, Talia, just as you did for me."

Her frown eased. "I cannot argue with that logic."

"No, you cannot."

He tugged at her neck and she leaned forward, setting her cheek onto his, the rough stubble on his jawline rubbing her skin. She inhaled, taking the scent of him into her chest, letting it fill her, warm her.

He was alive. Tremors still ran down her spine at how very close she had come to losing him. "Thank you for not dying."

His jaw flexed against her cheek. "I died, Talia. I was gone."

She inhaled sharply, his words instantly sending her body into a tremble.

He pulled his head from hers and captured her face between his hands, his fingers twining into her hair. His grey eyes found hers, his soul on full display. "I died. But then I heard your voice."

"You did?"

"It was darkness, and then your voice, telling me to fight."

"And you did."

"Yes. I did. I promised I would. A promise you demanded of me."

Her head dropped as tearless, silent sobs racked her body. Fletch's hands slipped to the back of her head, his fingers weaving into her hair, a silent comfort.

It took minutes for her to hold her breathing in check. For her to look up at him. "Promise me. If that ever happens again, you will fight just the same. You will come back to me. You know you can do it now." She smiled. "And I can beat your chest just as hard as Dr. Terrental, if needed."

"I do not doubt it."

"Promise me."

"I promise."

He smiled, the curious, wondrous smile he reserved for her alone. "Now, Talia, about this child of mine you are carrying."

A smile took over her face, took over the room, took over her husband.

"Yes, about that child. We have some planning to do, Fletch."

{ EPILOGUE }

FIFTY YEARS LATER
JANUARY, 1873

Talia's hand slipped over the smooth, well-worn pigeon with only minute traces of the gold gilding remaining, the ruby eyes long since surrendered to vanishing in the streets of London. But Aunt Penelope had always had it right. A cane was useful.

She lifted the stick, swatting the butt of her oldest great-grandson running by, who was gleefully terrorizing two of his younger cousins with a toad that had just squirted in his hand.

He stopped and gave her a look, sheepish, his head falling. His brown hair fell in front of his grey eyes as he looked at his toes.

"Edward, you know very well Penny has a fear of toads," Talia said. "Not to mention this is the drawing room and toads do not belong in the drawing room. Your mother will have a fit if she sees you inside with it. Put that poor thing back in the garden this instant."

He nodded, his eyes down. "Yes, MiMi." He was the oldest, but still young enough to take a scold with proper chagrin.

"Off with you, then." Talia swatted the side of his leg with her cane.

He scampered off, leaving the room, and within moments, Talia could hear the renewed squeals of his cousins from deep in the manor.

Next to her on the settee, Fletch folded his newspaper, looking at her over the spectacles on the edge of his nose. "The boy at least pretended to be contrite, Talia. I daresay he gets credit for that, in the least."

She chuckled, watching the same mischievous smile she had just seen on Edward appear on her husband's face. Wrinkles aside, Fletch was still the man she had fallen in love with fifty years ago, the dark flecks in his grey eyes still dancing bright. It was no wonder she loved him a thousandfold over now.

She sighed, shaking her head as she settled her cane alongside her leg.

"Talia?"

"Yes, Fletch?"

"You were right about the curse."

She looked to him.

The mischievous smile still played on his lips. She gave him a curt nod. "Thank you. Fifty years, that took you."

He shrugged. "I didn't want to tempt fate."

He lifted his arm, settling it along her shoulders as he pulled her into him. Their muscles had weakened, their hair had whitened, their voices had gone scratchy with time. But this. For all the change—this was still her most favorite place in the world.

She nuzzled her cheek onto his chest, into the well-worn curve that still fit her head perfectly. "Let it never be said I did not marry a smart man."

His kissed the top of her head. "And I, a smart woman."

~ ABOUT THE AUTHOR ~

K.J. Jackson is the author of *The Hold Your Breath Series,*
The Lords of Fate Series, The Lords of Action Series,
and *The Flame Moon Series.*

She specializes in historical and paranormal romance,
loves to travel (road trips are the best!), and is a sucker for a
good story in any genre. She lives in Minnesota with
her husband, two children, and a dog who
has taken the sport of bed-hogging
to new heights.

Visit her at www.kjjackson.com

~ Author's Note ~

Thank you for allowing my stories into your life and time—it is an honor!

My next historical in the *Lords of Action* series will debut in winter 2016/17.

If you missed the *Hold Your Breath* series or the *Lords of Fate* series, be sure to check out these historical romances (each is a stand-alone story): ***Stone Devil Duke, Unmasking the Marquess, My Captain, My Earl, Worth of a Duke, Earl of Destiny, and Marquess of Fortune***.

Never miss a new release or sale!
Be sure to sign up for my VIP Email List at
www.KJJackson.com
(email addresses are precious, so out of respect,
you'll only hear from me when I actually have real news).

Interested in Paranormal Romance?
In the meantime, if you want to switch genres and check out my Flame Moon paranormal romance series, ***Flame Moon #1***, the first book in the series, is currently free (ebook) at all stores. ***Flame Moon*** is a stand-alone story, so no worries on getting sucked into a cliffhanger. But number two in the series, ***Triple Infinity***, ends with a fun cliff, so be forewarned. Number three in the series, ***Flux Flame***, ties up that portion of the series.

Connect with me!
www.KJJackson.com
https://www.facebook.com/kjjacksonauthor
Twitter: @K_J_Jackson

Printed in Great Britain
by Amazon